HEARTSTEALER

∞ ∞

GRACE BRANNIGAN

P.O. Box 100
East Jewett, New York, 12424 USA

Heartstealer

Women of Character Contemporary Series
Echoes From the Past
Once and Always
Heartstealer
Wishing on a Rodeo Moon

Women of Strength Time Travel Series
Once Upon a Remembrance (Book 1)
Soulmates Through Time (Book 2)
Treasure So Rare (Book 3)

Romantic Short Stories
Two Babies, a Cowboy and Sara
Deception

Website: www.GraceBrannigan.com

Heartstealer
Cover Art By: Stephanie White of Steph's Cover Design: paranormal, fantasy, horror & more
By Grace Brannigan
Print Edition Copyright 2013   Elaine Warfield

ISBN: 978-1-939061-30-0

∞ **Chapter One** ∞

JACIE'S STOMACH CHURNED as she stared at the ground two thousand feet below. What insanity made her put herself through this punishment—just to prove she wasn't washed up as a stunt woman?

"Just do it," she muttered. "You've done it thousands of times before. Get your foot out the door and jump."

Automatically, she ran her fingers over her knee support and then the pull ring on her parachute harness. Lastly, she braced the toes of her boots against the door lip.

She had to jump. Skydiving was her life. It had always defined who she was; a member of her family's business, Aerial Antics. Her brother Con would pull her off this job if he thought she wasn't ready. She couldn't go home with her tail between her legs. Her family would try to put her back in cotton wool. Again.

How long did she have to pay for one dumb mistake—two—if she counted the one she'd made thinking Brad loved her.

With a low growl of impatience, she stepped out and an updraft pulled her up and away from the plane. As she plunged downward, a flashback to her parachuting accident thirteen months ago at Angel Falls came dangerously close. She could see again that mountainous ledge of rock, nothing but water and uninhabited jungle below her, the glorious release as she began her freefall, and then her parachute failure. . ..

Her chute opened. Years of training took over and the tightness eased inside her chest. Of course she could do this, she'd been jumping far too long to stop now.

As the ground drew closer she pulled the shroud lines of her chute, spilling air to control her landing.

Clustered dots took on the shapes of people. A lone figure with a cowboy hat stood apart from the rest. An imp of mischief surfaced in Jacie. She'd alter her landing slightly and land near the guy with the cowboy hat.

As her feet touched solid earth a gust of wind lifted and pulled her forward, past the camera crews, past the gathered crowd. She caught a glimpse of surprised faces and then she came to a dead stop as her body lightly impacted with another. She had a fleeting impression of a hat flying through the air and they both fell to the ground in a tangle of arms, legs and billowing parachute.

Arms closed around her and held tight. She squeezed her eyes shut and pressed her forehead into a hard chest. Spicy cologne tantalized her nostrils.

When the rest of her senses kicked in she was amazed to find she lay straddled atop a very male body. Hard chest and long, long legs. The cowboy.

"I guess I came a tad too close to my mark," she managed, barely suppressing her laughter. His arms were like hard bands around her back. She stayed unmoving against a soft shirt, her nose pressed into a dusting of nose-tickling hair. Scents mingled. Horse and leather, that subtle touch of man.

The flapping of her parachute forced her to stop thinking about the body beneath her. She opened her eyes. Her blue and purple chute swept upward, then gently settled to cover them in a cocoon.

"Can I help you, ma'am?" drawled a deep, amused voice in her ear. The hard body beneath her had a sexy-as-all-get out voice to go with it.

Her body did a head to toe shiver. "I think you've already helped me land." She levered her body upward. "It seems a shame to move," she added, but peeled herself from that broad chest partially covered by blue cotton. The impact must have torn his buttons loose, because the shirt gaped open. She stared at his flat stomach and then down to his hair dusted navel. They weren't buttons on his shirt, they were snaps.

Jacie studied the wide shoulders, square chin and slightly curved mouth. Lazily she moved on to lean, tanned features. His expression showed tolerance, amusement, interest . . . then a guarded look dropped as hard blue eyes stared at her. Well, it had been interesting until he got that guarded look on his face.

His arms were now straight out on the ground. A soft sound escaped her lips, but no words. Oh dear. She tried again. "S-sorry . . . " she managed faintly, trying not to laugh again. "What an embarrassing first impression this is turning out to be!" He didn't look amused now, but kind of stiff and probably too much of a gentleman to tell her to get off him. "I hope I didn't hurt you when I caught you," she said apologetically. "Actually, I guess you caught me." Literally. She suddenly realized her knee was in a rather delicate area.

"It's not every day I can lay claim to stopping a runaway female," the man professed, blue eyes framed by the blackest of lashes.

"Not exactly a runaway," she admitted, tilting her head and grinning widely. "Though it looks like I've made a slight miscalculation in my landing."

He swept his arm up to catch the folds of the parachute and began to pull it off them.

Jacie let her glance linger on his mouth and a barely noticeable dimple. A jolt of sexual awareness hit her. She immediately stifled it, gulping back a groan. The man shifted his legs and sensation rocked her. He was all hard muscles and long limbs. After Brad, she'd vowed no men. . .no way. But for a moment as her glance lingered on a rock hard jaw and wide shoulders, that vow felt about as substantial as fairy dust. The hell with Brad.

She rolled sideways and off him as he fully released them from the parachute's silky folds.

"Aren't you supposed to take wind shifts into consideration when doing a jump?" he asked. He sat up and dusted off his pants. His legs were encased in snug-fitting denims as faded as his shirt and he had well worn cowboy boots on his feet. He stood over her as he pulled off his gloves and stuffed them in a back pocket. Jacie measured his height against hers. Six three, maybe four to her five feet seven inches.

"Of course I take the wind into consideration." She told herself to focus, but it became impossible when his gaping shirt offered tantalizing glimpses of a man in superb physical shape. She tried to ignore the attraction nipping at her but for the moment gave it up as a losing battle.

His look turned questioning as he proceeded to snap his shirt. "Then you changed your target?" he asked with a hint of impatience.

"Guilty." She lifted her shoulders, thinking he looked like a man who had no time for nonsense. "Seemed like a good idea at the time." She didn't tell him he'd presented a challenge, standing off by himself like that, as if he wasn't impressed with her skydiving into the resort.

He did look pretty unimpressed. In fact, she guessed that right about now he was wondering who the fool was that had hired her to skydive into Timber Falls. Natural curiosity prompted her to ask, "Are you a guest at the ranch?"

"No." He looked past her toward the small crowd who had gathered for the jump. "Here come the others." With concern he quickly glanced up and down her scarlet jumpsuit. "You landed pretty hard, are you okay?"

Jacie saw him zero in on the knee support and then felt his sharp glance move up to her neck.

"You've hurt yourself," he added, reaching out a hand toward her.

She didn't wait to see if he would actually touch her neck but jerked her head back. "I'm fine," she said briskly. "The mark on my neck is old." She reached over to pick up a black cowboy hat on the ground. The shaped brim felt smooth under her fingertips. "Yours?"

"Yeah." He took it and held out his other hand to her. She let him pull her up and they stared at each other, each taking the other's measure. Jacie admitted she liked what she saw.

She stepped back. He put his hat on, tipping the brim forward the slightest bit, virtually hiding his eyes from her.

"Sloan." He shook her hand. "Welcome to the Catskills and Timber Falls."

"Thanks. Jacie Turner." She felt a measure of disgust when her voice came out breathless. She pulled at her sleeves and adjusted them. Men didn't usually make her nervous.

"Yeah, I know," he said.

That made her pause in buttoning her sleeve. "And

do I know you?"

"Nope. My brother hired you." He began to roll her chute, his movements swift and efficient. "Come on, we might as well see if that jump will satisfy the experts."

Jacie's leg muscles tensed. Back to business. She chewed her lip thoughtfully, knowing the jump hadn't been one of her better ones. "Your brother is James Wright? He was my contact for this job. Who are the experts?" she asked curiously. "Sounds like you're not lumping yourself in that category."

"James is my brother. He and his advertising agency are the experts." He threw her a serious look from under dark brows. "I didn't order a skydiving act. I think word of mouth is enough to put this place on the map."

She opened her eyes wide. "Whoa, okay, I get the picture that this wasn't your idea." She unclipped her harness and released the snap on her tight-fitting cap. "But since your brother owns Timber Falls, he's the one I answer to."

Sloan's blue eyes were intense as they settled on her, yet a slight hint of amusement lurked there. "Sorry to disappoint you, but we both own Timber Falls."

"Oh." A course of goose bumps raced along her arms under the jumpsuit. She gave him a full smile. That meant he'd be here her entire stay. There was something about him that rattled her just a bit. "Then you're my employer too. You know I'm staying here the month of August?"

"I know."

Two words with a wealth of meaning. He knew and was happy she wondered, or he knew and didn't like it? From everything he'd not said, it might be the latter. He watched the slowly dispersing crowd with a slight frown, as if he wished himself elsewhere. Jacie figured he probably had better things to do than pick her up and make sure she was okay. Well, that was okay with her.

She was here to do a job, not make friends with a guy who looked like he'd walked out of an old western. Sexy as hell, but an old western nevertheless.

Sighing, Jacie had to wonder why her hands shook as she slid the cap from her head.

Ω

Sloan knew he'd better not linger if he wanted to finish his workload by dusk, but his feet didn't move. He hadn't planned on staying this long, but curiosity had gotten the better of him when he'd seen Jacie arrive earlier with her brother. At the time he'd wondered if anyone that looked that good would risk ruining her perfect hair styling by jumping out of a plane. Sure enough she'd jumped and to his untrained eyes, she'd done it with flair.

Now as he watched her rich, reddish brown hair slide down her shoulders he could imagine a man burying his face there and getting lost. Fascinated, he stared as her slim fingers tangled in the strands. Her mouth was saucy, her big brown eyes lively. Her skin glowed and a touch of pink accented her high cheekbones. There was something exotic about her face with the slightly up-tilted eyes, yet he had a fleeting impression of shadows. Despite that, he guessed she was all sparks and fun.

He clenched the silky material of the parachute, discomfited by his thoughts. He didn't indulge in flights of imagination, but right now his brain was having a hell of a field day recalling her slim soft body on top of his. There was an undeniable charisma about this woman in the form-fitting jumpsuit. She exuded life and radiance with a smile that embraced the world. When she had veered from her landing mark, he'd feared she was in trouble and stepped into her path. They weren't close to the cliffs, but there existed a possibility she could have been flung that way; a fall no man or woman could survive.

"Sloan, I see you've met Jacie," his brother James said behind them.

Glad of the diversion, Sloan turned to his brother. "Yes." He let his glance move back to Jacie and he couldn't help but smile. "A quick introduction."

She tipped her head back, the lightly tanned skin of her throat exposed as her husky laugh rang out. His body tightened down to his toes.

"I guess the best thing is to make light of my less-than-perfect entrance," she admitted without apology, thrusting a hand toward James. "You must be James Wright. Luckily Sloan acted as a barrier, otherwise you'd still be chasing me across the field. What a series of camera shots that would be."

"I'm afraid that's typical of my sister," said a male voice dryly. "She likes to be the center of attention."

Sloan looked at the dark-haired man who came up behind James. His brown hair was cropped short and he was of husky build. The family resemblance between him and Jacie was unmistakable, especially around the eyes.

"Sloan, this is Con Turner," his brother said. "Con heads up Aerial Antics."

Jacie's glance at her brother was a mix of affection and exasperation. "Con's here to make sure the jump goes off without a hitch."

Sloan wondered about the hint of defensiveness in the angle of her body. Her glance at her brother seemed almost challenging.

Con shook hands with him. "Nice to meet you Sloan. As Jacie said, I wanted to make sure everything's in order."

Sloan met the other man's flint gray eyes. "I was under the impression you were the one handling this job."

"As I explained to your brother when we set this up, I have a commitment out of the country. Jacie is very capable of fulfilling the obligation."

"That's right," she said, stepping closer to James. "I was trained by my brother. I'm confident you'll be happy with my work."

James ran a hand through his already tousled red hair and smiled at Jacie. "The camera crew got several shots and they tell me they're looking good," he said. "I talked to the pilot and we won't need to do another jump today."

"Are you sure?" she asked. "That wasn't the best landing I've ever done. We can try a couple more."

"Actually, for the publicity pictures we're only using the shot from the plane and part of the freefall."

Sloan didn't miss Jacie's relief. She hadn't removed the knee brace and she seemed to be limping a bit. Was she worried they would release her from the job if she admitted she'd hurt herself? He frowned. Why take a chance on a jump if you're not up to it? He clenched his teeth, not happy with the picture he was getting. This skydiving gig might not be his thing, but he certainly didn't want to open the resort to any lawsuits.

"I have a good feeling about this publicity campaign," James said.

Jacie smiled. "I still think I'm getting the better bargain. A month-long stay at your ranch resort."

"One which I hope you'll enjoy. Here comes a member of the local news bureau," James said. "They asked me if you'd do a short interview."

Jacie looked toward the approaching reporter. "Of course," she said. "That's why we're here, right? The more publicity the better."

Sloan watched a cameraman approach Jacie and her

brother to position them for the impromptu interview. John Wilson, a local news reporter was there. Sloan had gone to school with John and now gave him a nod. "John, how are you doing?"

"Fine, Sloan. This place is really shaping up. You guys have done a great job." He turned his attention to Jacie and introduced himself. "Jacie, I've read the backgrounder on you. You've been on jumps all over the world. I'm curious why you're here in this relatively quiet area of the Catskills."

Sloan watched her give John a brilliant smile, noted the effect it had on the other man as John's usually reserved manner slipped a bit. Sloan wondered how often she used that smile to get her own way. It was the same one she'd given him.

"Look at this place!" she exclaimed, waving her hands to indicate the mountain ranges on three sides. "It's gorgeous. People should know about Timber Falls and all it has to offer. Aerial Antics is here to help them do that. As an added bonus, I get to stay here for a month. How could I refuse such a lovely setup?"

With cynical detachment Sloan watched John fall under her spell and take a step closer to Jacie.

"Has there been much interest in the skydiving lessons?" John asked.

"The guests are excited," James said. "We've had some response too from local people as you can see by the crowd that showed up."

"Jacie, it's obvious you enjoy jumping out of planes. Can you tell those of us who haven't dared that, what it's like? Is it really a thrill not to be missed?"

Sloan watched Jacie curiously as she closed her eyes and spoke softly. "When you jump the air catches you and whips you upward. It's like catching your breath on a wild carnival ride. Your heart rate is accelerated and the adrenaline's flowing. It's an incredible feeling of freedom."

The words were heartfelt; her love of skydiving came through loud and clear.

"Your film "Escape from Angel Falls" last year was a box office hit, despite the turmoil the film company has since experienced. Would you consider doing stunts for another film?"

Sloan didn't think that information was in the backgrounder. He saw a brief flash of anxiety on her face as she looked at her brother.

"That was a one-time thing," she said lightly. "Our specialty is film stunts, but usually my brothers handle those jobs. But who knows," she added, "I might consider doing another one if I'm asked."

"How did your company get into film stunts?" John asked.

Smoothly, she turned to her brother. "I think my brother can answer that question in more detail," she said.

She smiled and deftly sidestepped out of camera range so Con could take over. As Jacie headed his way with determination, Sloan watched her curiously, wondering what else might be beneath the surface of this woman.

"I'm ready," she said.

"I can wait. I don't want to take you away from the limelight," he told her briskly. "Some people just eat up that attention."

She lifted a brow. "Thanks for your consideration, but my brother can handle it from here. Publicity is his thing."

James joined them. "That pretty much wraps it up. Thanks, Jacie, for taking care of that. I'd say we're getting some interest stirred up." He threw Sloan a glance.

"Would you believe I signed up for a jump?"

Sloan knew what was coming as his brother gave him a speculative look and then said to Jacie. "Sloan's too down to earth to jump off anything more than a horse."

Sloan knew anything he said would probably be misconstrued, but James had it just about right. He was far from a thrill seeker.

Jacie looked at him and said earnestly, "If you're worried about it, Sloan, we can take it real slow. I explain everything in detail and show you how the equipment works. I promise you'd love it."

"I'm not afraid," he said, giving James an annoyed glance. "This ranch has an unlimited supply of work to keep me occupied. I don't have time to be jumping out of planes for a thrill."

She cocked a brow at him and slowly nodded her head. To Sloan's annoyance she and James shared an understanding glance. "Okay, I get it," she said. "You feel skydiving is a crazy thing to do."

"Guilty," he drawled, watching the determination narrow her eyes. He could almost read her thoughts, she had such an expressive face. She appeared undaunted, as if his opinion didn't bother her in the least.

"My brother likes to keep his boots firmly on the ground," James said with a laugh.

"Well, maybe by the end of my stay I can convince him otherwise," she said slowly, eyes sparkling.

For a moment as he looked into her eyes Sloan experienced a heady feeling, but he stood his ground. "You can try," he said laconically. "It might be fun."

"Yeah, good luck!" James said. "Sloan, can you drive Jacie in to get settled? I need to finish things up here."

Sloan bit back his impatience. "Sure." Work would have to wait a little longer. "My truck's over there by the gravel road." He turned and reached to pick up her parachute. As he straightened a hand clamped on his shoulder. Jacie's brother stood behind him.

"Do you mind if I talk to my sister before you leave?" Con asked.

Sloan threw Jacie a glance. "I'll be waiting in the truck."

Ω

Jacie gritted her teeth as Sloan and James walked away and left her with her brother. She knew Con meant well, but his attitude was beginning to get a bit smothering. When his unblinking stare got unnerving, she said, "What?"

"What was that landing about?"

She didn't pretend to misunderstand. "What's the big deal? So I altered the landing a bit."

"That guy could have been hurt."

"He wasn't. Anyway, how did I know he'd suddenly play hero and step in front of me?"

Con sighed, and ran a hand through his short cropped hair. "He thought you were in trouble. Were you?"

She opened her eyes wide. "No. I knew what I was doing. Are you having doubts now?" she demanded.

Con drew a deep breath. "If I did you wouldn't be here. I know you can do this, Jacie. I think it's more a matter of you convincing yourself. I just don't want you to get hurt along the way."

She stepped close and looked up into his face. "Listen, Con. We both know I made a mistake thirteen months ago. How long before you forget about that mess? I don't intend to be in that situation again, okay? Enough said." She crossed her arms over her chest.

Con put his arm around her shoulder. "Promise me you won't take chances," he said in a low voice.

"Con. You know me. Let it go."

"That's what I'm worried about." He dropped a kiss on her forehead. "Sorry."

Her irritability fled. "I'm here to do a job and I'll do it."

Con directed a worried glance back toward where Sloan waited by the truck. "I saw the sparks flying between you two."

She chewed her lip thoughtfully, knowing exactly what he'd seen. She still felt off balance by her reaction to Sloan. "It doesn't mean anything," she assured him, then sighed at the concern in his eyes. "I know you like to worry about me but I'm a big girl. Time for you to leave," she added fiercely. "I have to go."

"I'll see you in a month," he said. "Call me and I'll pick you up."

"It's all taken care of. Bonnie said she'd pick me up. She's even going to come and stay for a few days."

Con grimaced. He and her friend Bonnie had never quite hit it off. She stood on tiptoe and gave him a quick peck on the cheek. "Thanks for taking care of the interview. Have fun in Rio," she said, then turned and walked to the truck.

It was time her brother realized she could take care of herself. Making a fool of herself over Brad was a lesson well learned and she didn't intend to repeat. Being around Sloan for a month might give her a different perspective. But it would all be in fun, nothing serious.

∞ Chapter Two ∞

JACIE OPENED THE TRUCK door and scrambled onto the truck seat, sending Sloan a quick glance of apology. "Just finishing some business," she said lightly, pulling the door closed. "Sorry to have kept you waiting."

"It's okay. I had a few calls to make. Your parachute is in the back," he said, starting the motor.

"Thanks."

As they pulled away she waved to her brother and then turned her attention to Sloan. He looked relaxed in the driver's seat, one arm on the wheel, the other resting on the window. He was a darned attractive guy, but then she reminded herself looks sometimes went no deeper than the surface.

She stared out the window at the heavy growth of evergreens lining the road. "Everything up here seems so vibrant and lush in color. The Catskills are certainly a delight to the senses."

"I agree with you. There's no place like it." With barely a pause, he added, "I noticed you're limping."

She knew she had to deal with this now. "I have been for about a year." When he looked straight ahead, she realized she might have been too terse. "Sorry, I'm touchy about my leg. Suffice it to say it's an old injury and won't hamper my performance here."

"Sorry," he said crisply, sounding anything but. "I wasn't prying. I want to make sure we all understand what's expected here."

"My brother is very protective of our company reputation. He wouldn't have sent me on this job if I wasn't up for it," she said abruptly. "I'd never let the family business take a hit."

"James is satisfied with your credentials."

"The way you say that it's like you have doubts."

"You come right to the point," he said. "I admit this kind of stuff isn't my area, so let's just leave it at that."

When the vehicle slowed for a turn, she tipped her head back to stare at the rough-hewn sign overhead. "How did you come up with the name Timber Falls?"

"Logical choice. Timber used to be big business around here."

"And the falls?" she asked.

"We've got them," he said shortly, taking a turn into a large parking lot. A long gray-stained cabin sat on one side of the lot with a sign that read "Office."

"This is the main office," he said, slowing the truck. "There's a bar and restaurant with a small dance floor and there's rooms on the second floor." He drove through the parking area. "I'll bring you as close to your cabin as I can. We had quite a bit of rain this week and the road's taken a pretty bad hit. I'll have the dozer out in the next few days to smooth out the ruts."

He stopped the truck and she opened her door and cautiously stretched her legs. With a slow and easy stride, he walked around the vehicle and held her door. "Your brother put your suitcases in the back."

"Where's my cabin?"

"Just ahead. I have to warn you it's pretty small and rustic. Probably not what you're used to."

"It sounds charming. I'm not hard to please you know." She offered him a small smile. "I'm comfortable in most surroundings." She didn't get a smile in return. Jacie shrugged philosophically. It didn't matter what he thought of her. She studied his profile and then let her glance drop to his hands as he reached for her cases. She frowned, telling herself it didn't matter that he wore no rings on those long tanned fingers.

He caught her watching him. The impact and intensity of those blue eyes made her rush into speech. "If you point the way to my cabin, I'll find it."

He set her cases on the ground and dug a hand into his jeans pocket and pulled out two keys on a chain. They dangled a moment and then he flipped them back in his palm. "I'd be happy to show you."

"I'm sure you've got a ton of work," she said firmly. "I've already kept you too long."

"I'm the boss. The work will wait." His unexpected grin caused a fluttering in her chest. "The best thing about being the boss is I don't have to answer to anyone."

She gathered the chute into her arms. "We all answer to someone," she said smartly.

His grin was slow. "I'm the exception."

Emotion knifed unexpectedly through her midsection. God! His air of command combined with that hint of humor was unexpected. She recalled how being close to him had felt; wonderful yet dangerous to her equilibrium.

An image of Brad came into her head and sanity reasserted itself. Don't go there, she warned herself. He might be saying all the right things, but when push comes to shove some men just let you down. She had the scars to prove it. She had loved Brad and he had dumped her like so much garbage. Jacie squared her shoulders. That little reminder was what she needed to stay focused.

"Okay, then, I'd appreciate you showing me the cabin and I'll be off your hands." Absently, she pushed back a tangle of hair, feeling the fine layer of grit along her hairline. If she had listened to her father she would be home. Mentally, she shook her head. No way. She had had enough of being looked after.

His glance dipped to her leg and back up. "Follow me."

Maybe he had seen the grimace of pain on her face and guessed she was hurting. She needed privacy to deal with her pain. It wasn't open to public scrutiny. Her leg only bothered her when she was really tired. She had been up before dawn this morning thinking of what she had committed herself to. Was she insane taking on this job, ground and skydiving lessons? Before the accident, such a job wouldn't have daunted her, now she lived with a fear of failure. She had convinced Con she could do it, that she needed to do it. He was right on one score. She just had to prove it to herself.

Sloan was now waiting for her. With an unconcerned smile, she quickened her pace. "I'm right behind you and I won't land in a heap at your feet."

"I promise to pick you up if you do," he drawled.

She fluffed her hair back. "It's a deal." She entertained the notion of falling and letting herself be picked up by Sloan. *Tempting.*

They walked along a rutted path through dense evergreens. Someone had gone to the trouble of placing large wooden tubs with a profusion of bright colors along the narrow road.

She drew in a deep breath. "Mmm, I smell balsam. It's unexpectedly refreshing. I've been admiring the mountains rising all around me since I arrived. I already love the wild beauty of the Catskills."

"You're beautiful so you'll fit right in," he said.

"Well, thank you," she murmured, taken back, sidetracked by the unguarded expression on his face. It spoke of attraction. She gulped back a breath. Attraction. God! He felt it, too, then. She had been aware of it the first moment they had come body-to-body. She pressed her parachute more tightly against her chest as if the flimsy material could provide a barrier.

He grimaced. "That was pretty dumb blurting that out. No doubt I've made you uncomfortable."

Jacie laughed out loud. "Yup, that's my first thought when a good looking guy tells me I'm beautiful. Uncomfortable as hell. I'll let you in on a little secret. I'm the most laid-back person I know. Not much bothers me. Except lately, I find myself asking for help more than usual. It annoys me."

"Well, around here we're big on helping out. So if you need help, make sure you ask."

"We'll see." Her mother called it strong, but maybe there were times when you needed to lean on someone else. "With four brothers you grow up taking care of yourself," she said dryly. "Otherwise they take over your live."

"Well, just to remind you the whole idea of Timber Falls is relaxation. There's riding, swimming, hiking, whatever strikes your fancy when you're not giving skydiving lessons."

"I'll probably just hang out." She gave him a humorous grin. "You know, kind of balance things out." This place might offer her a chance to withdraw for a while, perhaps mend a little inner torment. "Who knows, maybe you'll be asking me for skydiving lessons."

He gave her a narrow-eyed glance. "Watch your footing, this next area is pretty rough."

He rattled her, quite simply. She placed her feet carefully, walking beside the ruts in the road.

"There's an activity schedule in your cabin. If any problems crop up let me know." She found his slight drawl attractive.

"Thanks." She steeled herself against that devastating smile. Surely she wouldn't keep reacting physically to everything he said, each gesture he made! Sloan reminded her of Con in a way. She loved her brother dearly, but he was the type of man who looked out for the women in his life. She did not need Sloan getting the idea in his head that she couldn't take care of herself.

Finally, the cabins were in sight. "Which cabin is mine?" she asked. The deep reddish brown cabins were small and arranged in a wide circle.

"The one on the end."

"I love it." The structure was set a bit apart from the others, almost hidden from view, but the setting was pleasing. With the cabin partially shaded by huge maple and oak trees and a row of red flowering bushes on one side, there was an aura of privacy.

"This place is everything your brochure promised. Everything I hoped it would be. I'm glad Bonnie talked me into taking this job."

"Bonnie is a friend, I take it?"

"Yes."

She had almost decided against the job. Since the accident she had been in a crippling apathy. Although she and Bonnie hadn't been friends that long, she'd proven to be a lifeline during her recuperation. She'd needed the buffer between her and her family.

"Have you been skydiving long?" Sloan asked.

"Eleven years or so."

He stared at her incredulously. "You must have started when you were a kid."

"Almost." She lifted her face to the sun. She couldn't talk about her job right now, not without getting into some maudlin history. "This is like its own little paradise—the isolation and raw wildness of the mountains," she murmured.

He looked at her and lifted a dark brow in amusement. "We're not really isolated. The closest town is only twenty miles away."

She smiled at him. "Having lived in a city most of my life, this is isolation. It'll suit me."

There was a skeptical curve to his mouth. She wondered if he thought she was trying to impress him. As he moved ahead she eyed his straight, broad back, the lean-hipped jeans, the curl of dark hair visible along his collar beneath the hat. She bit back a curse when the toe of her boot caught on a root. Catching herself, she gave him a quick look that dared him to say a word.

Apparently undaunted, he said quietly, "Are you okay? Maybe I could—"

"Would you like to rub my leg?" she asked deliberately, tilting one brow, a devil prodding her on.

His eyes darkened and she bit back the rest of the words, determined to curb her mischievous streak. "Sorry, my tongue gets ahead of me. It comes from growing up with only brothers."

"Should you be jumping out of planes?" he asked bluntly. "I keep coming back to that."

"The leg only bothers me when I'm tired," she said lightly, pushing sweaty wisps of hair from her eyes. "The brace is for added support."

She envied him his apparent ease with his surroundings. His stance was natural, effortless, while she knew she was almost at the end of her energy reserve. For a moment, she felt overcome by sheer hopelessness, not a feeling she welcomed. He fit here, with the mountains and the wide-open spaces. She used to belong in the family business but now she felt odd-man out. Since the accident it was as if she didn't belong anywhere, and she couldn't blame it all on Brad. The accident had been partly her fault, but it was too late to fix what was already done. She just wished she could figure out where she fit in.

She stared at the cabin as they drew closer. "It's beautiful," she said.

Ω

Sloan couldn't drag his gaze away from Jacie. He wasn't happy about the creep of sexual awareness that moved along his neck. He wasn't looking for a complication, at least that's what he told himself as he watched the smile transform her face. When she wasn't trying to be flippant, he sensed vulnerability. He reminded himself he didn't need to know anything about her, except that she could do the job she'd been hired to do.

"I'm glad you like the cabin." He wondered what else might please her.

He had annoyed her with his offer of help but it wasn't in him to be idle if there was a problem. He could see she was hurting, even though she acted offhand about it.

Despite the dust, the tendrils of hair curling around her forehead and the faint shadows beneath her eyes, she was a knockout. He had always considered guests off limits and he ruthlessly suppressed the urge to change that rule now. His knee-jerk reaction to her bothered him. He had the strangest desire to stay and find out all about her. He reminded himself there were chores to do. God and everybody knew they wouldn't get done until he saw to them. The ranch might be a resort for guests, but it was a working environment for him.

He knew this attraction could be a dangerous thing.

"Have you always lived here, Sloan?"

"Most of my life. I decided being in the mountains was my calling. Having lived a time in the city I wasn't impressed."

"I love the city. There's always something new."

He smiled. "I know, lots of thrills and excitement. I can't imagine you settling for a place like this."

"But I love it," she protested.

His fiancé Ilene had thought she could live here, but in the end the city had drawn her back.

Looking at her flashy scarlet jumpsuit, he'd give her two weeks tops before she was bored. He pushed the front door open and stepped back to allow her access to the cabin.

"What a perfect romantic getaway," she breathed. "Pure country, yet modern."

As her expression softened, his mouth went dry and his gut tightened. "I'm kind of curious why you picked August to come here," he said abruptly.

She gave him a quizzical look. "Why not?"

"Are you aware August is honeymooner's month?"

The surprise on her face gave him the answer he sought. "I guess you didn't know."

She put her hands on her hips and caught her lower lip between her teeth. "I can see you're dead serious." She gave a small, tired laugh. "How ironic, honeymooner's month."

"Why ironic?"

She waved her hand. "It's a long story."

Obviously, one she wasn't going to share. She spun

on her heel. "Did I mention that a friend may come for a few days?"

"That's no problem." He wondered if it was a male friend, then dismissed the thought. It was none of his business who she invited. Someone with her looks would have more than one guy hanging around.

He watched her run her fingertips over a wooden end table as if she enjoyed the feel of the smooth wood. He shifted his feet uncomfortably. "The kitchenette's in there." He indicated the small galley behind her as she placed her suitcases beside the sofa. "You'll find silverware and plates and anything else you might need, but meals are provided at the lodge."

She moved through the cabin, admiring as she went. "Don't mind me. I like discovering everything around me through touch." She stood on her tiptoes to look at the native bluestone mantle over the fireplace. "What beautiful stone work." She spun around. "I love those big windows along the wall. I bet this place is bright with sun early in the day."

"Those windows face west, so you do get the late sun."

Jacie walked over the mellowed oak floors covered by braided throw rugs. "The indigo blue rugs with a touch of pink are great, and the furniture goes so well with the rustic setting," she remarked. "Someone decorated this with a lot of thought."

"My sister-in-law Dotty. She used to be an interior designer. Glad you like it." He cranked open a casement window in the kitchen. "Maybe you'll want some air in here. It's kind of warm." She seemed oblivious to his presence as she stood by the picture window that overlooked the ravine below.

He wondered what she thought of the view. It was nearing sunset and the sky had lost its light, giving the mountains an eerie orange glow. He had seen the same light countless times but he never tired of looking at it. "This is the only cabin this close to the ravine," he told her.

She peered downward. "How strange," she said slowly. "It looks almost like a smoky mist creeping up the cliff. What are those strangely twisted trees clinging to the ledges?"

"Some scrubby pine. They're twisted because the wind blows through here like a fiend in the winter. Do you think the drop of the ravine will bother you?"

"No," she said quickly. "It'll be fine."

He wondered about the nervous blinking of her lids. "We figured since you skydive, it wouldn't bother you."

"Logical conclusion," she murmured. "I find it mesmerizing. It's like you look out into the fog and expect to see something take shape."

"If you decide being this close to the ravine bothers you, we have another cabin set further back." He watched her continued preoccupation with the view.

"I imagine some people like it . . . the height, the sense of danger."

"There's no danger if you use common sense. I've seen these mountains most of my life, but it can be frightening for some." He shrugged.

"I imagine the first settlers found them a challenge." She directed a bright-eyed glance his way. "I love a challenge."

He detected a trace of defiance. "I knew someone else who thrived on challenge," he murmured. "She died." He regretted the words the second he said them.

"I'm sorry."

"It was a long time ago."

"What type of challenges?" she asked with a gleam of interest.

He stifled a curse. When had he developed a loose tongue? "Everything and anything," he said abruptly. "I guess I'd better show you the rest and get back to work." Sloan strode quickly through the remainder of the rooms. "There's a bathroom through here and a bedroom."

Jacie stared at Sloan in surprise. He had seemed to be getting friendly and then the wall slammed down like a shutter over his face. Right after he talked about his friend dying. "This cabin is wonderful. I'll be fine."

He removed his hat and ran a hand through his hair. She noted the sun-bleached strands that fell carelessly from a middle part before he dropped the hat back in place.

Nervously, her fingers clenched the high back of the sofa. She had the idea he was trying to figure her out. He'd never guess how messed up she was. If he did, he'd be smart to run like crazy.

"There's a Jacuzzi on the deck." He nodded toward the atrium door on the back wall of the cabin. She acknowledged his words with a jerky nod.

"Thanks." She held her hand out for the keys.

He stepped forward, dwarfing her as he dropped the keys in her palm. Reflexively, her fingers closed over the metal warmed by his fingers.

"There's a listing of numbers by the phone. Dinner is over in the lodge. James has arranged for you to meet the guests tomorrow, although you might run into some of them tonight." He flicked back his cuff. "That's about twenty minutes. The lodge is the building I showed you earlier."

"I remember."

"See you at dinner, Jacie." His voice was low, impersonal. Glancing over her shoulder, she nervously swept back her hair and nodded. Finally, the door closed and she was alone. She had to wonder why Sloan disturbed her so but at the moment there were no ready answers.

She bent over to pick up her suitcase but suddenly realized she heard the murmur of voices so she crossed the room to look out a front window. With surprise, she saw her friend Bonnie must have just arrived and was standing outside talking with Sloan.

She opened the door. Bonnie, tall at six feet, was looking up into Sloan's face as they spoke. Bonnie's half smile made her wonder what they were talking about. Her light blond hair appeared a startling contrast to Sloan's darkness in the failing light.

"Bonnie!" she said. "This is a surprise."

They both turned to her.

Bonnie smiled with delight. "Jacie, hello. I know it's a surprise." Bonnie touched Sloan's shirtsleeve, her blood rail nails against the blue fabric. "Thank you so much for your help."

"No problem." He tipped his hat, stepped off the porch and left without a backward glance.

Bonnie walked up the steps, her black skirt and blouse looking a bit rumpled. "Jacie, good to see you." She gave her a hug and then pulled back. Bonnie's favorite fragrance enveloped Jacie. "I know you're going to think I'm crazy, but I had a rental to deliver in this area so I decided to stop and see how you were doing."

Jacie looked out toward the road. "Where did you park your car?"

Bonnie waved her manicured hand vaguely. "A parking lot back there. I had to walk in. Sloan just told me the road would be fixed next time I came. He seems very nice," she added. "Is he single?"

Jacie looked at the gleam of interest in her friend's eyes. "I guess so. Are you interested? What happened to Jim?"

"That was last week. You know how I like variety—and I like the look of Sloan. Why? Isn't he nice to you?"

"He's my employer. He took one look at my leg brace and I could see the questions in his eyes."

Bonnie gave her a direct look. "I'm sure you set him straight on your capabilities."

Jacie shrugged. "It's a matter of he'll see I can handle the job once I begin. Anyway, I'm glad to see you. Come inside."

They stepped into the cabin and she closed the door, anxious to get Bonnie's reaction. "Well, what do you think?"

Bonnie sat on the couch and reached down to rub one of her ankles. She gave her a rueful glance. "My heels didn't do too well walking up that road." She looked around. "This looks comfortable, if a little rustic."

Jacie laughed. "I know it's not your style, but I like it."

"As long as you like it." She surveyed the living area. "You have a kitchen, living room, bedroom and a bath, I presume. There's no outside outhouse?" she drawled.

"Very funny. Are you driving back tonight? It'll be dark soon."

"Yes, I have appointments in the morning."

"Who rode with you?"

"My new secretary is with me. Her name is Emily. She took one look at all the woods and opted to stay in the car."

"This must have been more than a little out of your way. I didn't know you brought rentals this far north."

Bonnie smiled, her red tinted lips curving just the slightest. "For the right money, Jacie, I'd drive to Alaska. Anyway, when I come to pick you up I'll know exactly where to go. How did the jump go?"

"I did it, let me put it that way."

"Nerves?" Bonnie asked sympathetically.

"Yes, but I didn't let Con know."

Bonnie looked at her thoughtfully as she swept the luxurious fall of hair away from her forehead. "I'm surprised your brother let you take on the job."

"He knows I was going stir crazy." She looked toward the kitchen area. "I think there's coffee in there. Would you like a cup?"

"Not unless it's Espresso." Bonnie frowned and stared at her long red nails. Then she gave a big sigh and said, "There's another reason I wanted to see you. Brad called me!" she blurted.

Jacie was pulled into the past, seeing Brad's wide smile, the dimple in his cheek. She gripped the back of the sofa. "You didn't tell him anything, did you? I don't need him waltzing back in my life when I'm finally getting things on track." She needed to put thoughts of him behind her. She had to, damn him.

"Of course not."

Jacie relaxed. "Good."

"Maybe if you talked to him, you could get this resolved," Bonnie said carefully.

Jacie looked at her incredulously, her nerve endings jumping. "You know he abandoned me in South America when I got hurt. I don't want anything to do with him."

Bonnie glanced at her expensive gold watch. "I understand exactly how you feel, but I just had to let you know what's going on." She came to her feet and brushed her black pencil skirt carefully over her slim legs. "I had better leave, it's getting late."

"You can stay the night."

Bonnie gave her a brief hug. "Thanks, but I always sleep better in my own bed. I'll call in a few days to check in."

"Let me walk you back to the car," she offered.

"I can find it. You look bushed. Get some rest." Bonnie wriggled her fingers, her gold rings glinting.

When the door closed whatever sheer force of will had sustained Jacie suddenly left. She walked to the couch and sat down quickly. She didn't rise even to reach for the pain pills in her suitcase.

She waited for the ache in her thigh and knee to ease. She tried to block the memories, but talking about Brad, however briefly, had brought the memories to the forefront. Scenes rolled through her mind like a video. Each detail of the accident had been burned into her brain. How had she missed the faulty shroud lines on her parachute that day? She had been so focused on Brad and her career that she had taken a stupid risk. It was a bitter truth.

Brad. She had been so optimistic about a future with him. It still hurt that he had thrown away her away so easily. In the end at the bottom of a cliff, all her dreams had come to nothing. She just needed to forget him.

Jacie saw again her helpless body, the bright splash of blood. The waiting had been endless as she dangled above the ground. Only her parachute lines tangled in the tree limbs had kept her from plunging to certain death.

She still found it savagely ironic that the faulty chute lines that had caused her parachuting accident, had ultimately saved her life.

∞ Chapter Three ∞

JACIE PULLED FUTILELY ON the shroud lines of her chute, closing her eyes as the trees rushed up to meet her and branches snapped against her face.

She bolted upright, her heart pounding. A cold sheen of sweat lined her forehead. Disoriented, she heard a door close. In the first hazy moments she wondered why the hospital was so quiet. Memory reasserted itself as her stomach growled a gnawing protest. She was not in the hospital for rehabilitation. She had fallen asleep on the couch in her cozy cabin at Timber Falls. She was here for a month to give skydiving lessons and relax.

Was she a fool to think she could do this? Would the past ever turn her loose? She wished Bonnie hadn't shown up and told her about Brad. Hearing he wanted to get in touch with her left her terribly unsettled. She wasn't still in love with him, was she? She had to be over him by now.

Looking at her watch, she groaned. "I missed dinner." She was starving.

A small lamp beside the couch lit the area, yet she didn't recall turning the lamp on earlier. Had someone come in while she slept? That thought disturbed her but as she looked around she found the cabin quiet and empty.

She tugged the Velcro loose on the brace and pulled it off, then cautiously stretched. She felt almost as good as new, but she needed a shower.

After her shower, Jacie admired the blue and cream Log Cabin bed quilt on her bed, the homespun touches throughout the bedroom. Unwinding her bath towel, she rubbed it over her still damp hair and then realized her suitcase was in the outer room.

Dropping the towel, she fastened her hair into a knot and walked back into the living room. She rubbed her arms as a chill touched her bare skin.

She lifted the suitcase onto the couch and froze at the knock on the door. Throwing a quick glance behind her she was relieved to see the lacy curtain was drawn.

Jerkily, she sifted through her clothes. Her hand bumped her bottle of allergy medicine, sending it flying onto the floor, hitting her in the ankle.

"Ouch! Darn." Grabbing the first thing that came to hand, she shoved her arms into the sleeves and belted the short robe around her waist.

She moved closer to the door, fingers nervously pleating the thin material of her robe. It was dark outside and she couldn't see a thing.

"Who is it?" she called.

"Sloan," came the terse reply.

"Damn, damn, damn," she muttered, looking around. She shrugged resignedly. "Oh, what the heck."

Leaning forward, she turned the knob and stepped back. "Come on in, the door's unlatched." She moved back toward the couch.

The door swung inward, admitting Sloan. In his hands he carried a tray with covered dishes. He pushed the door closed with the heel of his boot and walked past her, throwing her a quick glance as he placed the tray on the small kitchen table.

Bemused, she came up behind him and peered around him at the tray. For a moment the tang of horses and outdoors held her close to him. His scent, mingled with the food, made her mouth water. She stepped back quickly when he straightened.

"What's this?" she asked hastily and then laughed. "I mean—I just didn't expect it."

"Policy, ma'am, we don't let our guests go hungry." There was the slightest of grins molding his lips.

She couldn't resist looking under the largest cover. "Mmm, London Broil." Her stomach emitted an annoyingly loud growl. He pulled out a chair and invited her to sit. Self-consciously, she touched the lapel of her robe. "I—I really should get changed, that is, I just got out of the shower."

"Don't change on my account, I'm leaving." Indeed, he was backing toward the door, hat behind him in one hand.

On sudden impulse, she blurted, "Why don't you stay?" She bit her lip as his surprised glance shot up to her. No one was more surprised than her. The words had surely sprung from her lips all by themselves. She shrugged nonchalantly. "There's enough here for three people."

He looked at the plate and then at her. "That depends on your appetite," he said as he continued to study her. She knew what he saw. Her hair, tied in a careless knot, threatened at any moment to free itself, and her feet were bare. She rubbed her neck.

"I don't blame you. I don't have any makeup on."

"Thank you, ma'am, but actually I've already eaten and I have a couple horses to see to." He hesitated beside the door.

"Please call me Jacie. You did earlier." She sat, her shaking fingers playing with the napkin. "I do appreciate this. I didn't expect it, you know."

He pulled the door open. "Like I said, we don't like our guests missing meals." His lips curved upward and his voice dropped provocatively. "As it is, you look like a strong wind could blow you away."

She forced a mocking smile to her lips. "I'm stronger than I look."

"Good night, Jacie." He pulled the door closed and she stared after him, an unfamiliar yearning tightening the muscles of her throat. He had such a darned sexy voice. It made her want to get to know him. Maybe she could forget about her rotten luck with men. Maybe she needed an affair. A smile curved her lips as she mulled over that thought.

Jacie satisfied her immediate appetite with the delicious dinner. Re-covering the now nearly empty plates, she stood and crossed the room. On impulse, she pulled the front door open. The porch decking felt rough and warm against her bare feet and a slight breeze lifted the hem of her dressing gown.

She leaned against the waist-high porch rail, loving the warm draft of air that swept past her. Her door slammed closed.

"Great. Now all I need is to be nearly naked and locked out," she muttered. To her relief, the doorknob turned easily in her hand, yet she froze. Sucking in her breath, she saw exactly what Sloan must have seen earlier as he stood at her door. The lace curtains were insubstantial, a mere decoration. Anyone standing outside the door with the lights on inside could see directly into the living room.

Where she had stood stark naked.

"You look like a strong wind could blow you away."

She groaned, but then had to laugh. Hopefully Sloan wasn't under the impression it was on purpose. Trust her to make a great impression.

Early the next morning Jacie slid from her horse's back and looked up at the waterfall in wonder. Almost hidden in the woods, it fell about a hundred feet, splashing onto ragged bluestone with a small pool at its base. One of the ranch's employees, Michelle, had taken a group of them out on a horseback ride to show them the riding trails their first morning at Timber Falls.

Three of them had elected to come, she and vacationers Leo and his wife, MaryAnn, whom she met at breakfast. They occupied the cabin closest to hers. The other couple, John and Emma, had decided to stay beside the pool.

"He'll ground tie," Michelle called to Jacie now, pointing to her horse. "Just drop the reins."

She allowed the reins of her mount to trail to the ground, then knelt and dipped her hand into the cool water. With a delighted squeal, she cupped her hands and lifted them, letting the cool water run down her face and neck.

"Nice, huh?" Michelle queried with a grin. She had dismounted and now stood beside Jacie. "Boy, is it hot." Michelle pushed her wide-brimmed hat off her head. Sweat dampened her curly, dark hair.

"Any possibility I could stay here awhile?" Jacie asked. "I can't believe this is out in the middle of nowhere."

Michelle's dark eyes shifted a moment to where Jacie's hand rested on her outstretched leg. She nodded. "Sure, I guess so. We'll be back around this way after a bit. Once everyone's familiar with the layout of the ranch, you can arrange your own rides."

"I'd love that."

Michelle grabbed a handful of water and splashed it on her own face. With water running down her neck and dampening her T-shirt, she grinned at her. "Great idea. That feels much better."

"Is it okay to take a dip?" she asked Michelle.

The other girl gave her a wicked grin. "Sure. If I didn't have to work I'd join you." She bent close to Jacie. "Be quick about it though. We'll be back in half an hour." Michelle remounted her horse and led the other riders up the hill.

Jacie sat at the edge of the pool and pulled her boots off. Tentatively, she dipped her hot feet in the water. The coldness was a shock and a bit of heaven. The sun was sweltering today.

When the sound of the horses died away, there remained only the cooing of mourning doves and the nonstop splash and gurgle of the water. A small creature scurried in the underbrush but remained out of sight. She had wakened earlier to the sound of dove's cooing outside her bedroom window. It had felt so incredible, lying in bed, listening to the unfamiliar sounds. No cars honking or people in the street below her apartment as they made their way to work.

She looked at the top of the falls, marveling at the continuous splash of water over the rock ledges. She could feel the cool spray filming her skin.

Her jeans and T-shirt stuck to her as she stared at the temptation of the water. She checked her watch. Twenty-five minutes left. Never one to hesitate, she shucked her jeans and T-shirt. In her underwear, she stepped into the water. It covered her ankles and then her knees as she stepped further along the firm mud bottom. She ducked down and sucked in her breath when the icy water covered the heated skin of her stomach.

She dog-paddled to the heart of the waterfall. Here, the water was deeper and over her breasts. She lifted her face, enjoying the gentle pummel of the water. It made her feel lighthearted. Her laughter bounced off the rocks and echoed back to her.

Jacie put her back to the falls and looked at her horse. He stood with his ears perked alertly forward, looking toward the hill. She didn't see anyone and at this point didn't care if they came back early. She lifted her hands and embraced the gentle flow of the water, letting it stream down her body. It felt glorious.

Without warning, something hard glanced off her upper arm and then plopped into the water. With a muffled squeal, she stumbled back, lost her footing on the mud bottom and the water closed over her head.

Surfacing, she felt something brush her right breast. Hard hands gripped her under the armpits and pulled her up. Panicked, she drew in a deep gulp of air mixed with water, trying to find the bottom with her toes. Coughing, she stared in amazement at Sloan. Fully clothed, he stood in front of her, his hands holding her under the armpits.

"What are you doing?" she demanded when she could talk.

"Are you all right?" His features looked strained, his mouth compressed to a white line. He lowered her until her feet touched bottom and released her as she gained her balance. "I saw you go down. I thought you couldn't get up."

"I'm okay, although I'm not sure what happened." She rubbed her eyes to clear the water away. She coughed again, conscious of a prickling sensation on her arm. Lifting her arm to look at it she was surprised to see a swelling on the skin up near her shoulder. "It's cut."

Sloan stared at the area that had begun to purple around a jagged cut. "That looks like a fresh cut. Come on out and let me check it." He grabbed her hand and pulled her forcefully toward the rim of the pool.

"Wait a second," she protested, "Something hit me."

He looked at her. "Something hit you?" He looked up toward the top of the falls. "I suppose a rock could have worked its way loose," he said shortly, stepping out of the pool. He turned back to her and tugged her up the bank. She noticed then his horse stood close beside her own.

"I didn't see you come."

"I didn't know anyone was in the water until I saw the splash as you went under."

She stared back at him, bemused as water gushed from his clothes. "You're not exactly dressed for a swim," she said, unable to contain a burst of laughter, then she quickly sobered. "Your clothes and boots will get ruined."

He scowled. Standing on one foot he removed a boot, upended it so the water could flow out and did the same for the other. "They've been through worse," he muttered, sitting down on a large rock. He pulled the boots back on then stood and stomped his heels down. "What happened?"

She quickly grabbed her T-shirt and pulled it over her head, aware that her underwear clung to her as if she were naked. "I didn't hear anything. I was under the waterfall."

Sloan looked to the top of the falls. "You wouldn't hear anything with all the noise the water makes. It's kind of puzzling considering the creeks are low. I can't imagine how a rock worked its way to the edge."

She pushed her head through the shirt. "One minute I'm enjoying the water and the next thing I know something hits me." The bruising had now turned a deeper purple.

"Come to the lodge and get something on that. Part of it's raw. Does it hurt?" Moving closer, he gently pressed around the cut. "It looks pretty clean."

She pulled her arm away, disturbed by his touch. "It's only a scratch. It'll be fine."

"Scratches can get infected. It should be cleaned with peroxide and ice put on the swelling."

She dropped to a flat rock. "Thanks for pulling me out," she said, working her pants up over her wet legs. "It was a bit scary not being able to get my footing. How did you happen to be here?"

He gave her a quick head-to-toe appraisal. She wondered if he was reassuring himself she didn't have other injuries or was he just checking her out in her underwear? She discarded the latter notion. Sloan wasn't the type of guy to sneak a peek.

"I met up with Michelle and the others," he said. "She mentioned you were here so I rode back this way."

She felt the deep-voiced drawl sink to her bones. She noticed now he was dressed in a black T-shirt under an equally dark denim shirt. As she watched he pulled the tails of his shirt from his pants, unbuttoned the shirt and pulled it off. The T-shirt underneath pulled up, exposing the tanned expanse of a flat stomach before he pulled it back down. The wet material molded to each muscle and contour. Her mouth went dry, thinking he'd make a great entry in a wet T-shirt contest.

"What do you need from me?" She cleared her throat and resisted the urge to cross her arms self-consciously over her breasts where her bra had soaked through. "Why did you want to see me anyway?" she asked crisply.

"James needs your skydiving schedule. He wanted me to remind you."

Feeling she needed to get her thoughts and eyes off this man, she stretched along the rock and pulled her socks and boots toward her. "I have it at the cabin. I forgot to drop it at the office this morning."

"It's lucky I came along," he said. "You could really have been hurt."

"I appreciate the help, but I was getting my footing when you pulled me up. I hope you're not mad at Michelle. I asked her to let me stay here."

She sensed those light eyes missed nothing as they swept over her once again. She flicked him an unconcerned glance, telling herself she could handle his scrutiny. "Michelle gave us the general tour."

"It's standard procedure," he acknowledged. "After tomorrow, you're on your own, if that's the way you like it. If not, we can accommodate you."

Her breath came quickly. She wondered why she took everything he said so personally. Accommodate. That word alone she didn't want to think about in relation to this man.

Jerkily, she stood, shaking her legs, trying to get her pant legs straightened out where they clung to her wet skin. "I don't mind being on my own." She ignored the fact that her underpants would soak through her jeans as her bra had her T-shirt. The man never looked away, never batted an eyelash. She had four brothers, for heaven's sakes, surely one man couldn't rile her! But she knew he did. Whatever this attraction between them he had the power to make her nervous.

"Your friend Bonnie left already?" he asked conversationally.

"Yes." Was he interested in Bonnie? Somehow, that didn't set right with her. Dropping back to the rock, she dipped her head to comb her fingers through her hair.

"I'll be darned," he said, as if making a discovery.

She squinted up at him and then put up a hand to shade her eyes. The sun behind him made a curious halo around his head and shoulders. As if realizing this he moved slightly until his shoulders blocked the sun.

"All that hair, I wondered if it was real."

She saw his smile; cynical, gently taunting. Caught off guard, her toes curled. The feeling lasted but a moment. Genuine amusement came to the forefront. She threw him a mocking grin as she fluffed her fingers through the already drying strands.

"What were you expecting, hair pieces?" Quickly, she plaited her hair. "It's as real as can be."

She heard the creak of leather and half turned toward him. He fastened his denim shirt to his saddle with a latigo strip and turned back to her. A frisson of awareness licked at her nerve endings as he stepped closer.

"It's an unusual color." His voice was low and deliberate, bringing goose bumps to her skin. Several strands of her hair were dark against his fingers as he reached out to touch it. Seeing her hair twined around his fingers increased that shivery sensation at the back of her head, as if that curl were an electrical conductor.

"The color's pretty common in my family." Slowly, she allowed her glance to move up to his face. He had bedroom eyes. Did they still use that description, she wondered breathlessly?

"I'd venture a guess there's nothing common about you, Jacie."

He was so close she could barely breathe. She didn't want to breathe. She found she wanted him closer. Sloan bent his head toward her. His mouth touched hers and it was everything Jacie wanted and thought it would be, a swirl of heat centering right inside her stomach. She traced his mouth with her tongue, closing her eyes as the erotic sensation of fully alive nerve endings responded quickly to his touch, even while their bodies remained apart.

Sloan pulled back slowly. He frowned. "We'd better get you back."

Breathing evenly, telling herself his dark presence didn't alarm the hell out of her, Jacie moved back. She squatted to lace her boots. Carefully, she said, "Despite what you might think, I don't usually kiss strangers."

"We're not strangers anymore." He gave her a half smile. "You're right though. I don't either."

She didn't mention how good he was at it.

"So are you rounding up cattle or horses today?" she said, pulling her laces tight.

He turned his head and scanned the immediate vicinity. "Yeah, we've lost a few calves. The cattle are pretty jumpy. I figure a big cat or bear must have passed through last night and the calves got separated from the rest of the herd."

"Do you think they're in danger?"

"There's always the danger they could get up in the ledges and fall. Then again, if the cows catch a bear or cat's scent they might stampede. James spotted a good size sow yesterday foraging around."

She raised a brow. Fascinated, she watched that dimple appear in his cheek.

"A female bear," he clarified.

Her lips curved. "Of course. How do you know where to look for a little calf?"

"There are tell-tale signs. Around here, you can track just about anything, if you set your mind to it."

"Does that include humans?"

A dark brow lifted in amusement. "In most cases, yes. I figure he went toward the south pasture." He pointed toward the ridge where the other riders had gone, then reached his hand out. She let him tug her upright.

She heard the sound of approaching horses and turned to see riders were making their way down the hillside.

Tossing her hair over her shoulder, she moved toward her horse, pulling herself into the saddle from the right side.

"Wrong side." He kept his voice low. Coming up behind her he guided her boot into the stirrup.

"Easier on the leg," she said airily.

"You're pretty sure of yourself, aren't you?" He stared up at her.

"Does that bother you?" She found herself very interested in the answer.

He pushed his hat back on his head. "It doesn't hurt to be self-confident."

"But?"

He stared at her hard. "As long as it doesn't cross the line into foolishness."

"Hi, Boss," Michelle called as they reached the bottom of the hill. A wide grin split her face. "We were just coming back for Jacie."

"Jacie was smart, she cooled off," he drawled with a glint in his eye.

"Looks like you did, too," Michelle said meaningfully, running an eye over him. "Never known you to go swimming in your clothes, Boss."

Abruptly, he moved away from her and grabbed his horse's reins. "Sometimes circumstances warrant it. Jacie had a bit of trouble. A piece of ledge worked its way loose and hit her."

"It's nothing," Jacie said hurriedly as the others began to express concern. "It's just a scratch."

"We'd better get you back to First Aid and put something on that arm," Michelle said.

"I'm ready." She looked back at Sloan. "Thanks for the help. I'll be fine."

"See to your arm," he reminded her curtly, climbing

back on his horse. As she watched him ride over the hill in the opposite direction Jacie wondered if he thought she was a nuisance. That thought bothered her.

About an hour later Sloan walked into the ranch office in search of his brother.

James leaned back in the desk chair and ran an amused eye over him. "What the hell happened to you? As far as I know it hasn't rained today."

Carefully, Sloan removed his hat and pushed both hands through his still slightly damp hair. "It hasn't," he said sourly.

"Is something bothering you?"

"No—yeah. It's Jacie."

James smiled. "You've got to admit this is a great publicity slogan, 'People will try anything to get to Timber Falls.'"

"The jury's still out on that one," he muttered.

"So what about Jacie?"

Sloan carefully moved a crystal paperweight around on the desktop. Abandoning that, he stood and shoved his hands into damp pockets.

Mildly, James said, "She seems like a nice girl. Look how accommodating she's been, doing that jump and the lessons in exchange for time here."

"I'm still waiting to see how the lessons will go over."

"Look at the list." James pushed a paper across the desktop toward him. "We've filled all the slots for the skydiving lessons. I even had to give my spot to someone. I've already gotten positive feedback from the first ground lesson she gave this morning."

"If this company is in such demand, why is she out here in the middle of what's probably their busiest season? She didn't even know it was Honeymooner's month."

"That was probably just an oversight. She's here to do

a job so why should it matter to her? Maybe she needs a vacation. Why don't you ask her?"

"Maybe I will."

James narrowed his eyes. "Is there something more personal going on? You look like you're pretty worked up."

In his mind's eye Sloan saw Jacie when he'd pulled her from the pool. He had thought she was hurt or worse. He didn't want to think about what could have happened if she'd been hit on the head.

"I'm not getting worked up," he said impatiently.

James laughed. "Okay, whatever. I'll look the other way if you want to date a guest." James gave him a grin. "Sorry, I couldn't help throwing that in there. You've got to admit Jacie's a far cry from the women you usually see. She's probably a shock to your system."

"What does that mean?"

"Come on, you stick to the stay-home types, not that there's anything wrong with that, but Jacie seems like a woman who can put excitement in a man's life. She's out there. She's like a fresh breeze."

Sloan released an exasperated breath. "Tornado—more likely. I wonder how Dotty would feel hearing you say that."

James smiled, unperturbed. "My wife knows me . . . and you're trying to change the subject."

"Jacie was swimming at the big waterfall."

"This is a ranch resort, people swim."

"A piece of ledge came loose and hit her. She's lucky it glanced off her arm. It could have been really bad if it hit her head," he said bluntly.

James looked alarmed. "Is she all right?"

Sloan sat down and rocked the front legs of his chair off the floor. "Yes. I was out looking for those strays. When I rode by the waterfall she was in the water and had gone under. I pulled her out. She's got a scratch and some swelling on her arm. Michelle took her over to First Aid to have it looked at. As I said, she was lucky."

"So that's why you're wet. We better have Donny check the top of the falls to make sure there's no more loose stone."

"Maybe we shouldn't let people swim there."

"Come on, Sloan, it's a freak thing. We swam there as kids. I don't ever remember anything like that happening. It's a beautiful falls, you won't be able to keep people away from there."

"Well, we may have a real problem on our hands. I checked the top of the falls after Jacie left. I might be crazy but it looked like stone had been pried loose."

"Are you saying someone deliberately tried to hurt her?"

"I don't know if it was against Jacie or just general mischief."

"Come on Sloan, for what purpose?"

"If I knew that I'd give you an answer. All I'm telling you is it looked like someone dug a stone out."

"Maybe I should talk to her," James said with concern. "Is she upset?"

Sloan snorted. "Hell, no. I don't think much rattles her." The kiss they'd shared hadn't rattled her. He recalled last night at her cabin and what he had inadvertently seen. Long, slim legs, a smooth line of buttock, tantalizing curves. She must know he had seen her though not on purpose. He wasn't a damned peeping tom. Determinedly, he shook the images from his head. "I've got a load of work to do, I can't be worrying about the guests." He didn't want to be sidetracked.

"If it makes you feel better, I'll keep an eye on her," James offered.

Sloan stood, his chair legs dropping sharply to the

floor. He slapped his sodden hat against his leg. "You've got enough with your own family and running this place," he said abruptly. "I'll keep an eye on her to make sure she stays out of mischief." He'd find the time. They couldn't afford to have anyone get hurt. "I just hope she's not an accident waiting to happen."

"Come on, Sloan. It's got to be a freak thing. I'll talk to her about being careful when she's off on her own. I don't want to scare her away."

"She's going to be bored here."

"You're not giving her a chance."

With a self-deprecating grimace, Sloan shrugged. "You're right. I have no clue what motivates her." And he wasn't going to find out. "It doesn't matter anyway. She'll be gone in a month."

He had a feeling it was going to be a long month.

∞ Chapter Four ∞

AFTER HER GROUND LESSONS the following morning, Jacie walked toward the stables, thinking of the phone call she had received earlier from Bonnie. It had filled her with concern and then annoyance. Bonnie called her each day. After the accident, they had spent a lot of time together, but she wished Bonnie would stop talking about the accident and Brad. Both were in the past but Bonnie seemed convinced that since she'd first introduced her to Brad, she was in some way responsible for Jacie getting hurt.

She had taken the job with Brad's company on her own initiative. It had been bad luck.

Walking around the white pole barn with its blue trimmed windows, she saw Sloan's truck with a horse trailer behind it in the driveway.

Renee, one of the ranch hands, a gangly blond teenager, was backing an incredibly tall horse down the trailer ramp. The horse was a gorgeous sable color, but for every two steps he'd cautiously take back, he'd take a small hop forward.

Jacie stopped in the middle of the narrow track, not wanting to startle the already nervous animal.

Renee had him almost backed down the ramp when the horse suddenly swung his hindquarters to the right and his back feet dropped off the ramp. The horse jerked his head with fright, pulling the lead line from Renee's hand. The animal wheeled around and ran toward a fence where other horses were and then he spun and ran down the narrow track toward Jacie.

Instinctively, she spread her arms wide. When he reached her he came to a sliding halt and reared. Jacie looked up at him in awe. When he came down she was close enough to grab the lead line. She held onto the line and spoke to him as she gently ran her hand along his shoulder.

"I'll take him," Sloan said, coming up behind her.

Jacie turned toward him and saw the grimness of his face. "He's okay," she said reassuringly.

"You could have been hurt!" he snapped, taking the lead line from her.

"I wasn't."

"Don't ever stand in the path of a frightened horse again." He turned and led the horse back toward the barn, but his fierce eyes and angry expression stayed with her.

Renee hurried over to her. "Thanks, Jacie. The boss is going to have my head on this one."

"It's not your fault the horse was frightened."

"I was supposed to wait for Sloan, but I decided to get the horse out on my own. The boss doesn't like anyone taking chances."

"Well, no one got hurt," she said reassuringly. "Surely that counts for something."

"I can hope. Now, can I help you with something?"

Renee asked.

"I wanted to go riding. Am I too late?"

"Nope. I can get a horse saddled."

"I saw a chestnut out in the corral yesterday when they were evaluating all of us as to riding skill. I think his name is Dandy. Do you think I'd be able to use him?"

Renee twirled the ends of her hair, a look of uncertainty crossing her face. "Gee, I'd have to check with the boss."

"If you'd rather, I can ask him."

Renee grimaced. "No, I might as well face the music now. I'll be right back."

About ten minutes later Renee reappeared with the chestnut horse she had requested. From what she had seen of this animal, he would be a challenging ride.

"The boss said you could use him."

"Oh, great! When I saw him the other day, he looked like he'd be fun to ride."

"He is. He's quick and smart but too much for a beginner." Renee tightened the saddle girth.

"So I guess you're still working here?" she asked the younger girl.

Renee nodded. "Yeah. Sloan read me the riot act. You can be sure next time I'll listen up."

Jacie rubbed the horse's soft muzzle and led him from the barn. "You sound like my type, Dandy, quick and smart."

"Jacie."

She looked up and found Sloan walking toward her, leading his horse behind him. "I apologize for snapping at you. I thought the horse was going to hurt you."

"As I said to Renee, it came out all right."

"Still, next time don't take chances. If you'd like some company, we could ride together," he said as he climbed into the saddle.

She felt a shivery vibration at the back of her neck and slowly nodded her head in agreement. "Sounds like a good idea. It'll be fun to have a guided tour." She certainly would like to learn more about him.

They rode to the steel gate fence that led the way to the open pasture. Sloan maneuvered his horse's hindquarters away from the gate, opened it for both of them, then closed and refastened it. His horse moved up against hers. "It's obvious you've been around horses some," he remarked conversationally. "You're a good rider from what I saw yesterday."

"Thanks," she said nonchalantly. Indicating her horse, she added, "This guy here looks pretty athletic."

"He's fast and sometimes unpredictable," he cautioned.

She lifted a brow. "That's the best part. I look for unpredictability in all my males."

He let out a laugh, as if she had caught him by surprise. Still smiling, he removed his hat and ran a hand through his hair. "You have an answer for everything, don't you?"

"I try. So tell me about this horse."

"We use him sometimes in gymkhana games. He's got stamina, and he can take some rough play."

Stamina, a word with its own connotations. "All the better," she said huskily. With an inward groan, she wished his words didn't have such an erotic effect on her body. She knew the moment his glance fell to her tight T-shirt with 'skydivers do it in the air' written prominently in red across the front. She was very conscious she hadn't worn a bra. She cursed the heat that moved into her cheeks. It was ridiculous. She had worn this shirt countless times without thinking about it.

He shoved his hat down on his head and looked up the trail. "Not everybody can ride him," he muttered, clearing his throat.

"I'm honored you're letting me ride him then," she said with surprise.

"You wouldn't be if I thought you couldn't handle him." He nudged his horse forward and then turned in the saddle to look back at her. "By the way, you haven't seen anyone around other than the other guests, have you?"

"No, why?"

"One of the stable hands, Donny, thought he spotted someone this morning hiking on the trails. It's not a problem, but if someone's on our land I like to have them sign in at the office. From time to time hikers have gotten lost. It creates a problem because then we have to go and find them."

"I haven't seen anyone around. If I do I'll let you know. Where are we going to ride? I have about two hours before my next ground lesson."

"Follow me," he invited as he urged his horse into a trot. "If you think you're up to it."

She pressed her heels into her horse's sides and felt his quick leap forward. "That sounds like a challenge. I'm always up for a new adventure." She caught up with him easily as she was sure he intended.

The glance he gave her was hard to read. "I figured as much," he said. "After seeing you stop that horse, I've come to the conclusion you like to leap in with both feet."

She shrugged, sensing a deeper meaning behind the question. "What have I got to lose? If you don't try new experiences, you get stuck in the same rut, afraid of change." She chewed the inside of her cheek. "Everybody needs change." No matter how scary, but she didn't add that. She gave him a sly glance instead. "Even you might need a change. Think of the new dimensions you could add to your life by learning how to skydive. I could be your personal trainer."

He kept his horse at a brisk trot, but she had no trouble hearing what he said. "I think James has given you the wrong impression. My refusal to skydive isn't because I'm afraid. I appreciate your offer, but I've no interest in it."

"James said you jump off horses. I don't think I'd want to do that."

"That's different. Sometimes it's necessary when you're rounding up cattle, you have to get off in a hurry. It makes no sense to me to jump out of a plane. There's no real purpose."

"I suppose I could take that personally and feel insulted," she came back, amused. "But I'll overlook that little comment since you're taking me on a ride. Tell me, does everything you do have to make sense?"

He gave her a surprised glance before turning his attention back to the trail. "Usually."

"Don't you ever act on impulse?" she asked incredulously.

"Nope."

Jacie thought of the kiss they'd shared yesterday. "Hmm, well then, let me make some sense out of this business for you. Experienced skydivers are sometimes utilized in rescue missions where no one else can get in. Personally, I've been on two such assignments. The first one was scary, I'll admit that right off." She flipped back her hair, keeping her glance trained ahead. "But if my brother and I hadn't gone, a little girl might have died." It had been a touch and go situation, one she hadn't been asked to repeat. But if called upon again, she knew she would do the same.

"I appreciate what you're saying, Jacie, and I know there are times when such a profession would be very important, but I'm afraid it isn't going to make a difference. Most of the people here are doing this just for recreation . . . something new and exciting in their lives." As he pulled his horse to a standstill, she saw the tensing of his jaw. "Can you tell me there isn't some threat of death, no matter how small, involved in each jump?"

"Of course there's always that possibility, but that threat can lie anywhere," she came back. "I could get off this horse, fall, and land on my head on that rock over there."

His look was tolerant. "You're beating a dead horse if you think you'll change my mind."

"Anything's possible," she said, undaunted. "Why don't you tell me why you're set against skydiving? My family has always made a pretty good living at it. I just moved into it naturally but I'm not going to say I don't like it."

"I have nothing against the business."

"Then why?" she persisted.

He threw her an exasperated glance and shook his head. "You don't let go, do you?"

She shook her head. "Never." Silence fell between them, the only sound the metal clink of the horse's shoes on the stone ledge and the sigh of the wind through the trees. Jacie waited.

"I once knew someone who'd take risks without thinking of the consequences. She needed almost continual change and her needs hurt the people who loved her the most."

"You said that yesterday." She swallowed hard, feeling a tightening in her chest. "Was she an ex-wife?"

"No." His face remained expressionless, yet she sensed a deep vibration of emotion emanating from him.

She drew in her breath and then plunged ahead. "And you got hurt," she said softly, knowing it was the truth.

She wasn't sure she really wanted to know. It was getting very personal, to say the least.

He looked over at her with a set jaw, dark brows pulled together. "I was too young to really know much about it. My family got hurt . . . my father."

Her mouth opened in wonder. "Y-your father?"

"It was my mother." He looked at the trail ahead of them, then his watch. "It's not skydiving in particular, she never attempted that . . . not that I know of, anyway. It's the whole idea of living life looking ahead to the next challenge, laughing at the idea of death."

"I've looked death in the face but I didn't laugh. Life would get pretty boring if there were no challenges."

"Maybe." Her answer clearly had not pleased him. "I guess it all depends on the challenges you want. Now, if you're ready, we've got a demanding ride ahead. We're going to have to bushwhack our way through part of the trail."

She tried to marshal her thoughts but she kept thinking of what he'd said about his mother. Judging by his expression, however, he wasn't answering any more questions. She fought the temptation to probe, knowing it was time to back off.

"That sounds interesting," she told him instead. "Lead on, Sloan, I'm ready."

Sloan wasn't ready to move on. He was mulling over what Jacie had revealed to him about rescue missions. It put a slightly different perspective on the way he saw her. He realized his thinking about her up until now had been abstract and perhaps distorted. He didn't usually make presumptions about people, but in this case he had. Was he allowing his experience with his mother to color his perception of Jacie? She saw no problem risking her life and jumping out of a plane. She didn't see it in the same way he did. Jumping from a height of several thousand feet was crazy, no matter how you sliced it.

He shook his head with wonder. Despite her somewhat cavalier attitude, he sensed there were deeper currents to her. He still couldn't believe he had brought up the topic of his mother. It wasn't something he had ever talked freely about. At least she'd had the sense not to ask him any more questions. He nudged his horse into a walk. Good. He didn't need strangers knowing about his life. He should keep his thoughts to himself in the future. She was too quick on the pickup. He'd be giving her his entire life story if he wasn't careful. She had a way of watching you with an intensity that made you want to spill your guts.

"You know these trails pretty well." Her voice floated over to him. They were only about ten feet apart, but because of the rock over their heads, her voice sounded slightly disembodied.

He twisted in the saddle. "James and I explored these hills as teenagers, but we don't ride here that often anymore, the trail has pretty well disappeared."

"Some of it looks pretty hairy," she said, leaning over in her saddle to look at a vertical drop of about two hundred feet.

To Sloan's way of thinking Jacie looked natural in the saddle, her hair tossed by the wind with pieces of twig caught here and there, her cheeks pink.

"How did you feel about those narrow ledges we crossed?" he asked curiously. "Did they frighten you? I wouldn't have taken you down here unless I knew it was safe."

She gave him a broad smile as they reached a level area. Dropping her horse's reins, she spread her arms wide and lifted her face to the dappling of sun through the trees. "Heck, no, it was exciting. I've taken rides on ledges more frightening than these down in South

America. We used donkeys then. Of course," she added dryly, "I was more worried about the snakes and crawly things in the jungle."

"Come over here and let me show you something." He dismounted and waited for her to join him on a narrow outcropping of rock. He turned to the open expanse stretched out in front of them. "This area is loaded with maple, oak, ash and an occasional beech tree." Treetops with their deeply changing hues of green lay just below them.

He took a deep breath into his lungs as he looked at the valley below. "The view never ceases to amaze me. There's no air like up here." He reached out and gently turned her toward the distant horizon. "Do you see that ribbon of water down there? That's the Hudson River. The theory is that some of the ledge we're standing on matches ledge found way down there in the valley."

"That's amazing. I guess it must have sheared off a long time ago."

"Probably."

"It's beautiful up here, so real and simple, the view uncluttered. I can't thank you enough for showing this to me. It's so different from what I'm used to. Sometimes you forget about the wonders that can be seen just by looking around you."

"By the end of the month, you won't even notice it," he said with cynicism.

She turned to him indignantly. "I resent that. I've always appreciated beauty such as this. It should never be taken for granted."

He lifted a brow.

"Is this your overall opinion of women, or is it just me?" she demanded.

He swore he saw sparks shoot from her eyes. "Hang on, hang on. I guess I'm just cynical when I hear how beautiful it is, then someone throws away their food wrappers."

She held her hands up in front of his face and moved her fingers back and forth. "Look, no wrappers, nothing hidden."

Up close, he was reminded of just how tempting Jacie could be.

With one hand on her hip, she challenged him, "I promise you I'm like no woman you've ever known before."

"That's a given," he said immediately, allowing himself a chuckle. She was a ball of fire with a ready answer and a quick wit.

"We're even then," she fired back. "I know I've never met anyone like you." She spun away from him. "I do love the view," she said defiantly. "I would love to just keep riding. I've always enjoyed camping out. It would be magnificent to wake in the morning with a canopy of trees over your head."

"Well, your lesson starts in twenty minutes so we'd better get moving." Reluctantly, he walked back toward the horses and grabbed the reins. He made himself mount and then waited for her to do the same. She was right on one score, he'd never met anyone like her. He wondered fleetingly what depths might be revealed once you got to know Jacie.

"I appreciate you taking the time to show me some of this area. Riding along the edge of the mountain and seeing first-hand the valley below is exhilarating. I didn't even see a trail."

He pointed ahead. "We're coming up behind the barns now." Some of the excitement left her face. He wondered if she was sorry, as he was, that they were back already. The ride felt as if it had ended too soon. Before he knew he was going to voice the words, he heard himself say, "Maybe we could do this again."

Her reply came swiftly. "I'd love to."

She rode ahead. He stared after her, wondering what impulse had taken hold of him. Why was he setting himself up like this, spending time with Jacie? He shouldn't have opened his mouth and offered to take her out again, but the urge to do so had been too tempting.

He nudged his horse with his knee and headed in the opposite direction. She'd better not expect a tour every day, he thought grimly, or he'd be so far behind in chores he'd never catch up. For a minute, he wondered if that would be so bad.

Later the following afternoon, Jacie gathered her training material and equipment together. James had set up all her necessary equipment for the training sessions in a small field, and today was the last ground session before the actual jumps.

"Jacie, I have to tell you Leo and I are really looking forward to this jump," MaryAnn stated. "It's a great idea too that you're taking pictures. None of our friends would believe it otherwise."

"It'll be fun," Jacie told them, glancing around at the group of six. "I want everyone to relax. If you have any last minute questions I'm in cabin three, so feel free to come and see me. Tomorrow morning the list will be posted in the lodge for the jump times. We'll be doing two jumps tomorrow." The participants overall seemed eager but she knew from past experience that some would decline to jump. She had laid the groundwork for a safe and enjoyable experience, but when it came down to stepping out of the plane it was ultimately a personal choice. She wondered what they would think if they knew of her own pre-jump jitters.

"Do you need any help carrying this equipment?" Emma asked. Emma was a slim woman somewhere in her mid-to-late thirties.

"Thanks, Emma, but someone should be coming by any minute with a truck to cart this equipment back." She watched the couples disperse toward the lodge, which wasn't far away. Emma waved and then she and her husband walked along the dirt road, trailing behind the group.

Jacie would be jumping with some of the newcomers, offering assistance and calming fears. She had planned six to eight jumps this week, which was more than her leg had had to contend with since her accident. She recalled how difficult it had been the first few times she had jumped after recuperating from her accident. She constantly battled the fear that something would go wrong. If she gave in to the fear, she might stop jumping altogether. She had jumped eleven years without any major incidents, but her accident last year had almost crushed her confidence.

Hearing a motor, she looked across the small field. A tractor with a low wagon behind it was making its way toward her. As it drew closer, she recognized Sloan in the driver's seat. Leaving the machine idling, he jumped down and walked over to her.

"Hello, Jacie. James asked me to pick up your equipment."

"Oh, okay. I thought James would be by. I hope everything's okay."

"His eight-year old had a bike accident. My nephew's okay, but he's going to be taking it easy for a while. I'll bring your gear back to the lodge, but I'm kind of running behind so I have to get hay while I'm out here."

She had already begun to load her equipment on the low wagon near the front. "It's no problem, I'll walk back and help you unload this when you're through."

He picked up the last nylon bag and slid it across the

wooden planks of the wagon. "I can take care of this. If you want a ride the hay won't take long." His glance settled on her knee and the brace. "Is your leg bothering you?" He asked bluntly. "You're wearing that brace again."

"No, but maybe I will ride along." She sat on the wagon, stretching her legs out. "We've been simulating jumps today, so I use the brace for support." Nonchalantly, as if his presence didn't send little jags of excitement through her, she removed her hair band and pushed her fingers through her hair.

Shifting so she could watch him remount the tractor, curiosity got the better of her. "You know, Sloan, I get the feeling you might be even more stubborn than me."

Without pausing he dropped into the wide tractor seat. He twisted around in the seat to face her, a half smile stretching his mouth. "It might be real interesting to find out."

Since he had spoken of his mother she hadn't been able to get it out of her thoughts. Looking at him now there was nothing in the least vulnerable about him. Was it just the attraction that made her want to dig deeper or the man himself? "You're always working, do you ever take time for fun?"

Sloan looked back at her in surprise. "Of course."

"What do you do?" she asked impulsively.

He had a guarded look on his face now. "This and that," he said. "I have been known to go away on vacation."

"Do you head for hotspots or something totally different?"

"Something a little different. I like camping out but I've also taken my mother to Ireland."

"Very interesting."

"What about you?"

"I'll confess I have been to Cancun and the Bahamas a few times. But," she added as he nodded like it was the answer he expected, "I've also taken trips by myself to Montana and the Rockies."

"Beautiful spaces," he said. "Hang on now, I'm going to move ahead."

As the wagon lurched forward, he raised his voice above the noise of the tractor. "This path used to be an old logging road so it's a bit rough."

She braced her hands against the wooden bed. The dirt lane wound through a grove of tall silver maples. "Why don't you use the truck to get hay?"

"This wagon is lower to the ground and it's easier to load. You'll see, we're almost there."

The track curved down to an open pasture lot with mountains on three sides. The late afternoon sun was heated, yet along the mountaintops there hovered a faint blue haze.

As they drew closer to a row of large round hay bales she saw another gray and red tractor. He stopped beside the hay and climbed down from the tractor.

"How will you get the hay on the wagon?" Curious, she looked at the five-foot high hay bales.

He walked around to her side of the wagon, indicating the other tractor. "That has a special prong to pick up the bales."

She took the hand he held out and jumped off the wagon. He landed beside him, his breath warm on her cheek. She stared at him curiously, those light eyes, very conscious of her breath coming fast and her palms getting damp. She had the crazy urge to kiss him again. It had been so nice the first time.

He gave a low groan and reached forward with one hand to trace a fingertip down her nose. She took a half step closer or maybe she just leaned forward. When her breasts touched his chest, desire bit at her and she willingly abandoned herself to sense of touch and smell.

His hand gently cupped the back of her neck and he drew her close enough so she could see tiny flecks of dark blue in his eyes. His features blurred as his lips touched the corner of her mouth, then moved to pull at her lips. The contact was shocking, wonderful. She allowed her tongue to reach out and touch the outline of his mouth. Pure sensation rocked her. Her palms came to rest against his chest and all she could do was feel as he pulled her closer. There was no time for rational thinking. Being this close to him was an incredible sensory experience.

His drew back, his fingers splayed along her upper arms. She could step away but she didn't. Drawing a shaky breath, she kept her glance locked with his. Her legs shook and how the adrenaline raced!

His cool blue eyes seemed to see through her, yet a tiny vein throbbed in his temple and she knew he wasn't as calm as he appeared.

"Talk about chemistry and opposites attracting!" she blurted, unable to contain her tongue.

"That's probably all it is," he said in a hard voice. "Opposites attracting. It happens. God knows we're totally different."

She nodded quickly in agreement. "A fluke. You're a good-looking guy, Sloan, a great kisser, it's only natural we'd be attracted to each other. It doesn't mean anything more than that."

He looked for a moment like he was going to argue the point. Abruptly, he pulled her into him and dropped his mouth to hers. It was over in five seconds or less, too quickly for Jacie.

Sloan stepped back and moved quickly toward the other tractor. "Stand back from the wagon while I load the hay," he said brusquely. "These bales weigh about eight hundred pounds."

She shivered as clouds scuttled across the sky, stealing the sun. She was really at a loss. She pulled her sweat-dampened shirt away from her skin, yet his scent lingered in her nostrils. She saw again his face coming close, felt the touch of those lips. They had tasted slightly of licorice. She touched her lips and smiled. Licorice of all things.

She sobered, thinking she was a fool for being attracted to him, a fool to let him kiss her, no matter how good it felt. She stiffened her shoulders, reminding herself of one important fact. Her track record with men stunk. Hadn't she learned anything? In the past she had always been optimistic, thinking maybe this time it would work out; but it never had. Brad had stung her in the worst way. Could she risk going through that kind of rejection again?

While she wrestled with her thoughts, Sloan started the other tractor and moved forward to push the prong into a bale. She stepped well away from the wagon. As he drew abreast of her he looked at her for a brief, moment, and his blue eyes seared her with heat.

He tipped the bucket and the bale dropped. The wagon's wheels squatted under the weight. He prodded at the hay with the tractor bucket and the hay rolled over on its flat side. When he cut the engine it suddenly seemed very quiet in the field.

She moved to sit on the flatbed.

"You'd better move up here." He indicated a small seat behind him on the tractor.

She stared at the small space. "It's a short ride. I'll ride back here."

"It's not safe, the bale could shift." His voice brooked no refusal.

Surprised by his sudden sharpness, she moved to the front of the wagon.

"Sit behind me. I don't want to take a chance. If the bale should move that heavy metal bar will protect you," he said, his voice once more a normal, even tone.

Between her and the heat of his back there was nothing. She wasn't sure which was more dangerous. Deriding her own naiveté, she knew touching him was definitely more dangerous. "Will it move?" she asked.

"It shouldn't. Hang on." The tractor lurched forward, bringing her shoulder into close contact with his. She studied the back of his head. His hair was fine with a slight wave, the dark strands against his collar. The trace of gold from the sun was a natural look many women paid money to achieve. The back of his head narrowed smoothly to a strong neck, then the width of his shoulders blocked her view.

Absorbed in her sensory contemplation of Sloan, she didn't realize the tractor had stopped until his head turned. They were a hair's breadth apart. She could feel his heat, see the tiny fan of lines beside his eyes. She swallowed with difficulty, her mouth dry as she felt again their kiss, recalled his scent. What did he expect of her? What did she expect of him?

"Are you riding all the way with me?" he asked huskily.

Yes! Watching the slight curve of his lips, her mind screamed the answer.

"I'm going to the barn," he explained patiently. "Are you riding that far?"

She looked around and her eyes widened. They were outside her cabin. Quickly, she stood up. "I'll help you unload my things at the lodge."

"I'll have Donny take care of that, if you don't mind him handling the gear."

"Oh—that would be okay."

She put her feet over the side of the tractor. "Will I see you later?"

"Sure. I'll be around."

As her feet touched the graveled path, he said, "I guess I was right about you and Dandy."

"How so?" Surprised, she hesitated.

"You're a good match. He's half wild, too, sometimes unpredictable."

"Is that how you see me? I jump out of planes but I also grew up with a loving, stable family. Does letting you kiss me make me reckless and unpredictable?"

"If it does, I'm not complaining."

Sloan created excitement in her and she liked that rush of adrenaline that came with new relationships. She had never been attracted to a man like him before... someone rock solid and dependable. As he had said, they were truly opposites. She wondered how far it would take her and if she dared go down that road again.

∞ Chapter Five ∞

OUT ON HER BACK deck Jacie stretched with contentment. Despite a brief moment of dizziness earlier following a short nap in the living room, she felt incredible, physically and emotionally. It was only her fifth day at Timber Falls, but being here certainly agreed with her.

She had spent most of the morning sunbathing on her back deck. Luckily she had packed a few bathing suits. She felt more relaxed than she had in a long time. The resort had a wonderful setup. There was a hot tub on the deck, swimming pool by the lodge, a thousand acres of trails, numerous glens and ponds to explore. No matter where she looked, mountains rose on all sides. She could only surmise that the winter must be even more spectacular when snow covered the peaks.

If she had refused this job she would have missed all this. And Sloan.

She removed her sunglasses, forcing herself to look once more into the ravine below her. It didn't seem to bother her quite as much. She remembered a time when she hadn't feared any height.

The phone began to ring. She wondered if it was Bonnie calling again. Bracing herself, she decided to tell Bonnie to lay off the mother hen routine. Her concern had become a tad suffocating.

She lifted the cordless phone on the table beside her. "Hello?"

"Jacie! It's great to hear your voice. How are you?"

She clamped her fingers over her mouth. She knew that deep male voice, despite the fact she hadn't heard it in over a year. With detached curiosity, she saw her knuckles were white on the phone.

"What do you want Brad?" Was that cool voice hers? She marveled at her control.

"Now don't sound like that," he chided, as if he still had the right. "We haven't talked in so long. I've missed you, Jacie. I wanted to make sure you were all right."

"Isn't that funny, you missed me so much you haven't called in—what—twelve, thirteen months?" She knew exactly how long it was and was instantly mad she'd said that. It made it sound like it mattered to her.

"I did try to get in touch with you, Jacie. Your family blocked me every time. I've been working and I've really missed you—"

"How did you find me?" she demanded. She sat up and perched tensely on the edge of the lounger. She willed herself to stay calm. "I'm not letting you twist me up in knots again."

"I don't blame you for being furious, sweetheart, but give me a chance here. I'm trying to make amends. I got your number from Bonnie, she's worried about you."

Bonnie! "I'll remind myself to tell her to get lost," she muttered. If that was true she'd tell Bonnie more than that, but Brad could be lying too.

"Hey, don't say that, she's only got your best interests at heart."

"What do you want?"

"I don't want anything. I called to say I miss you. It's like you dropped off the face of the earth. No one has seen you. I heard you weren't working. I called Con."

"You called my brother?" she asked in disbelief. Her brother had never made a secret of his dislike of Brad.

"I was desperate. I couldn't find you, short of hiring a detective."

"Maybe that should have told you something," she said dryly. "It should have clicked that I didn't want you to find me."

"Well, I didn't get anything out of your brother. He was downright hostile, threatened to call the cops if I bothered you. Did anybody even tell you I've called? I tried to reach you because the insurance company needed information. I contacted them on your behalf, you know, to make sure they settled the case for you."

She stiffened. "You must've really pulled strings to get them to settle so fast."

"You don't know how responsible I feel. I would never have let you do that jump if I'd known the outcome."

"I don't have amnesia," she said skeptically. "I remember the time you came to the hospital in Venezuela."

"I was on sedatives. I was a wreck. I couldn't eat, couldn't sleep." He sounded convincing. "I still care about you."

Jacie stiffened. She had never told her family why she and Brad ended their relationship. Emotionally, she had felt humiliated. How do you tell anyone the man you cared about left you high and dry in a foreign country? She had fractured a leg, broken an arm. He couldn't handle the scars on her body.

"It's been a long road for me but I've recovered." Despite her intelligence, emotionally she felt scarred. She had miscalculated big time.

"Nobody was saying anything except Bonnie."

She exhaled slowly, counting to four. Bonnie again. "So what's the point of this conversation?"

"Well, how about we get together? I know I hurt you, and I'm sorry. I'm not trying to excuse what happened, it was just the surprise—the shock."

"For everyone," she said sarcastically. It was her body that had been hurt, not his.

"Come on, let me make it up to you."

He had a hide like elephant leather. Rejection meant nothing to him. The word no represented a challenge. How had she ever thought she liked this guy? How could she have been so blind? She couldn't help but compare him to Sloan.

She made herself laugh and her throat felt like sandpaper. "I'm seeing someone else, so I don't want to pick up where we left off. I'm not hurt either. I never was. You see Brad, you have to care to be hurt."

His voice dropped to that deep timbre she used to find irresistible. "Don't be like this, Jacie, remember how it was. We really had something. You're on the rebound with this guy. I haven't been able to concentrate, do anything, you're always on my mind."

"You said you've been working." She said dryly. "I know you wrapped up the Angel Falls movie. It was in the theaters. I presume you've moved on to other lucrative projects?"

Silence.

"You had time to get the movie out." Her voice rose. "It was a big box office hit."

"Come on, please understand. It was business, I was

under pressure, you know how badly those sharks wanted their money. I had borrowed too heavily—I had no choice but to get it out there as soon as I could. It killed me to have to do it—I knew you'd be hurting." He paused, as if waiting for her response. "So—can I drop by?" His voice sounded hopeful.

She took great delight in squashing that hope. "Sorry, I'm working."

"Working? Bonnie said—"

She tensed. "What?"

"Only that you needed a break."

"It is a break, a self-imposed break, but I'm also working. I'm not in the middle of a nervous breakdown."

"Do you mean you're skydiving again, doing aerial stunts?"

She gritted her teeth at the note of incredulity in his voice. "You know what? I have to go. There's another call coming in." The lied rolled off her tongue like silk unfolding.

"Jacie." He sounded urgent. "Don't hang up. I really need to see you, at least so I can apologize and get this off my chest—"

"I don't think that's a good idea." Gently, she touched the end call button, breaking the connection. "Because you see," she muttered, "I'm working on my screwed-up life and it doesn't include you."

"Bad timing?" a voice asked behind her.

Unnerved, she twisted around, half rising from her chair. Sloan was at the edge of her deck. She sank back down. "I-I didn't hear you . . .." She darted him a glance, wondering what he might have heard.

He stood with one foot resting on the bottom step of the stairs, his hat balanced on one knee. "I can come back later," he offered.

"No, no, it was just a phone call from a . . . er . . . no

one important." There was an awkward silence. She wondered if he believed her, then supposed it didn't really matter.

"An old boyfriend?"

She was going to deny that, but ended up nodding. "Yes."

"You're giving him the brush off and he doesn't get it?"

"Something like that. Is there something I can do for you?" she asked briskly. She felt uncomfortable discussing Brad with this man.

He held up a blue hair band. "I came to return this. It was caught on the bed of the wagon."

"Oh, thanks. I've got loads of those."

"Also, I told James I'd see if you wanted to ride into town tomorrow after your lessons. He's driving some of the other guests to check out local points of interest."

She gestured vaguely at the mountains behind them. "Sounds like fun, but I thought maybe I'd go for a hike to see North and South Lake in Haines Falls," she replied distractedly. The call had unsettled her, dredging up old wounds best left undisturbed. Brad hadn't changed. He was still selfish.

"It's a nice hike," he conceded. "Depending on how you want to do it on foot or horseback. In fact, there's a trail not many people know about . . . you can see both lakes from a vantage point on the ledges."

She shrugged off-handedly. "I haven't formulated any plans. I have a brochure about the area's history. Sounds like it used to be quite an attraction."

"It was. There were a lot of famous hotels."

"Here's the hiking map I was looking at." She leaned forward and pulled it out of the bundle of papers beside her. She handed it to him, pulling her swimming suit strap up as it slid down her arm. "It looks like I can hike to some of the old hotels."

He tapped the map with a finger. "There's another falls here."

She gave him an interested look. "I definitely have to see that. I'm a history buff, you know and I love taking pictures. I've even had some of them published."

"Then you've come to the right area. Actually, the falls is a double falls. We do overnight trips into the area."

She stood and pulled on an oversized shirt. Walking to the deck railing, she pulled her hair from beneath the shirt collar, her movements mechanical as she drank in the view. Haze hovered over the river far below, cloaking the valley in shadow. Dropping her chin she deliberately took in the ravine below and gripped the rail tightly. "I've never seen fog move in like here. It almost slithers across the ground," she mused.

"It could be sunny one minute and shrouded in fog the next. We have a saying around here," he said. "If you don't like the weather, wait a minute.'"

Sloan studied Jacie as she stood at the rail. He knew he was crazy to have come here. After their kiss he hadn't been able to get her out of his mind. She possessed uncommon grace, from slender bare feet to shining head, the sun glinting off reddish highlights. She fairly shimmered with life, yet right now a certain untouched quality about her drew him. It hadn't been urgent that he come and see her; in fact, James had been on his way over when he had waylaid him.

She intrigued him, there was no getting around it. She looked perfect with the river as a backdrop, long silky hair curling on her shoulders. His fingers itched to tangle in those reddish strands, remembering their warm silkiness, the feel of her lips moving beneath his.

Something inside him tightened, warning of his dangerous preoccupation. Fleetingly, he wondered if he was about to repeat a past mistake. She was a woman who seemed to enjoy what the world offered. Timber Falls, as beautiful as it was, was not the place to keep a woman like her happy. She was used to roaming the world.

As she turned from the deck rail she raised her face to the sky and smiled. He marveled at her apparent lack of self-consciousness. She suddenly swayed sideways. He stepped forward. "Jacie."

She blinked at him and her head bobbed.

He moved in close to her. "Here . . . sit down." Alarmed by her white face, he put an arm around her waist. She just stood there staring at him as if puzzled. He lifted her effortlessly. Surprisingly, she snuggled her head against his shoulder. He couldn't help but inhale her scent. Rose scented shampoo.

Gently, he set her in the lounge chair and she drew a deep, unsteady breath as she lifted a hand to her head. "Sorry, it's the ravine I guess. I got a bit dizzy."

"Is there something I can get you? Maybe I should call in a doctor."

"No. Heights," she murmured, tossing him a smile. "They bother me, seems I have no head for them."

Puzzled, he went perfectly still.

Her gaze suddenly sharpened. She gave him a quick glance and grimaced. "Oops . . . forget I said that, okay?"

"No head for heights? You skydived into Timber Falls. What game are you playing?" he demanded.

She pulled herself further up in the chair and clutched the shirt around her. "It's my job, my livelihood." Her voice bordered on the defensive.

"How can you do it if you have a problem with heights?" he asked impatiently. He shook his head. How could he understand this complex woman?

"Listen, it's related to the accident I had last year. The

more I do the jumps the easier it gets. Eventually, it will fade."

"Is that a doctor's prognosis . . . like Dr. Jacie?" he asked sarcastically. He moved away to sit on the deck rail. "Is this the same accident where you hurt your leg?"

"Yes, but I really don't want to talk about it."

Her hands gripped the chair's armrests. He wanted to know about her accident. Maybe he could understand what was going on. Was it safe for her to continue to skydive? "Take it easy, Jacie, you're as pale as a ghost."

"I'm fine." She sat forward and hurriedly rushed into speech. "So tell me, have you always lived here?" She fiddled with the chair arm and avoided looking at him.

He frowned and crossed his arms over his chest. "You're real good at evading answers when you set your mind to it. Yes, I've lived in these parts most of my life."

"Most of it?" the question came out quickly, nervously, he thought.

"I left for a while."

She looked at him in surprise. "You left? Did you want to explore new horizons?"

He shrugged. "I was young, just out of college. I thought it was what I wanted." It was what he had wanted at that time in his life.

"Where did you go?"

"Here and there. I lived in Philadelphia for a time, then moved to New York City for eight years. I was a sugar broker."

She made no attempt to contain her amazement. "You were one of those type-A personalities, buying and selling..." she shook her head. "I can't believe it."

"I wised up."

"And you came back."

He looked out over the vastness of the mountains. "I guess I've always known this is where I belonged, even though I fought it for a time. There's something about these mountains. It's in your blood. They call you back, sooner or later."

"I can understand, just being here this short time," she admitted quietly. "Whether you choose to believe it or not," she added.

"It gets a lot of people. They come to the mountains and never leave."

"They are exquisite, if I can use such an inadequate word, though it must be wicked when the snow flies."

"We manage," he told her dryly.

"I bet you always manage," she quipped, tossing him a grin.

He couldn't help but smile. This was the Jacie he expected to see. He pushed away from the rail and took a step toward her. "How about you, Jacie? You strike me as a survivor. Tell me about this fear of heights and the accident."

Before she could reply his brother walked around the corner of the cabin and called, "Hi, Jacie, Sloan." James stepped up on the deck and ran his eyes over Jacie appreciatively, "You look nice and cool. I hope you're enjoying your stay with us."

She shaded her eyes, looking at him and then his brother. Sloan wondered if she were making comparisons between he and James. James was easygoing, he was not. He moved across the deck and toward the stairs, knowing the answers he wanted would have to wait.

"I love it here, although I was just telling Sloan I can't imagine these mountains when the snow comes."

James laughed. "Sometimes we get snowed in but there's all kinds of possibilities, depending who you get stranded with."

She gave a husky laugh, and the sound rippled all the way through Sloan. What would it be like to be stranded in a snowstorm with Jacie? Images rose to his mind, entwined limbs and hushed voices. There was no doubt in his mind it would be interesting and thoroughly fulfilling.

"Actually, Sloan, I need to talk with you." James' voice snapped Jacie back to full awareness. How could she be daydreaming in broad daylight? She had had the most erotic thoughts about Sloan. What was the matter with her?

"Mom and Dad will be arriving in a few days," James said. "I want to set up some arrangements and I need your input."

"I was just heading back to the office," Sloan said. He turned back to her. "Are you going to be okay?"

"Of course," she told him.

"Are you ill?" James asked with concern.

"No, just a momentary dizziness. It's passed," she reassured him.

"Let us know if you're interested in the overnight in two days," Sloan reminded her as he stepped off the deck.

"Sure." As if she hadn't just had the air knocked out of her, she waved gaily at him and James as they left. From what Sloan had said, she had assumed his mother was dead. James said she and their father were coming for a visit. She would get to meet the woman who had given birth to Sloan, the woman who had hurt him. She felt a strange mix of antipathy and curiosity.

She picked up her hair band where Sloan had left it on the rail and stared out over the valley. The sun was almost completely down, the day nearly over. A soft sigh escaped her. Life sure took some strange turns. She looked to the heavens, staring at the rose and orange streaks placed there by nature. The sun rose and set, it remained constant. Why weren't people so predictable?

Once this job was complete and she proved to herself she was as good as new, she would move on and leave Timber Falls. Leave Sloan, a man she felt more and more attracted to each time they met.

∞ Chapter Six ∞

FOLLOWING DINNER THAT EVENING Jacie sat at the lodge bar and nursed a tumbler of Schnapps. Lifting the glass slowly, she took a small sip, relishing the icy peppermint as it slid past her tongue and burned down her throat. She twirled the glass, watching MaryAnn and her husband sway on the small dance floor. Other couples sat at the tables. A slow, romantic song by Willie Nelson played on the jukebox.

She half-closed her eyes, recalling another night. It had been spring, and she had just met Brad, a client from Bonnie's car rental company.

She'd let him talk her into a date and then taken him to a honky-tonk bar to give him a taste of her favorite music. She ran a hand through her hair, staring up at the dark beams supporting the ceiling. Brad had not been interested in the slow, easy pace of country. He wanted rock and roll and city sights. In all fairness, she'd been right there beside him, keeping pace.

"Jacie, can I get you another drink?" Michelle asked

from behind the bar.

Dragging herself out of the past, she glanced at the other girl. "I'm okay for now. By the way, how did you end up bartending?" she asked curiously.

"I go wherever the boss needs me," Michelle said with a grin. "They were short-handed so I'm filling in. I'm hoping to get into college next year, so I'm saving every penny. Of course, it helps that Sloan and James are first cousins. They give me a lot of overtime."

"You're a versatile woman, Michelle." The music ended and it became quiet. "This place is too quiet." She dropped her feet to the floor.

"Leaving so soon?" Michelle asked.

She gave Michelle a sly grin. "Nope. This place needs to be livened up, and I think I'm the person to do it."

Michelle's eyes widened. "Go for it, Jacie. I'm right behind you."

Jacie placed a ten-dollar bill on the bar. "First thing I need is some change for the juke box."

Armed with quarters, Jacie walked over to the juke box, fed the quarters into the slot and picked out lively country tunes. Even if nobody else decided to dance, she would. Dancing was something she thoroughly enjoyed. Strolling back to her seat she stood with her back to the bar, tilted back her head and closed her eyes to better appreciate the music as she waited for it to begin playing.

"Mind if I sit down?" Sloan.

A flutter began in the hollow between her shoulders. She couldn't mistake that sexy-as-all-get-out voice.

As the music began she waved a hand carelessly to indicate the seat beside her, but she felt anything but indifferent. His hair was neatly slicked back and his smoky gray shirt made his blue eyes seem more intense. She recalled the kiss they had shared and her insides melted. Michelle placed a long-necked bottle of beer on the bar in front of him.

"I love music." Jacie said, tapping her toes to the music. She gave him a questioning glance. "And I love to dance. How about you?" She gave him a long, slow look.

"I like to dance. I've been called pretty good."

She swept her arm and indicated the empty dance floor. "I plan to dance the night away." She pushed her glass toward Michelle. "I think I need something to drink." She swiveled her chair so she faced him. "Care to join me?" she challenged, rising.

"I'll have to pass right now. I'm waiting for a phone call." His voice sounded husky and his eyes, well, was it her imagination or did they promise something?

She tamped down her immediate disappointment.

"Michelle, Jacie's next drink is on me. Get her a—" he raised his brows questioningly.

"I've decided to switch over to soda," she supplied impishly. "I have a feeling I need my wits about me tonight."

"Put an extra cherry in it," he said, lifting his beer and taking a swallow.

She watched the strong column of Sloan's neck as he tipped his head back. Tanned and strong with a hint of a beard. She turned on her heel. "Thanks for the drink," she told him over her shoulder. "Now I'm going to get started on dancing the night away." On impulse, she looked back at Michelle. "Do you line dance?"

"No," Michelle said, "but I'd love to learn."

"Well, come on then, I'm just in the mood to teach you." When Michelle hesitated she ran behind the bar and pulled the other girl out by the hand.

"You don't mind, do you Sloan?" she called laughingly to him. Michelle sent him a questioning look and he waved her on.

"Go ahead, I'll take care of the bar for now," he said.

Quickly, Michelle pulled her apron off and tossed it toward the bar top as she joined her on the dance floor.

Fleetingly, Jacie wondered if he really was waiting for a phone call or if it had been an excuse not to dance with her. Maybe she imagined that hint of a promise in his eyes.

Never one to let country music go un-danced, she let the foot stomping, soul-stirring melodies take her over.

She and Michelle started out side by side. She showed her the basic steps to line dance, and then they were off. Before she knew it, others had joined them, people she didn't even recall seeing in the bar. They formed two lines from one end of the dance floor to the other.

After a time she took a breather and stood back to watch the dancers with satisfaction. Throwing back her head in pure enjoyment, she kept the clapping going in time with the music. The quiet night had turned into a hell-raising good time and everyone seemed game to join in.

She looked over toward the bar and studied Sloan. He caught her watching him and she smiled slow and easy. There was a lull in the music and Michelle flitted past her.

"I hear the phone," the other girl said on a breathless laugh. "It's probably for Sloan. I have to get back to the bar anyway, now that everyone's worked up a sweat and a thirst. You know how to get a party going, Jacie. That was fun."

"So much fun," she agreed, "that I'm going to start it all over again."

She moved across the dance floor and pushed the buttons on the jukebox and played more songs.

Looking across the bar she noticed Sloan take the portable phone into a back room behind the bar. Part of her felt lighter. Apparently, he hadn't been making excuses to avoid dancing with her. She fairly danced across the floor and joined the others as some line-danced, others were in couples, and the remainder danced in groups as they pleased.

The next song was slow, a favorite of hers by George Strait. Without warning, she felt hard fingers and a wide palm clasp her hand and slowly pull her around. She had danced with different male partners for the last hour, but she knew this time it would be special.

Jacie whirled on her toes in a half circle and found Sloan behind her, his chest against her shoulder as they danced to the music. Her heart flipped, excruciatingly slow, and then beat so much faster and faster. He pulled her around to face him and they moved, breast-to-breast, her head tucked under his chin, her one hand captured in his, the other resting on his shoulder. She felt ready to burn up in his arms, but she tipped her head back briefly and smiled at him instead, automatically matching her steps to his. By the end of the dance she didn't want to stop.

Ω

Sloan heard the music change tempo and he reluctantly released Jacie. When she stepped back he saw her vibrant face and the question in her eyes. He couldn't refuse to answer the question there. She loved to dance, he had seen it as he watched her teach the other patrons intricate steps.

"I've wanted to dance with you the last half hour." He'd finally decided he wanted the pleasure of holding her close. Following that thought with action he pulled her into his arms, inhaled the fresh scent that lingered in her hair. All his warnings about her to himself meant nothing. Life and energy fairly radiated from her, drawing him closer and closer. He wanted to discover more about Jacie, a woman who danced like a dream, who liked to keep life busy and energetic. She kept secrets that he wanted to unravel. He wondered for a brief moment if this was how his dad had felt back when he had met Sloan's mother.

The surprise on her face when he pulled her back to him gave way to pleasure. Smoothly he twirled her to the faster music.

"You're smooth," she said, laughing with delight.

"I feel like I've danced with you many times before." The tempo of the music sank down into his heart, his steps and movements attuned to her as he let himself drink in the beauty she radiated. His throat felt bone dry, his heart beat hard and loud in his chest, but he couldn't give her up, not even when the music stopped.

She stood beside him, her shoulder leaning into his chest. He held onto her hand and he was surprised by its smooth texture, the fine, small bones beneath the skin.

"For a woman who skydives and has strength in her hands," he mused, "you feel damned delicate."

"That sounds like a compliment." She tilted her face up to him and his immediate thought was to kiss her, taste those lips again. Temptation in the form of liquid brown eyes stared up at him. He took in the faintest of freckles across her nose, the full red lips. He wanted to taste them and make her breath his own. He dropped a slow kiss on her smiling lips. She responded immediately and then pulled back.

"I need a drink," she said.

Sloan stepped back and led her to the bar, still holding her hand.

Jacie took a long drink of her soda. "Sloan, I had no idea you were such a great dancer." She wiped her mouth with a napkin, her voice breathless. "I'd dance with you any time, Cowboy."

"I don't do it that often, but I do like to dance."

"What other accomplishments are you hiding?" she asked playfully. "Where did you learn to dance like that?"

"When I lived in the city. There's a lot of nightlife out there as I'm sure you know. The first year I lived there I was determined to sample all of it."

"I know what you mean."

She turned sideways and reached for her drink. "I've always been one to sample whatever was out there. I hate to miss out on any of the fun." She ran her finger around the edge of her glass. "I'll have to say though, in the last year I've learned a bit of caution the hard way but I've never been tempted to give up the night life. That sounds corny." She looked around. "I think about you living here year round, living in such an isolated area. I don't know if I'd like it."

"Well, at least you're honest."

She smiled. "Sometimes to a fault. You probably see me as too brash, maybe too independent. I'm not a woman who wants to be taken care of most of the time." She gave a big sigh. "It's a pity we can't get to know each other longer. I think it would definitely be interesting." She stepped away from the bar.

"Where are you going, Jacie?" he said.

She whirled to face him and continued walking backwards. "I'm all ready to start in again. I can't let that music go to waste." She held her hand out to Sloan and he didn't refuse her. He couldn't.

Looking at her watch, Jacie decided midnight was time to call it a night. What fun they'd had! Everyone had loosened up, the place was still hopping, and she had been designated the dance teacher. She didn't mind at all. She loved people! Poor Michelle, though, would be staying until the party wound down. Looking at the other girl's animated face, she had a feeling she didn't mind.

Knowing she had an early call in the morning to

prepare for tomorrow's preliminary jumps, she walked toward the door and called good night as she went.

"Jacie, hang on a minute." Sloan came up behind her. She had lost track of him in the last half hour and had assumed he'd left.

As she pulled on her lightweight jacket he came up behind her and lifted her hair out from under the collar. She turned her head to thank him, but the words became lost as his fingers traced fleetingly along the sensitive skin of her neck. She felt that caress clear to her toes. She stared at his hands bemusedly. Did this man have fire in his fingertips?

"Shall we?" he asked, opening the door.

She lifted her face and a refreshing breeze washed across her face. "Have you ever been drunk on life? It's a great feeling."

"Since I've known you Jacie, I've been asking myself all kinds of different questions. If the way I feel right now is drunk on life, I owe it to you. I enjoyed dancing with you."

"It was fun getting everyone in a dancing mood." They walked along the now level road to her cabin. "Do you live in the main lodge?" she asked idly. "I know some of the ranch hands have rooms upstairs."

"I have a cabin a little further up the mountain. There's a side road before the cabins that goes up there."

"How did you come up with the idea of Timber Falls? This entire vacation concept? Did you and James buy this place?"

"Our father bought it back in the forties when land was dirt cheap. He didn't move here until I was about four."

"So you made the transition from working farm to resort?"

"It's still a working farm. The resort is pretty much

James' baby. Mine is beef cattle."

"It was your brother's idea to have paying guests?"

"Yes. In the beginning the resort guests paid for the ranch and cattle. We're at a point now where the cattle are paying for themselves and I'm expanding the breeding herd, trying out an experimental cholesterol-free beefer."

Jacie was impressed. "I've read something of cholesterol-free beef. Seems like it would be a good idea for people with heart problems."

"The idea is certainly catching on."

"So you started importing guests?" she asked easily. "You don't strike me as a man who'd welcome strangers on his property."

He shrugged. "I don't have too much to do with the guests."

Jacie pondered his words. "That's interesting. You were there when I skydived into the ranch, then you took me riding and here you are tonight, dancing and now walking me to my cabin." With her usual curiosity, she had to find out what he meant. "So you're here tonight because . . .."

"What do you think?" he said simply. "Because of you."

She had sought that answer but now that she had it, she dug her hands nervously into her jacket pockets.

"Well, that's pretty straightforward." The attraction made her feel vulnerable. He had deviated from his usual routine because of her. Logic warned her to retreat . . . yearning urged her to step closer. She wanted to kiss him again. That small kiss earlier had only whetted her interest.

Sloan's hand clasped hers. She stopped and faced him. His fingers brushed wisps of hair away from her eyes and the light caress caused her heart to do a double beat.

"I'd like to kiss you."

"Nothing like following words with action," she murmured, her lips curving.

He leaned forward and touched his mouth to hers.

She closed her eyes, enjoying his touch, the sensation of his lips, the slight brush of his tongue along the rim of her lips.

His lips left hers and she reluctantly opened her eyes. "I think you're a straight shooter too, Jacie."

"I try to be." Right now she felt muddled, unable to get the taste and feel of his lips out of her head. "I feel like I'm addicted," she admitted a little shakily. "Every time we kiss it kind of catches me off guard. I've never felt like this."

"Yeah," he muttered. "I know what you mean."

Jacie's emotions were in a turmoil . . . emotions that had been on hold since her break up with Brad. Now with Sloan she kept thinking about giving in to the desire she felt for him.

She walked the remaining distance to her cabin, climbed the porch stairs and sat on the metal glider. Drawing her legs up, she stared up at the sky. "The moon came out," she observed, her chin resting on her up-drawn knees. "I've never seen it so big. Right now I can't imagine going back to my small apartment with no mountains in sight." No Sloan.

His voice was low-pitched and intimate, "Jacie, tell me about your life."

She felt a faint stir of panic and breathed deeply in an attempt to dispel the flutter. "There's nothing to tell, I lead a pretty boring life."

He walked up the steps and leaned against the deck rail. She could see his grin in the porch light. "I find that hard to believe coming from someone who jumps out of planes. Let me be the judge," he added coaxingly. "Tell me."

The warmth and interest in his voice drew her in. "We've moved from subtly lethal kisses to even more dangerous territory."

"Is that how you see sharing personal information?"

She forced a bright smile. "Yes—but I'm not kidding, I do lead a boring life. I didn't always think so," she added thoughtfully.

"What changed?" he queried.

She chewed her lip. "My job changed, my life. I went from being an active professional to doing hardly anything at all. It was after my accident that the bottom seemed to drop out of my life." She halted the rush of words, hating the underlying bitterness. "God, that sounds self-pitying. It could have been worse, I could be dead."

"What happened?"

She looked at his silhouetted profile, familiar now with the quiet strength he exuded. She wanted to open up to him, let him know about her but part of her still felt frozen inside. "As you know my family's skydiving business specializes in cinematography, film stunts."

"There's nothing ordinary about that business from my viewpoint."

She detected a trace of reserve in his voice. "You're right, of course."

"You travel a lot but you're mostly based in New York?"

"Yes, I've been all over the United States and a few places internationally."

"It sounds exciting."

Lifting one shoulder, she pushed her hair back with a careless hand. "I haven't done much of it lately."

"Do you want to do resume that life?"

She became still, thinking back over the last year, the

hospital, the pain . . . her family. She grimaced. Her family.

"I had an accident on a job, a freefall gone wrong. Since then everyone's pretty much avoided that question. I've been recuperating and just hiding out." She made the admission honestly, threading shaky fingers through her hair. "My friend Bonnie was another one I've been hiding behind, shielding my emotions even from myself. My family has been careful not to talk about that mistake in Venezuela. Something happened with my chute. I should have checked it one last time but I got careless. Since then, I've been afraid I couldn't handle the reality of my job." She met his glance directly. "I'm taking this on a wing and a prayer, hoping I'm not jeopardizing my job here by telling you this. This job is my first assignment since the accident. I've done jumps, but not a real job."

"I figured something was up with you but I wasn't sure what."

"I'm still the same professional I've always been, but again, everything is different. I have to get back into the routine so I can feel like I fit in the business again."

"Your brother seems to keep a close eye on you."

She grimaced. "Yes, it's a blessing and a curse. Con hasn't left me alone for a minute. It got to the point I felt as if he was babysitting me." She lifted her chin. "I love my family, but they're too protective."

"So you returned to work."

"I had to. I felt like I was in limbo. Con probably realized that if I didn't get back into skydiving, I might never do it again. As it is, I'm afraid I've lost that edge." She felt vulnerable to have revealed so much. "I've let fear creep in." She threw him a quick glance. "When I did this jump into Timber Falls, I almost backed out."

"How did you manage it, Jacie?"

She folded her arms and clenched her jaw. "I had to. I

couldn't admit defeat."

"There's no shame in admitting you're scared. I don't know if it's something I'd ever do," he admitted.

She crooked one brow and smiled at him. "You would if you had to, or if you wanted to badly enough."

"Sounds like skydiving's been part of your life too long to just let it go."

She emitted a half laugh. "I have four brothers in the business. There was a time I couldn't imagine doing anything else. At fourteen I did my first solo freefall. I don't know that I ever made a conscious decision to make it my career. I just did it; it happened."

"How did your parents feel about it?"

"Well, my mom had no problem with it, she's the one who started the business, but Dad wasn't keen on his only daughter taking up skydiving. Even so, he never tried to stop me." A smile flitted across her lips. "Dad is our manager, though in recent years Con has taken over most of that responsibility. I've been hell-bent on skydiving most of my life. My family is giving me space to sort things out."

"You seem to be working through your fears," he said slowly.

"I can't imagine you being afraid of anything, Sloan."

The rocking of the glider stopped. She looked down and saw his boot against the metal leg.

"We've all got our secrets," he said softly.

"Did your parents come?" she asked abruptly, deliberately changing the subject. It felt like he was getting too close to home. She wasn't sure how much she was ready to share.

"Yes, James picked them up. They'll be staying with him and Dotty at their place in town for a couple days. Myra . . . she's actually my step-mom. She and my dad live in Maryland. You'll probably see them around this week."

"Oh, I thought you and James had the same mother."

"My mother died when I was young."

The glider swayed crazily a moment as he joined her on the seat. She looked at him in surprise, the wanting curling tightly inside. His shoulder brushed hers and he dropped his head down until she could see the glitter of his eyes. His lips felt warm and tingling on her mouth. A shock of sensation hit her. All kinds of wanton feelings surged, making her forget the questions on the tip of her tongue about his mother.

Ω

Sloan had to touch her. Despite an inner struggle to end the night before it began he grazed her lips with his tongue, lightly, increasing the contact when her hands lifted and encircled his neck.

He had it bad. His attraction to Jacie blew to bits his good intentions to remain uninvolved. He was breaking his own rules. He had danced with her and been given another glimpse into the woman she was. Being with her felt like an exhilarating ride.

"After the day I had I should be bone-tired and dragging. Instead, being with you I feel alive." When she had roused his usually quiet vacationers into stomping and dancing down at the bar, he hadn't known what to expect from her next.

He had had plenty of unpredictability while growing up but his father had always been there to keep him grounded. His mother had been like a butterfly, flitting from one exciting pursuit to the next . . . usually at the expense of her family.

Being this close to Jacie right now he didn't care if all she wanted was a one-night stand. It wasn't his usual style, but he wanted to capture some of this woman's zest for life.

Caught in a spell, he let her mouth catch his more fully. She took his breath and his body's response was immediate and inflammatory.

Cupping her jaw with one hand, he let his fingers tangle in her hair as he threaded them through the fine strands. She leaned her head into his hand and her eyes drifted closed.

He pressed kisses along her forehead, his mouth loving the supple warmth of her skin. He drew the scent of her into him, fingers tightening as he enticed her mouth to his with slow, teasing pecks.

Sloan groaned. "I haven't sat on the front porch like this since I was a teenager." He captured her mouth again. He felt the smooth, muscled contours of her body, the flat belly and soft breasts. One of her long legs wound around his. He groaned in pleasure, liking the feel of her against him. The meeting of lips became more desperate and frantic. He could hardly draw a breath he wanted so much more.

She tipped her head back, her breathing as uncontrolled as his. He pulled a ragged lungful of air into his deprived lungs, letting his hands drop to her waist. Smelling the dampness of impending rain on the air, he wondered if his senses had ever felt so heightened or charged.

He pulled back, grimaced, looked at his watch. He reached for her hand. "I'm damned reluctant to end the evening, but morning will be here before you know it."

She moved away from him jerkily. "Y-you're right, it's late."

"Do you recall what I said a few minutes ago about secrets?" he asked. "Here's one. You scare the hell out of me."

"I can't believe that." Brushing back her hair, she said,

"You always seem so in charge."

"Well, when I get close to you my heart pounds and my mouth goes dry."

"Me, too." She pressed her fingers into the metal seat. "Maybe that reaction will go away if we keep doing it. Kissing," she added, one brow raised impishly.

Sloan grinned at her. "That's a theory I'd like to check out." He kissed the side of her neck.

Jacie put her arms around him again and let him half pull her into his lap. It felt so good being this close to him. His fingers moved under her jacket and lifted the hem of shirt, splaying across the skin of her back. His hands were warm and large, burning her skin. She arched into him, then put her hands behind his head and into his silky hair.

Sloan stood, bringing Jacie with him. She clung to him, locking her ankles behind his hips as they continued to kiss with increasing heat. He walked toward the door of her cabin and then leaned her back against the closed door. He pressed his body against hers, feeling the softness of her breasts against him, her soft moan in his mouth.

Leaning down he turned the doorknob and pushed the door open. Sloan jerked his head back suddenly as he got a whiff of the air inside the cabin. He turned so his back was to the cabin and pushed her down so she stood on her own feet. He urged her backwards away from the front door.

"What?" she asked, startled.

"It smells like gas. Wait here." He walked into the dark cabin. All of the cabins were laid out the same and he knew the layout like the back of his hand. He strode toward the kitchenette, but turned back when he heard her behind him. He gripped her wrist as she reached to switch on the living room lamp.

"Don't," he said quickly. "I think there's a gas leak." He pulled her back toward the door. "How long has it been like this?"

"I don't smell anything," she said hesitantly.

He hurried her out of the cabin and down the porch steps. "Are you kidding, you can't smell the gas? It's not real strong, but I noticed it right off."

"No, honestly . . . it's kind of a joke in my family, but I have on-again, off-again sinus problems. Sometimes I can't smell anything."

"I can't let you stay here. You'll have to spend at least tonight in the lodge. I'll have the gas supplier in here the first thing in the morning. Right now I'll get you set up in a room at the lodge. I'm really sorry about this, Jacie."

He walked around the side of the cabin and closed the valves on the upright gas tanks.

"I've shut the tanks off. That will give the air time to clear in there." He led the way back to the lodge. "My God!" he said, shaken. "How long were you in your cabin today?"

"On and off all day."

Sloan gripped her hand and led her back to the lodge. He felt like he'd been doused in cold water. Just outside the lodge front door, he stopped and pulled her around to him. "You mentioned earlier feeling dizzy?"

"Yes. It just came over me suddenly," she said slowly. "I had taken a short nap on the couch earlier and felt dizzy when I got up." She began to look scared.

A shudder passed through him. What would have happened if he hadn't come with her to the cabin? "I'm going to call a doctor—"

"No way!" she stated emphatically. "I feel fine now."

"I'll know you're fine when I hear it from the doctor."

She stepped back from him, her lips tight and her jaw obstinate. "You can go ahead and get the doctor out at this hour, but he won't be happy when I refuse to see him. I'm not dizzy anymore. No nausea. No symptoms."

He could see she meant it. "Dammit, I don't like the idea of you not being checked out."

As they reentered the lodge Michelle was washing glasses behind the bar. Sloan was surprised to see Donny, his ranch hand, leaning against the bar talking with her.

"Hi Donny, Michelle."

Donny looked a bit nervous, but Michelle greeted them cheerfully. "Hi. I thought you were both going to turn in. Are you back for more dancing?"

"Sloan discovered a gas leak at my cabin. He's giving me a room here tonight."

"A gas leak?" Michelle said. "That's weird."

Sloan pulled a key off the wall. "Here's your key, Jacie."

Good night again," Michelle said. "If you want, boss, I'll call the gas company first thing in the morning."

Sloan shook his head. "No, I can take care of it. I can't understand how it happened." He looked at Donny and Michelle. "Good night." He gripped Jacie's elbow. "Let's go upstairs. I'll show you where your room is."

He led the way up the wide staircase, stopping at the second door from the wide landing. "You'll have to share a bathroom with Michelle and Renee, it's the third door down."

"That's okay." She took the key from him and put it in the door lock.

"I'm sorry about the inconvenience. I'll find a way to make it up to you," he promised.

"That's not necessary," she said, looking at him over her shoulder.

"I'm sure I can think of something," he murmured, giving her a slow grin. "It's too bad our night was interrupted like this. Good night, Jacie."

Ω

When Sloan went back downstairs Michelle and Donny had disappeared. He locked the doors, left the lodge and cut back across the parking area to Jacie's cabin. He had a strange uneasiness about the gas leak. He entered the cabin and opened all the windows. Although he had turned the tanks off, there was still a faint odor inside.

Reaching for the flashlight hanging on the kitchen wall, he flicked the switch and lifted the porcelain top of the stove. Everything looked fine to his untrained eye. He maneuvered the kitchen stove away from the wall and immediately saw that the gas line from the tanks to the stove had worked its way loose. He pushed the flashlight closer and noticed scratches on the copper tubing that attached to the stove. A curl of unease wound through him. It looked like the line could have worked its way loose, but he didn't know for sure.

He pushed the stove back toward the wall. Why should he be suspicious that someone had deliberately disconnected the line? He had no reason to think any such thing, yet he couldn't shake the notion that this wasn't an accident. Each summer he had the gas company do any maintenance and check all the lines, but someone could have been careless.

A short time later he left the cabin and walked the short distance to his house. His mind went around and around. The low-down, anxious feeling in his gut wouldn't let go. By the time he walked inside his house he knew he had to make a phone call to Con, Jacie's brother.

He walked immediately to the phone and pulled a slip of paper from a nearby clipboard. He punched in several numbers and waited impatiently until a voice came on the other end. It was an answering machine.

"This is Sloan Wright out at Timber Falls. I want to talk to you about your sister."

He hung up the phone, feeling unsatisfied that he hadn't been able to talk to Jacie's brother. She'd said her brother would be out of town for awhile. Maybe he was overreacting, but he couldn't take a chance. Was someone intent on ruining Timber Falls or could they have a personal vendetta against Jacie?

∞ Chapter Seven ∞

EARLY THE NEXT DAY on a bright, clear morning, the small engine plane circled over one of Timber Falls' largest meadows. The wide, flat area had been designated for their skydiving jumps. Jacie turned her attention from the plane's window to Emma beside her. Emma had elected to do the first jump. Her husband John wasn't jumping but had accompanied her in the plane for support.

"Now, we've gone over all the basics," Jacie raised her voice so she'd be heard over the plane's engine and the wind rushing outside the open door. "I'll be jumping with you, Emma. Do you remember what we talked about?"

Wide-eyed, Emma nodded. "I think so. Yes, I think so."

"If you have any last minute questions or concerns, now is the time. How are you feeling?"

Emma shivered as she looked toward the open door. "Kind of sick, but okay."

"I've been there," Jacie said. Meticulously, she

checked her pack and Emma's one last time.

She stepped over to the door and braced one foot against the threshold. She looked back at Emma and held out her hand. "Ready?"

Emma gave her husband a quick kiss and then moved to join Jacie. Jacie admired her grit, knowing how the fear could make you exhilarated and terrified at the same time.

"We're all set, we'll just ease up to the door carefully." Jacie pushed back her own hesitation in this last moment.

The pilot gave the signal and she looked into Emma's excited, terrified eyes. They stepped forward together and there was no hesitation.

She breathed deeply, feeling the familiar updraft of air as it pulled them toward the heavens. They began their descent, swirling, the air rushing past them as the plane continued onward. She nudged Emma's legs into the proper position, knees bent, and smiled at her, delighted by the wonder on Emma's face. That had been the same exhilaration she had felt until the accident, and then she had lost it. But little by little, it was returning, filling her with the indescribable joy of a successful jump. It was the freedom and release that went with her occupation.

She released the chute and they shot upwards again. Jacie took a picture of Emma, the wonder on her face. Slowly, gently, they dropped to the green pasture where others waited to offer congratulations.

They landed without incident. She unclipped Emma's harness as fellow guests gathered around a stunned, smiling Emma. Jacie saw Sloan standing on the sidelines. She hadn't known he would be here today but she was glad he'd come.

Her heart beat faster. She stood in the midst of the chatter and the congratulations and hugged the parachute to her chest. She saluted him with one hand. He smiled and shook his head and she felt wonderful. Absolutely wonderful.

Sloan approached her. "That went very smooth," he commented, his face thoughtful.

"Yes."

"You're scheduled for one more today?"

"MaryAnn will be jumping." She flicked back her sleeve and checked her watch. "In about ten minutes, then we'll break for lunch."

"I'll hang around to make sure everything is set."

"I appreciate your vigilance Sloan, but I don't want to take you away from your other work."

"These jumps are part of my work. Anything on this property is my concern."

Some of her exhilaration faded. "Of course I understand that. I just didn't want to hold you up."

He threw her an assessing glance. "Jacie, if I didn't want to be here, I wouldn't be. I might not be crazy about skydiving but I'm going to make sure things go well and everyone is happy." He paused and he gave her a slow once-over. "I'd also like to mention you look great in that outfit."

"Sometimes you say the nicest things, Sloan. I'm tempted to throw my arms around your neck and kiss you."

"I'm not stopping you."

Jacie moved close and reaching up, dropped a kiss on the side of his jaw.

The plane flew in and landed further up the road they used as a runway. "Okay, I have to go," she said cheerfully. "I'll see you after the next jump."

"Sure thing," he said.

When the plane was once more in the air, Jacie watched Sloan's figure become smaller below them.

Jacie turned her attention to Maryann beside her. "Jacie, I can't believe I'm doing this. My friends won't believe I'm doing this," MaryAnn said excitedly.

"You'll have the pictures to prove it," she reassured MaryAnn, but was surprised in the next moment to feel the plane begin an ascent.

She stood. "Be right back," she said cheerfully.

She walked to the front and found the pilot trying to right a coffee cup he had tipped over. She leaned past him and set the cup in its holder. "Bill, what's going on?"

His round face was pasty white. "Sorry, Jacie, I'm heading back. I've got a touch of the flu or something. It suddenly came on me."

With concern, she noted droplets of perspiration on his forehead and his dark hair was damp. "Bill, are you okay? Are you going to make it?"

He nodded. "Yeah, but I want to get out of the air." The plane bumped a little and she grabbed the back of his seat. "We'll land in a few minutes. Don't worry, I'll get us down safely."

Bill was a good pilot. There was no reason to worry but she went back to sit with MaryAnn, she rubbed her palms nervously down the side of her jumpsuit.

"Unfortunately, we'll have to postpone your jump," she told MaryAnn. "The pilot has a touch of flu or something. To be on the safe side he's bringing us down."

"Poor guy."

To her relief MaryAnn didn't look duly concerned but Jacie kept a furtive eye on Bill. Moments later they landed smoothly. MaryAnn exited the plane while Jacie moved quickly back toward Bill.

His cheeks now had a faint flush.

"You need to see a doctor," she told him quickly. "I'll see about a ride for you." She didn't like how shaky he looked.

"What's the matter?" Sloan asked, appearing around

the back of the plane. "Did MaryAnn decide not to jump?"

"Bill's sick."

Sloan looked at Bill as he too exited the plane. "I'll take you into town."

Bill didn't protest. "I think it's a flu or something." He held his stomach and grimaced.

Sloan unhooked a radio attached to his belt and spoke into it. "James, call Dr. Adams in town and tell him I'm bringing someone in to see him. Bill is in pain, might be the flu. We're on the way now."

Jacie touched Bill's arm reassuringly. "I hope you're okay."

"Sorry, Jacie," he said with a grimace.

She watched Sloan run across the pasture to get the truck.

"Don't worry about it. Here comes Sloan now. Let him get you to the doctor. You'll be feeling well in no time."

She helped him into the truck and watched it drive away. Hopefully Bill would be feeling better in a few days. As the truck moved down the road, she pondered the suddenness of the pilot's illness. She hoped no one else caught it.

Ω

The next day Jacie burrowed into her jacket, trying to ward off the chill morning air. She was glad she had decided to go on the overnight camping trip to Haines Falls. Since Bill was out of commission for a few days there would be no skydiving jumps. The doctor had declared it a case of gastric upset. Apparently he had eaten something that didn't agree with him. She thought it was kind of odd, considering everyone had eaten bagels and cream cheese from the same breakfast buffet as Bill and no one else became sick but the doctor also conceded it might have been another place he had eaten.

James, Michelle and Donny had led them along trails of rock and through dense evergreen and hardwoods for over an hour before they reached a clearing on the mountain.

She had elected to ride the horse Dandy, yet he seemed out of sorts today. The longer she rode, the more uneasy his behavior. Snorting, sidling, he acted like a totally different horse from the previous times she had ridden him.

"Jacie, maybe we'd better switch horses," James said again, casting a worried glance at her. "I don't like the way he's acting."

Jacie shrugged. "I'm okay, maybe he's just in a bad mood. I'm sure he'll be okay until we get there."

"We're almost to the camp," Michelle said.

They had left quite early, before the sky had had a chance to lighten the sky. The supplies for the trip had been packed the night before so all they had to do was climb on their horses and take off.

Right now as they crossed a wide-open ledge the rising sun bathed everything in an eerie half-light. They were offered a pure, unobstructed view of trees and mountains. The ragged ledge below them cast interesting shadows into crevices and hidey-holes along the escarpment trail.

"This place is gorgeous," she murmured. "I'm going to have a hard time leaving."

"That's the magic of the Catskills," James asked. "I think the bug has hit you."

Mentally shaking herself, she agreed with his assessment. "It amazes me I guess that where I live there are taxis and lines to contend with, humanity on all sides and you guys have constant access to the total opposite.

Nature at its best."

"The camp is right around this bend." James stopped and let everyone pass by him. "Go on ahead. Unsaddle your horse and then we'll take care of them while you get breakfast."

He fell into line behind her. "I'm starving," she told James as she dismounted. She swept a soothing hand over her horse's neck. Nervously, Dandy tossed his head and pawed the ground. "I wish I knew why this guy was so ornery today."

She removed his saddle and tack and Michelle led the horse to the sturdy camp corral. James and Michelle conferred on the animal and then released him into the confined area. Dandy immediately whisked away, bucking across the fenced area.

Everyone helped pitch the tents. She chose an area outside the clearing, close to a growth of white birch saplings. Beside the small corral was a pipe with a tap that made use of an underground spring.

"Coffee's on," James said.

Donny had already started a fire. She dropped to sit cross-legged beside the small blaze, holding her cold white fingers out to the flames. "That was quick work, Donny." She threw the long-haired teenager a smile.

"Can I get you coffee or tea, Ms. Turner?" Donny asked shyly, brushing a stray lock of dark blond hair off his forehead.

"Make it Jacie, and I'd love tea."

"Sure thing."

She held the warmth of the mug between her fingers as he prepared eggs, bacon, potatoes and ham.

"Have you worked at Timber Falls long?"

"The last two summers." He flipped the eggs, then looked up at her. "This is the first summer Sloan let me help on the overnight trips."

Her interest perked up another notch at the mention of Sloan. She hadn't seen him since he'd taken Bill to see the doctor yesterday.

It had been James who told her the gas leak at her place had been due to a fitting that had worked its way loose. It had been taken care of and she had been able to move back into her cabin.

She ran a finger along the rim of her mug. "It must be like a working vacation," she said to Donny. "Living and working up here."

"I love the summers," he said. "Everyone at Timber Falls is like family."

"Especially Michelle?" she asked impishly.

Donny looked at Michelle where she stood across the clearing talking with James. His ears immediately became red. "Um, yeah, Michelle is okay."

Realizing she had inadvertently embarrassed him, she said casually, "I like Michelle too. Does Sloan ever do the overnights?"

"Sure. James expects Sloan to show up. He got back late last night from a buying trip. I heard he picked up twenty new heifers."

"I didn't know that." She kept her voice level, trying to tamp down feelings of anticipation. She had missed him.

"Hey, Donny, we're starving!" James called out good-naturedly.

The rest of the party gravitated toward the campfire.

"Pass me a cup, will you, Jacie?" James said.

She reached over and picked up a mug, then handed it to him. "You've lived here all your life?" she asked him now.

"I was born here in the Catskills. Sloan, on the other hand is a transplant. Our dad moved here permanently from Texas when Sloan was little."

"Yes, he mentioned that."

James looked surprised. "He told you that? My mom married Everett Wright when Sloan's mother died. Sloan was around nine. I came along about a year later."

"You seem very close. That probably has a lot to do with the success of Timber Falls."

"I have to admit the last two years have been the best yet. Dotty, that's my wife, well, she thinks we should expand and build a dozen more cabins."

"You sound like you don't favor the idea?"

"Not entirely, Sloan and I think Timber Falls is fine the way it is. I want to bring in more revenue, but not to the extent that the ranch loses its quaint appeal."

"I agree with you, James. You might lose something if you catered to too many at once."

Emma joined them as she precariously balanced a full plate of ham and eggs. "Hey James, what's on the agenda for today? If I don't get moving soon, I won't want to."

"We'll hike to the falls then meet back here for lunch. By then Sloan should be here."

Jacie was aware of heat enveloping her from head to toe at the mention of Sloan's name. Tensely, she ran her palms over her jeans. Disturbed by her reaction, she spied a bright growth of Morning Glory and walked across the clearing to inspect the delicate blue flowers. They had wound themselves tightly around a nearby sapling and the effect of the flowers against the slim trunk was startling and unexpected.

"Penny for them." A pair of dark brown boots appeared beside her. She lifted her eyes slowly . . . dark jeans, silver belt buckle, faded green shirt, stopped at devil blue eyes.

"Hi, Sloan."

Sloan had a slight smile curving his lips. Leaning close, he plucked one of the blossoms and offered it to her. She looked at the fragile bloom lying in his calloused palm, her heart turning over. The gesture was so simple, yet touching.

She had worked with all types of men, been wined and dined by a few, but none affected her as this man did. Her relationship with Brad paled in comparison. He had never made her feel so intense, yet secure. Sloan was outside her realm of experience; she had the sense he played for keeps. Did she want to be in that league?

"Thank you," she said simply, a satisfying warmth coursing through her. She plucked the flower from his palm and touched it gently to her nose.

"How was the ride here? Did you enjoy it?"

She nodded. "I loved it. This is the best scenery and James is a great guide." She added the last for James' benefit as he appeared beside Sloan.

"You must have hustled to get here," James said, his glance moving between the two of them.

"I brought the truck and trailer," Sloan said.

James nodded. "Good. You've got perfect timing. We're getting ready to leave on the hike."

"Sometimes, I get lucky," Sloan murmured, his eyes on her. She watched him drop his pack to the ground and look around their group. "Are we ready?" he asked.

"Here." James tossed his brother a backpack identical to his own, which Sloan caught deftly. "You can carry the bag with the juices and water. We'll be leaving as soon as we finish eating."

Emma looked over at the horses where they stood in the corral. "Will the horses be okay here by themselves?" she asked doubtfully.

"Sure," Sloan answered. "Donny and Michelle will stay behind to keep an eye on things."

When everyone was ready Sloan and James led the way toward a dense growth of short pines. "Watch out for the briars," Sloan warned, holding back a tangle of vine.

Jacie skirted around him. "Thanks." She stopped beside a huge stone monument located halfway up a steep bank. She touched the precisely placed stones with her hands. They felt cold and damp yet seemed to have held together well through time. Slinging her camera around to her back, she climbed to the top of the stone mound.

"This is an old railroad bed," James said, climbing up behind her. "When we climb out of this shallow knoll you'll see the clearing where the Laurel House used to stand. Below it is where you'll find the falls."

"Be careful going down toward the falls," Sloan cautioned. Everyone paused beside railroad ties that had been sunk into the earth above the creek to stabilize the bank. "The ground has washed out. It's always slippery."

His hand closed around her arm as he guided her down the small slope, then he did the same for Emma and MaryAnn. When she stood on a flat rock at the top of the falls, she drank in the one-hundred-eighty-degree view stretched so magnificently before her.

"This is magnificent. The falls is at our feet."

James came to stand beside her. "It gashes its way through the mountain to the clove at its base."

Jacie stood perfectly still, aware only of the hushed quiet and the long drop to the top of the trees. She pulled her camera out and slowly, methodically began to take pictures. "Can everyone face me?" she called out. "I want to get everyone in this picture with the mountains as a backdrop." She specifically wanted a picture of Sloan as a memento of this time.

Jacie snapped several pictures. Sloan joined her by the edge of the falls. "This height doesn't bother you?" he asked.

She lowered her camera. "No."

"The top of this falls used to have an observation deck about a hundred years ago." Sloan touched the toe of his boot to a circular bit of metal that appeared embedded in the rock. "They used to lower drinks down to hikers at the bottom of the falls."

"A hundred years ago?" Emma asked. She looked carefully over the edge, holding on to her husband's arm. "I don't see a trail."

"There's a really steep trail on the side of the falls. It used to be maintained a bit more back then. Women used to hike with their long skirts and dresses."

"Amazing," Jacie murmured, snapping more pictures.

"The area's hotels used to be host to quite a few famous people," James remarked. "The biggest hotels were the Catskill Mountain House and the Kaaterskill. We'll be riding to those sites later."

As a group they moved away from the edge of the falls and up the creek, hopping from rock to rock.

"Look at these rocks!" MaryAnn exclaimed. "There's dates chiseled in the rocks."

"Some of them go back into the 1800's," Jacie marveled. "Do you ever come here in the winter?" Jacie asked Sloan curiously.

"I haven't in a few years but it's accessible by car. In the middle of winter the falls freeze on top but the water still runs beneath. The upper crust of ice is thick and looks blue."

The group scrambled up the small incline and walked back through the pines. As they fanned out she found herself between Sloan and James.

Jacie pulled a hair band out of her jeans pocket. As twisted her hair into the band she studied Sloan's face. "You look very serious."

He leaned close. "I should have thought about

bringing you here, just the two of us." He took her hand as they pulled up the rear of the group, winding a path through balsam trees.

Jacie tilted her head. "What a sweet thing to say." She drew in a deep, appreciative breath. "My head feels clear today. I don't think I'll ever smell balsam again without thinking of this wonderful trip."

As they emerged from the trees, Jacie looked around the clearing doubtfully. "It's hard to imagine there was a large hotel here."

"For anyone interested, we have pictures back at camp," James said. "You'll be amazed by the differences between past and present."

When they arrived back at camp they had a quick lunch and the horses were saddled and ready to go. Jacie persuaded James to let her ride Dandy. He seemed to have settled back to his normal self. As a group they rode a state designated horse trail to the next site.

About an hour into the ride Dandy started hollowing out his back and crow-hopping sideways again. When he brushed her up against a tree, Sloan moved up alongside her with his horse. "Jacie, dismount and we'll switch horses."

"Okay." In that instant Dandy kicked his hind feet out, narrowly missing Sloan's leg. The horse then reared up, a frantic whinny tearing from him. He jerked his head forward. Caught by surprise, the reins were pulled from Jacie's fingers.

Sloan lunged forward. The reins caught for a second on the horse's ears and then slid over his head. Nose almost on the ground, Dandy leapt forward and tore swiftly up the narrow path and away from the others.

"Jacie!" Someone shouted. There was nothing she could do. She sat upright as best she could, afraid the horse would catch a foot in the reins and they would both go down. The animal continued to do odd little hops and she lost her left stirrup. When the horse plunged and became more frantic, she swayed off balance to the left.

Jacie had only seconds to consider the best way to get off. Two horses came abreast of her as the path grew wider. James forced his mount in front of Dandy, forcing the horse to veer toward Sloan's horse. What happened next was a blur. Sloan's arm snaked around her, pulling her from the saddle. James slowed his horse, jumped off and grabbed Dandy by the bridle.

Jacie felt the biting strength in Sloan's arms. His muscled arm cut into her side as she bounced against him painfully. He slowed his horse to a walk and then the animal stopped and stood still. Gripping the corded muscle of his leg, she dangled from the side of his horse. Her legs hit his horse's legs but the horse remained calm.

Unclenching her shaking fingers, she slid down until her feet touched the ground. Her legs shook and she held onto his boot, afraid she'd collapse.

"Jacie, are you okay?" he asked urgently.

"Yes." She pushed her hair out of her face. "What was that about?"

Dandy now stood quietly, sides heaving and foam flecking his belly and legs. The rest of their party caught up with them and began nervously asking questions.

"What happened to him?" Jacie stepped away from Sloan's horse. "My legs are shaky."

Sloan dismounted. "Jacie, come and sit down." He urged her over to the side of the path, but she shook her head and pushed away from him.

"I'm okay. What's the matter with Dandy?"

James spoke softly to her horse as he unsaddled him. In minute detail he and Sloan examined the saddle pad and then the saddle.

She crossed her arms over her chest, feeling a chill chase across her. "What are you looking for?"

Sloan dropped the pad on top of the saddle where his brother had dropped it on the ground. "I don't know, Jacie, I just don't know. I can't see any problem with the pad."

"Or the saddle," James offered quietly.

She saw a strange look pass between the brothers. "What's going on?" she asked stiffly. Neither of them answered. Sloan ran a gentle hand over the horse's back. The animal trembled, yet now stood unmoving.

She touched a light finger to Dandy's neck. "He's been acting strange all day, but this was the worst. He was out of control."

"Geez, Jacie." MaryAnn's voice was hushed, "I don't know how you stayed on. He acted like he was crazy or something. You're lucky he didn't throw you."

Jacie sensed anger in Sloan, but she didn't understand why.

"Are you sure you're okay?" he asked tightly, a closed look on his face.

"Yeah, I'm just glad Dandy's not hurt." She reached forward and grabbed the horse's reins. "I'm going to walk him back."

"No," James said. "I'll take him. If you think you're okay, you can take my horse. You've come this far, you might as well go on to the next site."

Trying not to let what had happened dampen the fun of the day Jacie explored the Kaaterskill Hotel site with the others. There wasn't much left, a few traces of foundation, an old concrete swimming hole and what was left of a bottle dump. She couldn't rid her mind of the bizarre way the horse had acted.

"You're still white, Jacie." Sloan had watched her like a hawk since the incident with Dandy.

"I'm worried about the horse."

He expelled a harsh breath, shaking his head. "Forget the horse. I'm worried about you."

As they started back to camp they followed a narrow footpath overgrown with bright green foliage. Jacie recognized it as Mountain Laurel, but her mind was still focused on the horse. Was she an accident waiting to happen? Why did all this stuff happen to her?

The path grew narrower and she moved her horse closer to Sloan. "You must have ideas about what caused this. You haven't said much since it happened."

"Sorry, I know my brother's a better guide."

Exasperated, Jacie said, "I'm not talking about that! If you're worried I'll hold you liable, don't be. Even animals have off days."

Sloan gave her an impatient glance but kept his voice low. "Don't you think it's strange these accidents keep happening to you?"

"I did think about that."

"I'm wondering if this was deliberate," he said. "I'm wondering if the gas leak in your cabin was intentional."

"The gas line was a fluke. It came loose, unless you know something I don't." She tried not to panic. "No one would want to hurt me." The track became steep and she concentrated on the trail ahead.

"There's just too many things going on here, and they're all happening to you."

As the path leveled out they trailed the other riders and rode side by side. After a few more feet she pulled back on her reins and let the others move further ahead.

"Explain what you mean about the gas leak."

"Maybe the gas line did pull loose. Maybe the rock hitting you was a freak occurrence. Dandy has never acted like this before."

Her heart raced into her throat and beat hard, almost

choking her. "When you add them up, it sounds like a case, but then again maybe it's crazy even saying something like that." She rubbed her forehead, feeling flushed and nervous. No, she admonished herself, don't let fear take hold. Surely there was a reasonable explanation.

"It just sounds incredible. I've always been kind of accident prone, but I've been lucky enough to pull out each time." Except for last year. She shivered. She had just about died that time.

Perhaps he saw her fear because he muttered a curse. "When we get back I'm calling the sheriff. For your safety and the reputation of Timber Falls I need this investigated."

She didn't say anything. In all honesty, she didn't know what to say.

Sloan spurred his horse to the front of the ride. "Okay, everyone ride through the stone pillars and into the clearing. Donny should be waiting with the horse trailer."

The group moved into a wide, grassy expanse and found Donny was there with their transportation.

"We'll load the horses and drive back to camp," he said.

Jacie's legs ached. She wasn't' accustomed to spending hours in the saddle. She looked around the field and some of the tension eased from her. The area abounded with colorful wildflowers. "This is incredible."

"You're incredible," Sloan murmured. "That ride you took. I'll tell you what—I got this God-awful feeling when I saw the reins trailing and you flying by."

"I was scared, but I didn't have time to think about it. It turned out all right, though. I've been in worse scrapes." It was over with and she felt a feverish need to move on.

"The outcome could have been different, especially with a horse like Dandy. We won't know anything until the vet sees him."

Once the horses were loaded into the trailer, the group moved toward a wide-open area where the Catskill Mountain House had stood.

Jacie pulled out her camera again. "The view is spectacular!" she exclaimed. "The lower Hudson Valley is at our feet."

"The Mountain House stood on the edge of this ledge," Sloan said. "Boats traveling up the Hudson River could see the hotel standing here like a beacon."

"How did people get here?" Emma asked, her voice full of awe.

"In the early days they brought horse drawn carriages up the front of the mountain. Later on, they built a railway called the Otis Incline. It worked on the principal of weights and it was quite an ingenious idea. When you look over the edge here, you can see the straight-as-an-arrow scar down the mountain to the valley where the rail line ran."

Jacie snapped Sloan's picture. When he looked up and stared at her, she zoomed her lens and snapped another picture. He lifted a brow tolerantly.

"See, I'm just like any other tourist," Jacie said. She moved away with a grin and shot the remainder of the roll on the group.

Sloan followed her. "I can see you appreciate our mountains the way I do, Jacie. They're beautiful, aren't they?" he asked.

"I envy you," she said softly. "With all the traveling I've done, I've never felt like I belonged anywhere the way you seem to fit here."

"People rush through life. I've chosen to stop and look."

"I know what you mean. I have a tendency to rush ahead."

"Look." He pointed toward the sky. "There's a red-tailed hawk."

The bird flew gracefully over their heads then zoomed down toward the grass a fair distance away. She captured the bird with her camera as it landed and then almost immediately took off again, a snake clutched in its talons.

They walked back toward the waiting truck and everyone climbed wearily into the extended cab for the ride back to camp.

The return trip to camp only took ten minutes. It was over paved road, winding through heavy woods. At the camp, Jacie carefully climbed down from the cab on her sore legs.

"Everybody okay?" James asked as they unloaded the horses from the trailer. "Any saddle sores?"

She managed a laugh. "It's been a while since I spent this much time on a horse. Some of my muscles have tightened up."

"Need help?" he asked, closing the corral gate behind the last horse.

She waved him on. "Go ahead, I'll be fine."

An arm encircled her shoulders, sending a jolt of heat through her. She turned her head and came eye-to-eye with Sloan. "Mmm, I believe I'll lean on you."

"Come on, old girl." His mouth crooked in amusement as he tightened his arm around her. "We'll never eat if we have to wait for you to amble into camp."

"Very funny." A wry smile touched her lips.

"My brother has a weird sense of humor," James said as they joined the others beside a small bonfire. He handed each of them a plate. "The food is behind you on the small table. Drinks are in the coolers and there's coffee set up next to the grill."

Jacie smiled. "I'm so hungry I'm forgetting about how tired I feel."

During dinner around a brightly glowing fire everyone discussed the day's events. James had an album of old postcards depicting the hotels in their heyday. The manicured lawns, carefully tended carriage drives and the immense size of the wooden structures was amazing.

Jacie took in the chatter but remained quiet. In truth, she still felt jittery over what had occurred earlier.

After dinner the atmosphere felt very relaxed. Jacie helped clean up the trash and pack the food away in the coolers. Skirting the camp fire, she carried the last of the trash to the truck's garbage container. She felt a bit of an odd man out since the rest of the party was couples. Sloan, James, Michelle and Donny were all either cleaning up or attending the horses.

Jacie washed her hands and swiped some bottled water from a cooler, then moved to the edge of the camp, admiring the sky as the sun faded from view. She heard a step behind her and looked over her shoulder at Sloan.

"You look wiped out," he said.

She rolled her head on her neck and lifted her shoulders. "Pleasantly so. Do you have a Jacuzzi hidden somewhere?"

"Aches, huh? I think I can help."

When his warm hands touched her shoulders, gently at first, then more strongly, she was lost in pure sensation. The tenseness in her shoulders and neck eased as his strong fingers massaged her. Hard, sure, smoothing, exotic. Erotic. "Is that helping?" he murmured.

She stifled a moan of pure pleasure. "I have the strangest desire to purr like a cat. I think I'm out of shape."

"Looks pretty good from where I'm standing," he murmured provocatively. Jacie just about jumped out of her skin when his mouth touched the back of her neck.

His hands across her back and shoulders made her clench her stomach muscles. "How curious. I feel relaxed and tense at the same time."

Images floated just beyond the perimeter of her vision. She and Sloan. She closed her eyes to enjoy the power of her imagination.

"How does that feel?" he asked, his voice husky and low. Intimate, she thought.

"Bring out that Jacuzzi."

His hands on her shoulders tightened, then slid down her back and away.

She twisted around and studied his face in the firelight. His cheekbones were prominent, his eyes partially hidden in shadow. "You're magic," she said sincerely, slowly rotating her shoulders. "Don't tell me you're a masseuse, too?"

"I used to do it for my mom," he admitted quietly, sitting back on his heels. "She was bedridden several months before she died."

"Oh." She felt an instant welling of concern. "How frightening that must have been, since you were only a child."

He looked away from her, searching the darkness beyond the perimeter of the camp as the horses whinnied to each other. "You learn to deal with losses. In time everything loses its sharp edges."

"Does a child ever get over seeing his mother suffer?"

"Not entirely, I guess."

"Well," Jacie said quickly, not wanting him to think she was being too probing. "It was a great massage. You've got the touch." Her shoulders weren't the only part of her body that had responded to his touch. Did he guess that? Of course he would. He was a man who looked like he knew what women wanted. She sighed. Now all she needed to figure out was what she wanted.

She drew him over to a fallen tree. "Here, sit down." She knelt behind him. "Now it's your turn." She grinned slyly. "Don't look so surprised. Fair is fair," she added lightly.

She clasped the warm skin of his neck, feeling the fine hair at the base of his skull as she kneaded gently. She moved down his shoulders. The muscle beneath her fingers was hard and well defined. Her mouth went dry. He'd look fabulous without a shirt.

She leaned into him, moving her hands down his back, working at the muscles. "Boy, are you tense." She touched his side, kneaded her fingers along his ribs and he scooted sideways and grabbed her hands with a low growl. She laughed in delight. "You're ticklish! How very interesting. This could be fun."

Just then someone clapped their hands. "Now that we've eaten, I think we should get the low-down on everybody," MaryAnn said.

"Sure," John said. "Sounds good to me."

Jacie looked away from the heated look in Sloan's eyes. For a moment she wished they alone.

"Come on." Sloan held his hand out and Jacie took it, following him back toward the campfire. She dropped into her vacated seat and Sloan pulled another camp chair over to the fire next to her. She needed time to wind down from the sensory experience of touching him.

MaryAnn laughed. "Since you're all bashful, I'll go first."

"She's never at a loss for words," her husband Leo agreed.

"Leo and I own a computer business. We heard about Timber Falls through a friend. We've been trying to take a break for a while, so here we are. It's like a second honeymoon." MaryAnn turned to Emma and John. "Your turn."

"Emma and I hail from Vermont where we run an inn. We're on our honeymoon. It's a second marriage for both of us."

Jacie let the lighthearted banter wash over her. It reminded her of home and late night camp-outs in the backyard with her brothers. A dab of homesickness touched her. She hadn't talked to her family since she had come here. They were off on a job, but she missed them suddenly.

Aware of silence, she looked up and found expectant faces staring at her. Reluctantly, she said, "I suppose it's my turn? I live about an hour and a half outside of the city and I'm not married." Her eyes slid past Sloan's speculative glance.

"Well?" MaryAnn prompted.

Jacie looked at her and raised her brows. "What? Oh, I love photography. If I wasn't skydiving I'd probably be a photographer."

The other woman wore an openly curious expression. "I'm not trying to pry, but when I first met you I kept thinking I knew you. It's not every day you meet a celebrity."

"I'm not a celebrity," Jacie protested.

"I saw a documentary about five years ago about skydiving and exhibition jumps. I remembered because you were the first woman to do a certain type of stunt."

Jacie shrugged. "Yes, I remember that, it was filmed to document parachuting as a sport. But it wasn't me they highlighted, it was my mother, who is also Jacie. Back in the sixties she was a member of the US Army women's team. In sixty-four they won individual championships in parachuting and spot jumping."

"Wow," John said.

The entire group seemed awestruck. To break through that, she said lightly, "My father feels pretty much the same way. He's never jumped out of a plane. I have a really unconventional family."

"It was exciting watching you parachute into Timber Falls the first day," MaryAnn said. "Before last week I would never have imagined myself jumping out of a plane. It terrified me, but now I'm really looking forward to it."

Jacie studied Sloan intently. He poked at the fire, his face absorbed as he watched the flames.

"It grabs you and doesn't let you go," she agreed.

She was disturbed by the closed look on his face, his features harsh and drawn. Had talking about her skydiving put that look on his face?

"What's the next job after this, Jacie?" someone asked.

She deliberately watched Sloan's face, which was half-turned away from her. "I'm sure there will be something in the works when I get back." He jabbed at the fire with a long stick, causing sparks to fly upward.

"Do you ever get afraid up there?" John asked.

"You'd be crazy if you didn't have some healthy fear. The business is a risk. You know it and you live with it."

Sloan stood up and disappeared into the shadows. She felt a momentary chill, but ignored it and continued to answer questions as best she could. People were naturally curious about her work; she didn't hold it against them.

Jacie finally decided to call it a night about nine o'clock. Early by any standard, after riding and hiking most of the day she was beat.

Once in her tent she reflected on the day's events. Perhaps there was no significance, yet a strange ache twisted through her as she recalled how Sloan had left the group. She knew it had something to do with her. He had returned to check the fire at a later point, but he had not joined in the conversation. He had reservations about her line of work. He regarded jumping out of planes as something foolish.

Listening to the sizzle and crack of the dying fire, Jacie began to drift off to sleep. Suddenly, she suddenly heard a different noise. Recalling what Sloan had said about bears when she first arrived, she rolled over and looked through her tent mesh. Beyond the glowing embers, on the edge of camp, she could make out a dark silhouette by the horse pen.

An odd, warning prickle touched her. Sloan and James had set up their tent on the opposite side of camp. Was it her imagination or was there someone over by the horse pen? She concentrated her attention on the shadow, but it seemed to melt away. Quietly, she crawled out of her tent and hurried over to where Sloan and James stood talking.

As she drew closer perhaps her expression must have alerted Sloan something wasn't right. He stopped mid-conversation and stepped forward, a hand going out to her arm. "Jacie, what is it?"

"I had the strangest feeling someone was over by the horses. Something was crouched down in the brush. Then it disappeared."

Sloan and James walked to the area she indicated.

When Donny suddenly appeared out of the brush Jacie gave a small screech. Sloan jumped toward her and grabbed her arm.

"Donny, it's you" she said with relief.

"Sorry," he said sheepishly. "Just checking everything before I turn in." He shifted his feet nervously.

"Did you see anyone out here?" Sloan asked with a

frown.

"No. What's going on?"

Jacie put her arms around herself. "I thought I saw someone crouched down in the brush."

"What were you doing out there, Donny?" James asked.

Jacie saw Donny swallow as he looked back and forth between the brothers. "N-nothing."

Sloan and James produced flashlights and combed the immediate area. After several moments she joined them at the fenced corral.

"Maybe I'm seeing things," she said ruefully. "It's been a long day."

Sloan swept his flashlight over the ground one more time, then abruptly stopped. He crouched down. "Maybe not," he said grimly.

She followed the light beam, her eyes widening as she saw a syringe and needle lying in the grass. Fear ripped through her. An indrawn breath had her turning to Donny, who stood behind her. With dismay, she noticed Donny's frightened expression.

"Donny, have you ever seen that before?" Sloan asked quietly.

"No, I swear I haven't." Donny looked beseechingly at Sloan. "I swear," he repeated, his eyes darting back and forth between them.

"I believe him," she said quietly.

Sloan threw her an impatient glance as he stepped closer to the teenager. "I'm not accusing you Donny. You've been with us two years and I've come to trust you. Just explain to me what's going on that's making you so nervous."

Donny nodded quickly. "I know I was in a lot of trouble when you hired me on two years ago Sloan, but I've kept my nose clean." He clenched his fists and stared earnestly at each of them in turn. "I like working here." He looked down at his feet. "I've been seeing Michelle. I know I'm not good enough, what with all the trouble I caused back then, but I like her and I'd never hurt her."

Sloan clasped Donny's shoulder. "I know you wouldn't harm her. There's no reason you can't see Michelle, Donny."

Jacie smiled, expecting nothing less of Sloan. He wouldn't accuse anyone unjustly.

Donny gave him a look of relief. "Michelle said that too, but I figured since she's your cousin and all, that you might not want me hanging around with her. We were down by the creek, you know, just talking. I thought it would be better if nobody saw us coming back together so I had her go on ahead."

"Okay, Donny, why don't you turn in," Sloan said. "God knows it's been a long day."

"I'll get a pair of pliers and a plastic bag for that syringe," James said grimly when Donny ambled off to his tent.

Sloan kept his flashlight trained on it. "Good idea. We'll have to have it looked at. Maybe it's something as innocent as an insulin needle from the last set of campers."

Jacie wished it was something as simple as that but she had a bad feeling about it.

Using the pliers Sloan gingerly placed the syringe with the needle inside a plastic bag. "I'll keep this in my tent," he said. No one argued.

She didn't want to be anywhere near it.

"In the morning we'll see if anyone lays claim to it."

"Why don't you turn in for the night?" Sloan said to her.

Troubled, she knew he was right, but wondered if she'd be able to sleep.

"I'll keep watch during the night, so don't worry about anyone coming back."

"We'll split the watch," James said. "I think we should break camp earlier than we planned in the morning."

"Do you think that needle could be the cause of why Dandy acted so strange?" she asked hesitantly, finally voicing the fear which had steadily grown. "Could someone have given him something?"

Sloan looked at her sharply. "Anything is possible, but we won't know until it's tested." As if he sensed her apprehension, he put his arm around her. "Come on, I'll walk you to your tent."

"Thanks, Sloan."

"Try to get some rest, Jacie. One way or the other I'm going to get to the bottom of this."

He leaned down and gently, firmly placed a kiss on her lips. The brief contact wasn't enough. She reached up and gripped the collar of his shirt on both sides. She held him close to her for a moment, savoring his scent. She placed a lingering kiss on his firm mouth, then a quick kiss on his jaw. She watched his mouth curve into a smile.

"Thanks, Sloan."

He waited until she was settled in the tent, the mesh flap zipped and snapped. Even under the tense circumstances, he showed her consideration. She watched him walk back toward the dying fire as she burrowed into her bedroll, shivers of reaction taking over as she wondered what was really going on out here. Who would want to harm her or the horse?

∞ Chapter Eight ∞

WHEN JACIE WOKE DAYLIGHT was just beginning to break and the sky beyond the mountains was a fiery orange red.

She had never thought of herself as a person who scared easily, but between her skydiving accident last year and the suspicions Sloan had voiced about someone trying to hurt her, she began to feel incredibly paranoid.

She looked outside her tent but she didn't see anyone stirring. She quickly put on some clean clothes and climbed out of the tent, wondering if coffee was available. She reached down to close her tent flap and heard a noise behind her.

"Were you able to sleep?" Sloan asked and she almost jumped out of her skin.

She whirled around with her hand to her chest. "I didn't see you there. I'm about ready to jump out of my skin. I must have dozed off and got an hour or two of sleep."

He reached forward and gently cupped her cheek.

"I'm not going to let anything happen to you Jacie. I stayed close to your tent most of the night."

She swallowed, touched by his concern. "You didn't get any sleep at all, did you?"

He shrugged it off. "Right now I've got other priorities." He moved toward the portable grill on the back of the truck tailgate and retrieved a pan of boiling water.

"Coffee?" he asked.

"Yes."

"Sorry, it's only instant today."

"That's fine." She looked around, stretching, feeling cramped muscles protest. The morning air was quite cool and she shivered as she accepted a cup of coffee with a murmur of thanks. "Is anyone else up?"

"James. Donny and Michelle are around here somewhere."

"That was really well done, you know, the way you put Donny at ease last night." She felt she had to tell him that. "Anyone else might have jumped down his throat."

"Donny's a good kid."

"So, you're going to tell the rest of the party what's going on?"

"We have to. They should be aware of what's been found. I'm still hoping for an easier explanation than the one that's been running through my head all night."

She felt the tension build up again. It had been a pressure in her chest since the night before. "I know, I've been trying to figure this entire thing out too. It's making me crazy." She traced the rim of her coffee cup. "I'm really sorry and that's so inadequate. If it turns out this is my fault in some way, I hope I haven't done harm to Timber Falls."

"It's not your fault," he said gruffly. "You didn't ask for this to happen. We'll get it figured out."

Before it's too late. He didn't say the words but they were inside her head and she read them in the grimness of his expression.

She heard the murmur of voices. The others were beginning to stir. She looked at him, not envying him the next half hour.

After a quick breakfast Sloan and James gathered everyone together and showed them the syringe and needle. She watched the varying reactions of horror and concern and was certain no one in their group was involved, yet she felt a measure of relief when they finally packed to leave.

"How are you holding up, Jacie?" James asked.

She managed a laugh, but she didn't know how convincing it sounded. "I'll be fine."

"We're worried about you, Jacie. We're getting the authorities involved. There have been too many coincidences."

She nodded. "I know and none of it makes sense."

"We're not taking any chances. It's almost time to leave so if you want to see the lakes before we head out Sloan is going to take the group. It's about a five-minute walk."

She placed the last of her gear beside her bedroll. She looked over at the rest of the group gathered by the horse corral and thought they looked pretty subdued.

"Jacie." She looked up as Sloan joined her. "This has been a poor introduction to our mountains, I'm afraid."

"We couldn't know there's some kind of crazy out there." She hugged her arms around herself.

"It gets my back up that we don't know anything," he said grimly.

She sensed he wouldn't back away from a tough situation. Unbidden, the thought intruded...there was a world of difference between he and Brad. He didn't like anyone messing around on his territory. When she'd got hurt, Brad had virtually disappeared and left her to fend for herself.

"Are you coming to see the lakes?" he asked abruptly, stuffing his hands into his pockets.

"I wouldn't miss it." She forced a bright smile to her mouth. She looked around at the somber group and on sudden inspiration clapped her hands several times. "Come on everyone, it's not the end of the world. Maybe there's an innocent explanation here. Let's not assume the worst." With determination, she joined the others. "I would love to see the lakes, but I haven't the foggiest idea which way to go!"

Sloan, watching her, took over as if on cue. "Come on, everyone, I'll show you the path."

She began to breathe easier as they walked in single file behind him. Third in line, she watched him forge ahead, admiring his broad back and long legs. The man possessed a potent sexuality she couldn't ignore. His concern was touching, but there was still a possibility the explanation was quite simple. She shook her head at her own naiveté. And maybe there wasn't.

In the past, her leap-before-you-look attitude had at times led her into trouble. For a moment she wondered if Sloan was the next bit of trouble she was heading into. She stifled a groan and decided sometimes the trouble was worth it.

The wind seemed to suddenly pick up. The branches of the evergreens around them swayed and dipped the further they went.

"Watch out for your eyes and face." He held back a heavy branch as one by one they moved along weather-beaten rock. They came to a small, clear ledge and she swept an appreciative look at the twin lakes lying far below them. She lifted her camera and zoomed in on the scene.

"The trees are so short and twisted," she murmured. They clung to bare rock, their roots reaching out like gnarled, arthritic fingers. They reminded her of the trees outside her cabin window.

"Up here, they don't seem to have much chance to grow, yet they've adapted," MaryAnn mused.

"All it takes is one determined seed or vine," Sloan said.

"If the conditions are right anything can adapt," she said.

"Sometimes," Sloan conceded.

As the rest of the group meandered back along the path she buttoned her flannel shirt and hunched her shoulders against the wind. "I'll catch up in a few minutes," she said.

Sloan looked ready to argue, then he nodded and led the group back into the trees.

She sat on the smooth rock and dangled her feet over the edge, closing her eyes as the wind hit her face. It was exhilarating. . .it was peaceful and she let the feelings fill her totally. Voices died away and she was alone.

Suddenly aware she wasn't alone, she looked behind her and saw Sloan circling back toward her. A deep yearning clutched her. Quickly, she swiped at a lone tear. "The wind is making my eyes tear," she said. She looked back to the view. "You kept your promise," she said, raising her voice.

"What promise?" he was close beside her, his husky voice in her ear.

"The view...you promised a great view."

"I never renege on promises." He indicated the lakes below them. "So, was it worth it?"

Without hesitation she gave him a provocative smile. "It's always worth it."

He squatted beside her. The feel of his fingertips against her cheek felt right, causing a tremble to begin in her shoulders. His hand cupped her chin, guided her face around to him. She met the intensity of his eyes and swallowed hard. He said something low, but it was lost against the wind.

Closing her eyes, she acknowledged the power of his touch over her. He elicited responses in her, responses she reveled in. Her lips lifted, met his hardness, his gentleness, the wonderful heat of his mouth. It was an experience like no other, as elemental as the wind whirling bits of leaves and dust just beyond the ledge. She felt as if they were closeted in their own world, the moment of tenderness forever imprinted in her mind. How many others had come to this place, she wondered, with someone special.

Sloan abruptly pushed himself back away from her and retrieved his hat. He pushed the hat down on his head and stood. Lips which had made love to her for an erotic moment now pressed together in a grim line.

She wondered what made him look so bleak. Did his thoughts mirror her own... that they were from two different worlds, and any encounter between them would never be more than brief?

Sloan stared at Jacie and fought the struggle within. The expression on her face looked so expectant, as if she wanted something more from him. Part of him longed to bring her over to the bed of ferns beneath the pines and forget about everything else. God! He wanted to make love to her. The urge was so strong, so vital; it took him several moments before he could control it.

"Should I say I'm sorry?" he asked unexpectedly. His hands shook so he shoved them into his pockets.

"Are you?" With her head thrown back he could see the vulnerable skin of her throat.

He admired her brass and nerve. He shook his head and felt himself smile. "No, Jacie, I'm not sorry I kissed you. There's something about you..." He let himself take in the full wonder of her, head to toe, all too aware of the reaction of his body. Ruefully, he admitted, "Sometimes, like now, I find I can't help myself, but I know we're opposites," he added. "Come on, it's time to go," he reminded her.

Without answering she drew her knees up and circled her legs with her arms.

"Jacie." He struggled and almost gave in to what he wanted. He wanted to let her get close, let her see what was inside his head. She looked alone sitting on the ledge, the wind whipping her hair around her head. Dammit, he wanted to protect her, make her happy instead of forlorn.

"I'll be there in a minute."

He walked away and each step he told himself he was doing the right thing. People like Jacie didn't settle down to a normal home life. They hankered after the next illusion of a rainbow, whether there was one there or not. He knew it too well. Up until the time his mother had died he had seen her break his father's heart time and again. He didn't want a life that involved that kind of heartache.

He waited for her just out of sight. He was afraid that long after she had left Timber Falls a part of him would be empty without her.

Ω

Jacie jogged to the horse barn early the next morning. Unlike most mornings, the air was already warm. It felt like it might be a hot day later on. A vehicle with large plastic boxes affixed to either side of the truck bed was parked outside the barn. There was a name lettered in black, followed by D.V.M. on the door. The veterinarian had arrived to check on the horse Dandy.

She walked into the cool barn, her running shoes quiet on the packed dirt floor. As she drew closer to a cluster of box stalls, she heard voices.

"Doesn't sound good, Sloan. Someone might have done this deliberately," an unfamiliar voice said.

"That's what I was afraid you would say," Sloan said.

She came to a standstill in the barn aisle.

"Let's not jump to any conclusions. I'll call you as soon as I get the blood test back and the results from the syringe. Once we know what we're dealing with, we'll take it from there.

"As for the horse, even though the affects seem to have worn off, I don't want him ridden and make sure anyone working around him uses caution."

"I'll take care of him myself, Tim. I can't believe someone would try something like this. How could this happen!" Sloan sounded furious.

"No ideas?" the other voice asked.

She heard a stall door open and saw Sloan and a tall blond-haired man exit a box stall at the end of the aisle.

"I've never had a problem with anyone tampering with the horses." They hadn't seen her yet. "I'm as stumped as you, Tim."

The bag of carrots she carried slipped from her fingers and fell to the barn floor. Both men turned.

"Jacie," Sloan said. He looked none too pleased to see her.

The man he'd called Tim said, "Hi...Jacie, isn't it?" He stepped forward, a smile on his lean, attractive face as he held out a hand. "I'm Tim Wells. We're just about finished here if you're looking for Sloan."

She shook his hand and introduced herself. Seeing no reason not to jump in, she said, "I couldn't help but overhear your conversation."

Tim looked at Sloan, then back at her.

"So you think someone did something to my horse the other day?"

"The behavior Sloan told me about could be caused by numerous factors, one of which could be a chemical reaction to certain drugs. I don't want to speculate. I'd feel better with the test results in my hand. It could have been something as simple as a bee sting."

That explanation gave her a slight rise in spirits but then she wondered if she was just fooling herself. Tim turned back to Sloan. "If the chestnut horse is the only one I have to see today, I'll be on my way."

Sloan held out his hand to the other man. "I appreciate you getting here so quickly. Let me know as soon as you have the results."

"I'll call you, although with the weekend coming up, it might be next week." He nodded at her and then walked down the aisle and out the barn.

Sloan turned to her. "Eavesdropping?" he asked, his mouth tilted at one corner.

She looked at him with wide eyes and let out her breath. "Not on purpose, but eavesdropping has its uses," she said without apology. "What was that about?"

"He drew some blood but we won't know anything until next week."

"But you suspect something," she said. "And it has to do with that syringe." She reached up a hand to grip the iron bars on one of the box stalls. "Tell me I'm being paranoid and that this has nothing to do with me."

He moved down the barn aisle as the veterinarian had done. When he was about three feet past her, he turned back. Rubbing a hand along the back of his neck, he muttered a curse. "No, you're not being paranoid. I think this does have to do with you. At first I thought someone was trying to get at the resort, but I have this feeling it's you this is all aimed at."

She felt a sick welling in her stomach. "I know I asked for it, but I don't have to like the truth."

He came back to her and grabbed her by the arms. "Do you know why anyone would want to harm you?" Anger and concern laced his voice. The line of his brow was pulled into a frown. "Because I think that's what's happening here. We think...and we don't know for sure, that your horse was given a shot of something. That's why he flipped out. Then there's the gas leak in the cabin."

"You keep coming back to that."

"Dammit, it can't be ignored! Maybe someone wanted to hurt you. I've notified the sheriff's office. They're coming today to talk to you."

She pulled back. "Wait a second. If someone is trying to hurt me I sure as heck don't know why. How do we know the gas wasn't an accident after all?"

"That place had been thoroughly checked out."

"James told me a fitting or something had worked its way loose on the stove."

"It had. I didn't voice my suspicions right away because I might have been reading something into this that wasn't there. I didn't want to frighten you."

"Well, you're doing a pretty good job of it right now."

He tugged her by the hand into the tack room and closed the door. He lowered his voice. "Listen, Jacie, I don't want to believe this either, but with this last incident, it's past that point. We've got to find out what's going on." With a gesture of frustration he pulled his hat off and pushed the hair off his forehead. "This isn't coincidence, not three separate incidents."

"Three!" she said in outrage.

"That day at the waterfall...your first week here. Donny and I combed the upper stream. There was no reason for that rock to come over the falls. We found a spot where it looked like a rock could have been pried loose from the muddy bottom. It takes a pretty good current to move something that size. Do you remember seeing anyone around that day?"

"Other than the regular guests, no, but then I wasn't looking for anybody lurking in the woods. You're convinced that was deliberate, too?" She couldn't prevent the fear that raced through her.

"Of course I'm not sure, but I want to cover all possibilities. I can't let these questions go unasked. When we got back yesterday from the campout one of the housekeeping girls told me she had gone to clean the unoccupied cabin. Someone had been staying there. She found empty food wrappers."

"There could be a reasonable explanation."

"I'll concede that maybe the piece of ledge that fell was coincidental. We had had a lot of rain the week before; it's possible it worked its way loose. Maybe even the gas leak could be explained...but not Dandy's behavior. I've had that horse six years and I've never seen him act like that. I sure as hell wouldn't let anyone ride him if I had the least suspicion he'd blow up."

"There's no motive."

"There has to be."

"What would be the gain? Why is this happening?"

"I'm hoping you could clue me in."

"I haven't got anything..." she let her voice trail off.

Sloan narrowed his eyes. "What?"

She shook her head vehemently. "No! You're making me paranoid." She turned away. "If something happened to me, anything I have would go to my family." Impatiently, she pulled open the tack room door and exited the room, emotion bursting inside her.

"I'm not accusing anyone in your family," he called

after her.

"You'd better not. It's ridiculous and insulting." She swung around to face him.

He let out an exasperated growl and put his fists on his hips. "Hell, I can't dismiss what happened. I have to get to the bottom of this. I tried calling Con."

Fury raced through her. "You called my brother?" For a moment, a feeling of helplessness washed over her. Her family thought she would mess up again and this would further reinforce that notion.

"Of course I did, but I couldn't reach him. Apparently he's still out of the country."

With an aggravated mutter, she turned and walked out of the barn. She felt the burning at the back of her throat. Tears wanted to let go, but she blinked hard and kept them at bay. When would everyone learn she could take care of her own life?

A hard hand on her elbow pulled her around. She looked at Sloan, blinking furiously. "Do you have any idea how this makes me feel?" she demanded. "I don't need my brother checking up on me, and I don't need you helping him."

He released her arm as if she'd burned him. "Now hold on, Jacie. I'm doing no such thing. I don't know about your brother's motives, though I suspect they have something to do with love, but I'll be damned if I'll sit around and watch you get hurt and not do anything about it!" His voice was hard, biting at her.

She shook her head and waved her arms. "I have to leave, I can't talk rationally about this now." She needed time to think. She was an adult. Eventually, her family would realize her decisions, right or wrong, were her own. She had to make her own mistakes and face the consequences.

"Did my brother tell you to call if I screwed up?"

He looked at her hard-eyed, his mouth in a straight line. "No."

She turned on her heel. A dark silhouette stepped into the barn almost in front of her. She came to a skidding halt with an exasperated groan, stopping just short of running into a uniformed officer.

"Sorry, miss," the officer said, putting out a hand to steady her. "At the office they told me Sloan was down here."

She looked at the badge pinned to the officer's chest. In that fraction of time Sloan moved forward and shook hands with the officer.

"Hi Arnie, thanks for coming by. Don't go, Jacie," he said. "This is Arnie Bryant from the sheriff's office."

"Hello Jacie," the officer said pleasantly, his green eyes almost on a level with her own beneath his wide-brimmed hat. Black hair brushed his collar and his dark brown eyes appeared sharply inquiring. "I'm Deputy Bryant. I need to ask you some questions relating to incidents that have occurred recently at Timber Falls."

She nodded with resignation.

Deputy Bryant looked over at Sloan. "Is there someplace where we can sit or we can go out to my patrol car?"

"Let's go into the tack room." He led the way.

She followed and the deputy brought up the rear. She just wanted to get this over with.

Once she was seated in the lone chair, the deputy removed his hat and took out a small notepad and pen. Sloan leaned against the massive desk beside her.

"Now Jacie, let's start with closest living relatives."

"My parents are Jacie and John Turner. I have four brothers."

"On your second day here you had an accident while swimming?"

"Yes. A rock hit me from the stream above."

"Did you see anyone?"

"No." She thought a moment and took that back. "I thought I heard something. My horse looked back toward the hill where Michelle and the other riders had gone but I didn't see anyone."

"That's when the rock hit you, just after you heard a noise that sounded out of place?"

"Yes."

"You came to Timber Falls to give the guests skydiving lessons?"

"Yes."

"Any incidents involving those lessons?"

"Nothing unusual. We did our first jump without problems and there was another one scheduled but the pilot got sick."

"The pilot was sick? Is he okay now?" The deputy's question seemed idle enough, but she again took note of the sharp inquisitiveness of his eyes.

"They thought he'd eaten something that didn't agree with him. He's going to resume our flight schedule tomorrow." She glanced at Sloan.

"The next incident involved a problem with the gas stove where you're staying?" The deputy looked at Sloan for confirmation.

"I opened her cabin door one night and the gas odor hit me in the face."

"Jacie, you didn't notice it?" the officer asked.

"No, I have allergies and at times it affects taste and smell."

"How long have you had allergies?"

"I don't know, probably eight, nine years."

"Who knows about your allergies?"

She looked at him helplessly and shrugged her shoulders. "Everyone in my family, some of my friends."

"Now the last incident was yesterday? The horse you usually ride started acting strangely?"

"Yes. Maybe he was just having a bad day, but his behavior was pretty unusual."

"The horse was virtually uncontrollable," Sloan put in grimly. "He was wild-eyed, then trembling and disoriented. He's never acted that way before."

"I saw Tim Wells as I was driving in. Is the horse being treated?"

"Yes, Tim drew blood and he's sending it to be analyzed. We also found a syringe and needle when we went on that campout where the horse acted up. Tim has that too."

"I understand you were involved in an accident last year?"

She had no wish to rehash that incident. "I was in South America doing a film stunt. I was hurt."

"How did that happen?"

She hesitated. "My parachute was faulty."

"How long have you been skydiving? Has that ever happened before?"

"About eleven years and that's the first time."

"Any reason to think someone might want to harm you?" the officer asked quietly.

"None."

"If something happened to you, who would benefit?"

That question again. Coldness crept over her. "There's only my family." She glared at the officer. "As I told Sloan, there's no way they're involved." She stood up. "I think this has gone on long enough. I've answered all the questions and we're no further ahead."

Deputy Bryant stood also. "It's understandable you're distressed but I have one more question."

She let out a long breath. "Go ahead." At least it was almost over.

"Do you have anything of value that someone might want if you were out of the picture?"

She clamped her lips together, looked at Sloan and then back at Deputy Bryant. "No."

The deputy put his pen and notepad away. "Thank you for your time Ms. Turner, I'm sure this has been very difficult. We'll be in touch." He looked at Sloan. "I'd like to do an informal interview of each of the guests. Can we arrange something?"

"Of course," Sloan said.

She couldn't believe this mess was escalating out of control.

"One more thing, Ms. Turner," Deputy Bryant said. "I'm going to need the names of the film crew from South America."

"That's something you'd have to get from Brad Carlton. He's the film producer who took care of the arrangements down there."

"Will you be able to give me a number?"

Jacie wondered if they could hear the heavy pound of her heart. She looked at Sloan and licked her lips, then looked back at the deputy. "I might be able to get it from my friend Bonnie."

She stared at Sloan with bewilderment after the deputy left.

"James and I have decided to take precautionary measures," he said. "I'm canceling the jumps for tomorrow and maybe the day after."

"You can't do that, it will throw my entire schedule off."

"I am doing it," he said in a hard voice. "I'm not taking chances with you or my guests."

She looked at him impotently. Could this get any worse? He was right. They couldn't take chances.

"Do I have to start looking over my shoulder?"

"Why are you holding out?" he asked suddenly.

"What?"

"Arnie asked you if you had anything of value—I got the feeling you're not telling us everything."

She turned away, but he pulled her back toward him.

"I'm trying to help you here, help me." His voice was a demand.

"It's not important," she said fiercely.

"Trust me, Jacie."

She trusted him but there were other factors involved. Reluctantly, she admitted, "When I had the accident the film company's insurance carrier settled money on me."

"How much?"

"Half a million," she said reluctantly. "I think they were afraid I would sue. I didn't tell the deputy because I didn't want to plant a seed of doubt about my family!"

"The police should be made aware."

"You can't tell them!" she said angrily. "I won't have my family questioned over this. I'll give the money away before I'll let that happen."

"Cool down, Jacie. There's got to be something we're missing."

"There is. It's called a motive. Now if you'll excuse me, I'm going to take some pictures before the light is lost."

She left the barns, feeling angry and unsettled and wishing Sloan would stick to ranching instead of trying to interfere in the job she had come here to do.

She slowed down her hard pace, knowing that was unfair. Sloan was trying to keep her safe, that was all. She had no reason to be angry with him.

∞ Chapter Nine ∞

SEVERAL HOURS LATER JACIE walked toward the apple orchard situated behind the main lodge. The interview with the police deputy still weighed heavily on her mind, and she had almost forgotten about the barbecue tonight.

Sloan was convinced someone was out to hurt her. God knows her brother Con had questioned her enough times about the circumstances surrounding the accident in Venezuela and now they wanted to rehash that. There had been major chaos following the accident. The Venezuelan authorities had had big smuggling problems at the time and details about the skydiving investigation had been sketchy.

Sloan had asked for Con's number, but she felt it wasn't necessary at this time to call her brother back to the states, especially now that the authorities were involved.

As she rounded the lodge she heard the sound of festivities; music, people talking and laughter. She planned to enjoy herself, even if Sloan was being pigheaded about protecting her. She didn't need another big brother.

She flipped her hair back over her shoulders, tucked the hem of her halter-top into her jeans and sauntered into the light cast by the floodlights. She was determined to have a spectacular time.

People milled around a food-laden buffet table set beneath a rainbow-hued awning. Off to one side a pig roasted in a charcoal-embedded pit and lights were strung in the tree branches. She said hello to the various ranch hands, then noticed James standing with his wife and two boys and his mother Myra Wright, who Michelle had pointed out to her that afternoon.

She felt her breathing quicken when she spotted Sloan. He stood with Donny and Michelle. Michelle was cozied right up to Donny's side and the teenager had his arm around Michelle's slim waist. She smiled, once again applauding Sloan for his handling of that situation.

"Jacie! Come and join us!" Michelle called. She approached with a full plate of food. "Isn't this great? They're having live music later. Did you just get here?"

"Just now," she acknowledged.

"Well, settle in and have something to eat. There's dancing later, some crazy games for prizes and then maybe a ride."

"You're going riding tonight?" she asked.

"Sure. A couple of us figured we'd go for a moonlight dip...you remember that little pool you liked? Well, after a hot day like this it should be great. There's even a full moon."

She found the idea incredibly tempting. "Count me in."

She looked across the orchard at the older woman she knew to be Myra Wright...Sloan's stepmother. Myra had bright red hair and was dressed in a gaily colored gypsy skirt and wide-sleeved blouse. Jacie didn't see Sloan's father, whom she had also seen briefly earlier. Everett Wright was a striking older version of Sloan, his full head of hair steel gray.

"Jacie, have you met Myra?" Sloan's voice sounded almost in her ear, his breath warm on her neck. She turned and stared into his face. Warring emotions leapt through her as he reached for her hand and drew her with him. She clasped his hand.

"Your mother and father were pointed out to me this morning," she said coolly, "but no, I haven't met your mother."

He stopped and studied her face. "At least you didn't pull your hand away," he said in a low voice. "Does that mean we're still friends?"

"We'll have to see what the evening brings, won't we?" she said.

"Why don't you come and join us? I'd like to introduce you." He watched her a moment. "That is, if you'd like to meet Myra."

"Certainly."

"You look great," he murmured as he walked beside her.

Jacie had never been one to hang onto anger and she really didn't want to stay mad at him. He was doing what he thought was best.

"Mother, I'd like to introduce you to Jacie Turner." Myra Wright looked around at she and Sloan. "This is Jacie," he continued. "She's giving the guests skydiving lessons."

"Except for today," Jacie inserted smoothly.

"Except for today," he conceded.

Myra smiled warmly and extended her hand. "How nice to meet you, Ms. Turner."

"Very nice to meet you, and please call me Jacie."

"So you give skydiving lessons. I might come to your class, what would you think about that?"

"I'd say you were welcome to join us." She threw Sloan a quick glance and then looked back at Myra. "I'm always willing to recruit new fans to the sport, although some people are very resistant to change."

Myra smiled. "I was joking. I don't think I'd have the courage to jump out of a plane."

"You might surprise yourself," she told her with a wink.

"Mother, is Dad coming tonight?" Sloan's voice seemed abrupt.

"Not tonight. I'm afraid he's not feeling that well."

"Maybe I should go and check on him," he said.

"No, he's fine, Sloan, really. He overdid it today with the kids when he took them to the circus." Myra turned to Jacie and laughed. "Everett won't admit he's getting older. He wants to keep going as if he were twenty, even though he'll be sixty-five next year. Now Sloan, you have a good time and don't worry about your father. It's a pleasure to meet you, Jacie."

"Likewise," Jacie murmured.

Sloan's hand tightened around hers. Before she thought about it, she returned the pressure.

"The band is setting up now, Mother, I know you're waiting to dance. Excuse me, won't you, I need to talk to Jacie."

Jacie lifted a brow as he guided her away. She quickly waved goodbye to Myra, wondering what he had on his mind.

"Are you still mad?" he asked once they were out of the immediate range of the crowd.

She tilted her head to the side and put her hands on her hips as she considered him carefully. "I might be, but

I know you have to look out for everyone's best interest."

"Your best interests," he corrected gently.

"Nothing will happen, and I'm going to prove it to you tomorrow."

"What's tomorrow?"

She widened her eyes innocently. "Why, I'm resuming my skydiving jumps, didn't James tell you? We had a nice chat about it tonight."

"I don't know that that's a good idea."

She firmed her jaw. "I do. I'm not canceling another flight. If you're so worried then you can come up in the plane with us and keep an eye on things."

"I have cows to move tomorrow."

She gave him a little wave and then turned and walked away, calling over her shoulder, "If you took your play time as seriously as you do your work time, you'd loosen up a little and have some fun. You might like it." She stopped dead in her tracks and turned back to him. "In fact, I'll give you lessons in loosening up! All you have to do is ask."

Sloan watched her sashay away from him, her playful/serious words taunting him. He liked fun as much as the next guy. He used to, but lately he had forgotten about enjoying himself and had let himself become immersed in business, his thoughts never far from the bottom line. The business was in the black, he admitted to himself, he didn't have to micro-manage every decision any more.

Jacie stopped beside a group of people and joined in on their conversation. He marveled at her ease in making herself comfortable in her surroundings. The thought came to him of how much she reminded him of his mother. His mother had loved parties and gatherings. She had been the most vibrant person he had ever known, but she had died and left him and his father alone. Jacie had the same vibrancy and zest about her, it shined out of her eyes. He felt envious of the way she embraced each new situation, trying to turn it into something favorable.

Since she was determined to resume her skydiving lessons and his brother had agreed, tomorrow he would make sure everything was checked and rechecked before the jumps took place. If he had to follow her around, he thought grimly, he would do it.

Deliberately, he followed Jacie and came up behind her. He had a feeling she knew he was behind her, but she didn't given any indication. Suddenly, he needed her to be aware of him.

When there was a lull in the conversation, he leaned closer and said, "So, Jacie, are you in on our little ride tonight?" His nostrils flared as he picked up the scent of her skin. She smelled good. He was tempted to touch his lips to a spot on her shoulder left bare by her halter strap, but he restrained himself. She might swat him if he did that. But what a temptation.

"Sure, I'd love to go riding." The smile she gave him seemed reckless. "I wouldn't miss it. When do we leave?"

"At ten."

"I'll be ready," she literally purred, touching a finger to the front of his shirt.

Desire bit sharply at him. He caught that finger and raised it to his mouth. Gently, he kissed it, running his tongue across the pad, then turned and left, but not before he'd seen her eyes darken with desire. He knew the others in the small group observed his actions, but he was really past the point of worrying about it.

As he walked away to get himself a cold beer, he was convinced they would drive each other mad, but what a way to go.

Sloan thought the moonlit night was perfect for a horseback ride. He flicked back his cuff and hit the light button on his watch. Ten-fifteen.

Five horses and riders picked their way across loose gravel. The air felt humid, an unusual occurrence in the Catskills where the nights usually cooled even in the dead of summer. He let his glance stray over Jacie, who rode in front of him. When she glanced at him, she looked sultry, her eyes lidded, as if she had a secret. He found he wanted to peel her secrets away one by one.

Their group of riders included Jacie, Donny, Michelle and Renee. The women had changed into swimming suits and wore jeans over them, but he wore a pair of old swimming shorts under his jeans and had left his short-sleeved shirt unsnapped. It felt too airless to do otherwise.

When they reached the small pool, the water appeared silvered in the moonlight, the surface smooth and undisturbed.

Curiously, he watched Jacie as she flashed her wide grin and then threw her leg over her horse and slid to the ground.

"I'll beat you all into the pool!" she cried. In a mad dash she kicked off her sneakers and wriggled out of her jeans, the sight of her hips wriggling making sweat bead on his forehead. She hit the water mere seconds before Michelle and Renee did the same. The sounds of their laughter floated on the air as he dismounted from his horse. Captivated, he stood and watched them play in the water. Donny still sat on his horse and when Sloan glanced at him he saw the teen watching Michelle like a lovesick kid. He wondered if his face wore the same expression when he looked at Jacie. He told himself he wasn't lovesick, just...just curious.

She was fascinating, fun to be with, but that's as far as it went.

"I suppose you think we're crazy, you guys!" Jacie

called out.

"What else?" he drawled.

She floated closer to the edge where he stood and threw him a grin. "You wouldn't think so if you were in here cooling off." Threateningly, she reached out and grabbed his boot.

"Are you ready for the consequences of your actions?" he asked, curious to see how far she would go. He felt her tug again on his boot and shifted his feet, feeling the give of the moss beneath his weight as he went down on his haunches.

"Are you?" she asked mockingly, her voice for his ears alone. In the next instant, she pulled herself from the water and literally launched herself at him. He put out his hands to catch her and lost his balance. He fell onto his back, his palms sliding along her slippery wet flesh as she followed him down with a muffled squeal, landing between his legs. The warmth of her breath was in his face, then the heated touch of her lips touched his mouth. It happened fast and then she began to slide away, but he captured her and pulled her back to him, feeling the wet skin of her belly contact with his. He groaned and settled his mouth more firmly on hers, enticing her lips to open to him. She melted into him, and then he let her go and she slid back into the pool. She splashed as she swam away. It had all happened in the span of seconds.

Ω

Jacie pulled herself from the water and lay exhausted on a flat rock. She admired the feathery clouds that drifted in front of the moon. "This must be heaven," she murmured. Heaven, and she was here with Sloan. Thinking of her impulsiveness in kissing him, she felt warmth creep over her, and it had nothing to do with the night. She supposed the others might have seen her do that, but she couldn't summon the energy to care. It had felt right and Sloan hadn't seemed to mind her impulsiveness.

Lazily, she turned her head as someone came to sit beside her.

"Stay still," Sloan said as she began to get up. "You look comfortable right there." His fingers slid along her arm.

"I am," she said dreamily. "I could lie here all night. Why didn't you go swimming? The water's just right." Impulsively, she added, "You should relax more."

He looked at her, one brow up. "So you said before. I will admit I get caught up in work."

"What do you do to relax?"

He seemed to hesitate a moment. "I like to garden."

She smiled. "Really? That's one thing I've never had the space or time for. I love the flowers all over the ranch. They're so bright and welcoming."

"Thanks. I admit it's my green thumb."

"You did all the flowers? I'm impressed."

"I'll have to show you my place. I'm still working on the landscaping and the flower beds." His smile seemed intimate. A shiver raced across her water-cool skin, almost as if he had touched her again.

"I would love to see your cabin. It's been a really fun night," she added. "The barbecue, the ride and swim. I don't know when I've had a better time."

"This is pretty simple stuff. I'm sure you must've had more excitement in all your globetrotting." She could make out his profile as he stared at the others in the pool.

"My type of globetrotting as you call it, if you're around long enough to know the time zone, you're usually so tired from working you don't feel like socializing."

"Yet you've done it with your family?"

"About eight years, give or take a month." She shrugged. "It was a job."

"The risk...cheating death, you loved it." It wasn't a question, more a conclusion. She sensed a stiffness in him now. Restlessly, she sat up. "At times...many times, I loved my job, but I don't look at it as cheating death." She put her hands out, then let them fall to her sides. "Don't you love your job, as back breaking as it can be?"

"There's no comparison."

"In a way there is. You could get hurt working with the horses or the cows. Even with machinery there could be accidents."

"It's not the same." Abruptly, he rose to his feet.

She moved to stand with her fists on her hips.

"You are so hung up on my occupation. What is your problem?"

"Your life is your own. I guess I'll never understand how you don't think twice about jumping out of a plane."

She balked at the hard tone. "Skydiving is a skilled science. Every jump is calculated, the risks considered. Look at you...working with animals is unpredictable. There's so many variables to consider," she said in exasperation. "If I make a mistake on a jump, I know where to look, there's only one variable to consider, myself. Animals can spook, or have a bad day, and you get the brunt of it."

"If there's danger in my work, it's because it finds me, not because I court it." Abruptly, he walked away.

"That's not fair!" Perplexed, she wondered what had just occurred. His face was set, his back rigid.

Vaguely, she noticed the others were leaving the water. There was a hushed silence on the group, almost as if she had somehow touched on a sore subject everyone else knew about.

She bent to retrieve her jeans.

She mounted her horse. Sloan had ridden several yards up the path to wait. When everyone was ready she hung back to the end of the line. Her horse knew the way, she didn't even have to think as the animal automatically fell into step behind the others.

Michelle nudged her horse over to her. "You couldn't have known," she said in a hushed tone.

She looked at her with surprise. "Known what?"

"Sloan's mother was a loose cannon."

"He mentioned something about it once."

"She breezed through life and did as she pleased, regardless of anyone else. My mom always said it was like she thought she'd live forever. She and her friends used to race their cars on the back roads at night. One time she had an accident and almost got killed. Sloan's father found her in time and got her to the hospital. She pulled out of it that time, but I don't think it stopped her."

"God." Jacie felt pain for Sloan, the little boy he had been. "How did she die?"

"She developed a blood disorder from an infection."

Jacie felt her stomach turn. "But her life is nothing like mine."

Michelle shrugged. "I don't know...maybe Sloan is equating you in some way with his mother's lifestyle."

All the way back to the barn she mulled over what she had learned. After the horses were taken care of, she caught up with Sloan.

"I have one thing to say to you!" she declared.

He looked at her intently. "And that would be?"

"I'm a responsible person from a loving, stable family background. I've had a job since I was fifteen. Don't go comparing me to someone else." She stomped away. At least she had gotten that off her chest, for all the good it would do her. Sloan seemed to have a problem with the very occupation she was trying so hard to resume.

Ω

Sloan felt as if he had been ridden hard and put away wet as he sank into his favorite chair. He rubbed at the ache in the back of his neck and wondered why the devil he had thought avoiding Jacie and working his butt into the ground the last two days would solve anything.

He felt rotten, no getting around it. He was finally ready to admit she was getting to him, and she probably could give two hoots about him. He wanted her and to hell with her lifestyle that was so different from his. He needed to know if she would be interested in a relationship. That's what he had figured out in the last two days since her last jump, which luckily had gone off without a hitch.

Since her arrival he'd never felt so confused in his life. Her fun-loving nature drew him, yet at the same time it troubled him. He slumped into the chair, knowing he needed a shave and a shower. His mirror testified to the fact that he wasn't looking his best.

Growing up, he had loved his beautiful, fun-filled mother dearly, as only a young boy could. He remembered, too, the dark times. As a child of eight, he had seen the pain his father tried to hide, seen the evidence of sleepless nights, the worry over his mother who would sometimes be gone for days. She always made up for it when she returned, lavishing attention and love on them, but somehow it hadn't made up for the time in between.

Scrubbing his hands over his face, he reached forward and slid a plastic DVD case across the oak chest that served as his coffee table. He stared at the video inside the case, experiencing again a sense of urgency. That same feeling had gripped him earlier when he had driven into town.

He had gone to see Tim Wells to talk to him about the test results on the horse. A foreign substance had been found in Dandy's blood. It could only have gotten there by injection. Tim had already notified the sheriff's office and sent them a report of the findings.

His second stop had been the video store. Escape from Angel Falls. He placed the DVD in the player. After the credits the scene cut to a mountain of reddish rock which seemed to shoot straight up into the sky, a waterfall of frothy white plummeting a tremendous way to the base. He knew Jacie's stunt involved a freefall from the top of the falls. He fast-forwarded almost the end of the movie and Jacie's jump. The scene showed the top of the towering precipice. He watched her leap from the ledge, seeming to fly out into the air and his stomach did a sickening plummet. He backed it up, watched the descent over and over. The jump was shot from different angles, above and below.

When her parachute finally opened, it seemed to his untrained eye almost too late. The closing shot showed her dangling in a tree by the lines of her parachute.

Swallowing hard, he stared up at the ceiling. A paralyzing numbness held him immobile, knots twisting his gut.

A knock sounded on his front door. "It's open!" he called. Footsteps crossed his foyer. Sloan turned and saw his father. He jumped to his feet. "Hi Dad."

"Hello Sloan," Everett Wright said. "I haven't seen you all day so I thought I'd see what you were up to. Mind if I help myself to a beer?"

"Go ahead."

His father walked into the kitchen and then came into the living room and tossed him a can. "I thought I'd come over since it's been a while since we talked. James filled me in on what's been going on since the last time I was here. What's happening with this woman Jacie Turner?"

"What do you mean?" he asked guardedly.

"The business with the horse."

"I got the results from the vet today." He stared at the television screen through half-closed eyes. Popping the top on his beer, he took a gulp. "It's not good. The tests turned up traces of fluphenazine enanthate, a potent behavior modifier. Once injected, adverse reactions can occur, sometimes up to twenty-four hours later. I'm trying to piece together who had access to the horse during that time period."

"That explains the bizarre behavior. What about the syringe?"

"Same chemical."

His father's face reflected his shock. "I can't believe anyone we know would harm this young woman. Are you sure this isn't aimed at the ranch?"

"I've thought of that, but I don't think so. This is just one incident on top of others concerning Jacie. I've gone around and around with this. Whoever's responsible has to be familiar with horses and injections. Who would gain by doing such a thing?"

"Maybe someone is stalking this young woman."

"That's a possibility. What's really strange is Jacie only decided to go on that overnight at the last minute and she's the only one who's been riding Dandy. Just about everyone here knew that."

"Sloan, you're talking attempted murder—"

He clenched his jaw. "I know what I'm saying Dad. I've talked to Jacie, and so have the police, and to tell you the truth we haven't come up with a motive. The only ones who would stand to profit if she died are her family, which is out of the question. There might be money involved. Apparently, the film's insurance company settled a sum on her after the accident. From what I gather her family has kept pretty close tabs on her since then. It bugs the hell out of me to think someone's on the ranch sneaking around."

"What are you going to do?" Everett asked.

"Keep an eye on her and hope the police come up with something or I can catch somebody out."

Everett reached for the DVD case. Escape from Angel Falls. Is this the movie Jacie was in?"

He nodded. "I was trying to see if I could get any ideas watching it. She does her skydiving jump at the end, and that's when she got hurt. I'll play it again, if you want to see it."

"Go ahead."

When the movie was over, his father gave him a speculative look. "Wow, that is some lady. I've seen the jumps she does with the guests, but they seem tame in comparison. She made that jump look real."

"It was all too real," Sloan said, still feeling his tense reaction to watching the movie. "That producer must be some kind of inhuman jerk to use that footage after she was almost killed."

"Is Jacie someone special, son?"

Sloan looked into blue eyes so like his own. He simply nodded.

"I have met Jacie," his father said with a smile, "though only briefly. She reminds me of your mother."

Sloan felt his throat go dry.

"You probably don't remember much, but your mother was a woman who embraced life, Sloan," his father said. "Those years with her were ones I'd never give up. You don't find many women like that. She loved with a passion I've missed since the day she died."

"But if you could turn back the clock and live

through the uncertainty, not knowing what she would do next, would you do it all again?"

His father gave him a surprised glance. "Of course I would, son. I loved her."

He felt his father's answer seep into him. It sounded so simple, but he felt it wasn't.

"What's the matter, Sloan?"

"I guess I'm surprised to hear you say that. You never really talked about Mom after she died."

"That's because it hurt so much to know that light was gone."

"I might have been only a kid, but I remember what it was like."

"I remember the good times, when your mother was with us, and the amount of love that woman could hold. She had boundless energy. She could drag you out of the lowest mood. Don't get me wrong, I love Myra, and we've had a good life together, but your mother was unlike any woman I've ever known."

Feeling suddenly lighter, Sloan grabbed his hat from the table.

"Where are you off to now, son?"

"I've got cows to pen."

"It's getting late. Why don't you call it a day and do them tomorrow."

He pulled his hat low over his forehead. "Nope, I told my buyer the cows would be ready first thing in the morning. I'm gonna round them up and make good on that promise."

"How about if your old man comes with you? Between the two of us we'll have it done in half the time."

As they walked out the door together, he gave his father a mocking glance. "Are you sure you remember how to round up cows?"

"I know it's been awhile, but I think I can handle a few ornery steers," his father said, chucking him in the arm.

He grinned and threw his arm around his father's shoulder. He suddenly didn't feel so glum anymore. Maybe there could be a chance for him and Jacie.

∞ Chapter Ten ∞

LATER THAT AFTERNOON JACIE walked through a dense growth of pine and came upon a small clearing. A woman sat in the tall grass with an easel in front of her. She turned as Jacie's boots snapped pine needles underfoot. It was Myra Wright.

"Hi." Jacie halted. "I didn't see you. I don't mean to intrude."

"Don't be silly, stay." Myra put out a hand, multiple bracelets jangling on one slim arm. "The sun has gone down and it was that last minute of sun I was trying to catch. I'm through for the day."

Jacie glanced at the canvas admiringly. Myra had done a credible job of depicting the fading brilliance of the day across the mountains. Looking at the picture, she could feel the silence and vastness.

Myra retrieved brushes and paint tubes and she knelt to help her.

"Actually, I'm glad you're here, Jacie. I could use help carrying the easel." The older woman rubbed her hands.

"When I hold the brush for very long, my arthritis bothers me."

"I'd be glad to help."

When everything was stowed in a pack, Jacie slung the pack over one arm and picked up the lightweight easel. "Can you carry the canvas? I don't want to smudge it."

"Yes. My car is over there." The older woman indicated an area behind a thick growth of trees.

"You drove?" she said with surprise.

"It's just a narrow track, but Sloan keeps it graded so my car doesn't have any trouble. He knows I love to paint while I'm here."

"Have you always painted the ranch?"

"My goodness, no. When I lived here, I was too busy...accounts, the farm, raising two boys. Everett encouraged me, but I never seemed to get around to it."

They placed everything in the small gray car.

"Will you ride back with me, Jacie?"

"Sure, thank you."

They settled themselves in the car. She watched Myra competently reverse the car.

"Are you out walking?" Myra asked.

"Just getting back. We did a jump this morning and then I decided to go for a walk. This area is kind of awesome." They left the clearing. "Do you miss living here?"

"Yes. Life may have been hectic, but it called to something in me." Myra shook her head ruefully. "It's different now. We've adapted to our new life in Maryland."

"I suppose it's easier to adapt if you're born here. Sometimes it seems so isolated."

Myra laughed like a young girl, her face lit with amusement. "I was a city girl, Jacie, just like you. I'd never lived in the middle of such isolation as it was then. When I found myself in between jobs, I came to visit a friend, Miriam Wright, Sloan's mother." She sighed. "Miriam was so much fun to be around, the life of the party, almost desperately seeking out adventures. Miriam always said the worst thing she could do with her life was be boring." Myra shook her head sadly. "Miriam never really grew up."

Troubled, Jacie said, "But she had Sloan and a husband, surely—"

"I loved and envied her, most people did. She was easy to love, but she didn't stick around. After Sloan was born, she went back to her partying ways. Everett loved her desperately, and in her way, she loved him also." Myra's face changed and grew sad. "I believe everyone is capable of one truly grand love in their life. Everett is mine. Miriam was his. We both knew it...I knew it going into marriage with Everett, but I loved him regardless. We have a good life. We married a year after Miriam died. Sloan was almost nine, he needed the stability."

She could sense Myra loved Sloan dearly. Sympathy created a lump in her throat, sudden understanding hitting her. Did Sloan think she jeopardized her life by jumping out of planes just for the risk of doing it? She grew up in a skydiving family, she went into it naturally, but she wouldn't deny she had always liked the thrill, catching that first updraft of air.

"Sloan doesn't take risks. He regards my jumping out of planes as a foolish gamble."

Carefully, Myra pulled her car into a parking place by the lodge and turned to her. "You have to understand he was a small child. He loved his mother dearly. When she was around, she devoted all of her time to him. Nevertheless, as young as he was, I'm sure Sloan saw how Miriam's lifestyle hurt his father.

"One day Miriam was out early moving those big hay bales. She helped Everett on the farm from time to time. In her brash style, she had often declared she could operate the farm equipment as well as any man. She lifted the loader bucket too high and the bale rolled back. Somehow, she escaped being pinned in the seat and she walked away with only a few scratches. It was terrible justice that she died from what started as a simple infection."

"It must have been awful for them to lose her like that, someone so full of life."

"Sloan and his father were close, at least they had each other. Families are very important in times of crisis. Do you have family, Jacie?"

She looked down. "Yes, and I'm not proud to say I've kind of pushed my family away lately."

Myra gently touched her arm. "Family is very important, my dear, as I'm sure you know."

"Yes I do."

As they exited the car in the lodge parking lot Myra commented, "Skydiving must be an exciting occupation."

"It's an exacting type of work and it can be totally consuming."

"You've been in this business a long time?"

"Yes. My brothers run the business. I love my family, but sometimes it's too much. They think they have to keep an eye on me."

"Haven't you ever been scared?"

Chewing at her lip, she looked toward the deepening orange of the horizon. "Not until I got hurt this last time." She shrugged, pushing her door closed. "I came face to face with my own mortality. It sobers you up pretty quickly."

"That's difficult for anyone, I would say," a voice behind her said.

She turned quickly to find Sloan walking around the front of the car. His dark jeans were covered in dust, his dull red shirt unbuttoned and hanging open. Her eyes flicked the dark furring of hair running down his chest and across a hard, flat stomach to the waistband of his jeans. She imagined running her hands up that sculpted chest. Licking her lips, she lifted her eyes to his and felt the tell tale color surge into her cheeks.

Jacie hadn't seen him in two days. She had wondered why, but now all she could think about was how dark and sexy he looked.

"I see you found Myra." He opened the back of the car and retrieved the canvas. Carefully, he held it upright.

"Lucky for me," Myra said. "Jacie helped me load the car. I thought this painting might go nicely over the fireplace in the lodge's game room," she added.

"I'd rather have it over my fireplace," he said, turning it this way and that for a better look.

"Feel free." Myra waved a hand. "There's plenty more. Just be careful, it'll take a few days to dry." She rose up on her toes and kissed Sloan's cheek. "I'm going to have a quick nap before dinner." Without saying anything further, Myra left them and walked into the lodge.

Placing the painting on the hood of the car, he tucked the tails of his shirt into his jeans and began to button his shirt. "Thank you for helping my mother." He studied her intently.

"I happened to come on her while I was hiking to the swimming hole."

"Did you make it to the swimming hole?" His regard was warm as he did a slow perusal of her. She met those light eyes head on. She wasn't sure what it was, but something seemed different about him. He seemed less tense.

"No," she said lightly. "But of course there's always tomorrow."

"Great idea," he surprised her by saying. "What's your schedule like?"

"I'm taking tomorrow off."

"Since you missed out today, I can show you a place not many people know about."

Her interest peaked.

"It's also my way of apologizing," he added softly. "I was out of line the other night. I had no right to question the way you make a living. It has certainly benefited our business and you're very good at what you do."

"I am," she agreed.

Removing his hat, he brushed his hair back with his palm. The movement made his half buttoned shirt billow out, exposing hard-muscled ribs. Quietly, he said, "So what do you say, would you like to go?"

"Sure."

"We'll take the horses, it's a good day's hike otherwise. I'll be your guide."

She thought she would like to have Sloan as a guide again. Her fingers twitched, longing to touch him, but she curled her fingers behind her back. "Okay."

"Good," he said huskily. "I've got someone coming to look at some hay, then I'll meet you at the stables in the morning...say nine?"

"Okay." With a brief flick of her fingers, she turned on her heel, releasing her breath slowly as she put distance between herself and Sloan.

She conceded her father was right. When she had been younger he had claimed trouble would find her. If not, she would go looking for it. Every instinct warned her to steer clear of Sloan, but she intended to move full speed ahead, regardless. She could not ignore the excitement between them. It called to her. She had to find out where it would take her.

Early the next morning Jacie paced the floor, trying to calm an escalating anger as she listened to Bonnie on the phone. "Bonnie, I left you a message that I needed Brad's number for the police, not that I wanted him to come here."

"I know," Bonnie said quickly, "but I'm really concerned with everything that's been happening out there so I decided to ride out early. When I told Brad, he volunteered to speak with them personally. I know this is a surprise, but I'm en route now." Bonnie paused.

"What!" Stunned, Jacie could imagine Bonnie taking a deep draw on her cigarette.

The other woman rushed on. "Brad feels terrible, he wants to resolve issues so both of you can get on with your lives. He thought this was a good opportunity."

"There are no issues!" She wanted to scream in frustration. "However well meaning your intentions, I resent your interference. You can turn right around. Brad knows I don't want to see him. I don't know why you're getting involved, Bonnie, but I don't want you calling me again and I certainly don't want you bringing him here." Abruptly, she hung up the phone. Her hands shook and she felt incredibly panicked. The last person she wanted to see right now was Brad.

Pacing the cabin, she fumed, rubbing her forehead as a headache threatened. Why was Bonnie trying to bring her and Brad together? It was history she didn't want to repeat. Her glance fell on the kitchen clock and she groaned.

She was supposed to have met Sloan fifteen minutes ago. She wondered if she should just tell him to forget it. She wouldn't be very good company today.

Fiddling with the camera strap around her neck, she walked from the house and stood on her front porch. She suddenly heard the sound of horse's feet. Sloan came into view, riding his horse and leading one behind him. He halted on the drive in front of her cabin.

"Morning, Jacie." Her heart dropped to her feet at the gravelly warmth of his voice.

"Hi. Sorry I'm late, but I had a phone call."

"Problems?" he murmured, holding out the reins of her mount.

Taking the reins, she resisted the urge to confide. If she talked about it, she'd get mad all over again. "Nothing I can't handle." She looked askance at the pack on his horse.

"Lunch," he said, grinning.

"I'm hungry already," she quipped, mounting her horse, a sturdy gray with dapple marks on his hindquarters. Sloan had not let her ride Dandy yet, not until he was certain the horse's system was flushed of the drug he'd been given.

"Lead on."

"Okay." His smile was a killer, his eyes heating her through. "Let's go."

They rode through a small stand of evergreens and up a track she hadn't explored yet.

"My place is up ahead," he said, twisting in the saddle to look at her.

As the trees thinned, she saw his home. It was gorgeous, like a picture advertisement. His cabin was much larger than her own, with a semi-circular deck on the gorge side, set in amongst the trees.

"Wow—what a beautiful place, Sloan."

"Thanks. James and I put it together."

"Did you cut your own logs?"

"No, I hired a company from Maine. I gave them the plans and they delivered the pre-cut logs a few months later. If you like, I'll show you around some time."

"I'd love that."

The logs were reddish-gold, and it looked perfect in its setting. A two-tier flowerbed bordered the front of the house, drawing the eye toward the brilliant colors. "You did these flowers also?" She asked, impressed.

"I like to play gardener in my spare time," he murmured, shrugging. "My mom loved flowers, maybe that's where I got it from. This is my home."

She looked away, ignoring the ache in her chest. She had never wanted a place to call home, so why the sting of pain now? "So where are we going?" she asked brightly.

"Over on the far end of our property. It's really a well-kept secret, hardly anyone goes there since it's off the beaten path."

She returned his smile, anticipation warming her. Miles from anywhere with Sloan. The day was already looking brighter.

Jacie increasingly enjoyed the warm day and beautiful surroundings. They followed a thin trail through a heavily wooded area and then broke out into a clearing where they rode through frothy ferns. It seemed a shame to walk on them. At the edge of the clearing she drew her mount to a halt as Sloan stopped where the ground dropped sharply.

He waved his arm. "Look ahead, we're almost there."

She urged her horse closer, catching her breath as her eyes swept the valley below. The trail became grass and at the base of the small hill was a large pond surrounded by orange and yellow water lilies. A small wooden dock had been built on one side of the pond where massive maples shaded it.

"Come on," he said.

Anticipation rippled through her. She thought; what a romantic spot!

Following him, she drew her camera out and began to take pictures. He looked back, one brow raised and she pointed the camera at him.

He put up a hand playfully.

With a delighted laugh, she took his picture. "Sorry, you're a captive audience so you have to bear with me."

They dismounted by the pond.

"Let your horse have a half dozen gulps of water, then we'll put them in the fenced corral."

She looked over at the split-rail pen, the edge of which went into the woods, providing grass and shade.

"Sloan, this is incredible."

"When I was a kid my dad used to let me camp out here. Later, when James was old enough, I would bring him here. Each summer we'd clear brush until it looks the way it is today."

Removing saddles and bridles, they turned the horses loose in the corral. He carried the lunch pack toward the pond while she lingered a moment, watching the horses drop down and roll in the grass.

"Coming, Jacie?" His voice washed over her like a slow caress.

She nodded. "Be there in a minute," she called. Drawing a deep breath, she pushed herself away from the fence and made her way to Sloan.

"How about a swim and then lunch?"

She was momentarily disconcerted and then she started laughing. "Actually, I just realized something." Her mirth spilled over. There was nothing else she could do under the circumstances. "I...uh...kind of forgot my bathing suit." In her distraction over the phone call she had left her suit on the dining room table.

He removed his hat, his eyes on her. "All indecent proposals aside, you could swim in your underwear and T-shirt. It's not like you haven't done it before."

His words reminded her of the time he had caught her near naked at the pool. A spark of awareness snapped through her.

"I can't imagine you making an indecent proposal," she said, laughing. "You'd just come out and say what you had to say, like it or not." She looked down at her extra-long shirt, then let the sparkle of the water draw her attention.

"Maybe I will," she mused. "I'm not one to let a swim pass me by." She moved to the water's edge and dipped her fingers into the cool depths.

"I'm going to get the horses more water. I'll be right back," he said.

"I'll help." She moved to follow him.

"No, you go ahead. It'll just take a few minutes." As she watched, he pulled his shirt over his head and let it drop to the grass.

She understood his ploy or thought she did. He was giving her time to get in the water. Determinedly turning away from the sight of his long, tanned back, she pulled her jeans off and walked toward the water once more. Her shirt more than adequately covered her, and her underwear was more or less like a bathing suit.

Bypassing the small dock, she ran into the water and then dove. As she tread water her legs stirred cooler undercurrents. Catching her breath, she swiped the water from her face. She swam on her back, closing her eyes against the sun, floating and just relaxing. She even lost track of time she felt so relaxed, until like a great sea beast, Sloan rose up beside her. She squealed in surprise. Water ran down his face and across his chest. He pushed his hair back, a grin playing about his mouth. "Sorry."

"Uh-huh." She splashed water at him, twisted and dove away, but he caught her by the waist, lifting her from the water.

"Sloan!"

He held her above the water, one hand at her waist, the other under one leg. "Say you're sorry."

"No way." For a brief, still moment, she looked at him, her eyes taking in the water-spiked lashes. They were long and dark, his eyes an intense, serious blue.

He grinned wolfishly.

She groaned.

He dropped her in the water.

Spluttering, she surfaced. "You've got an unfair advantage! I can't touch bottom."

One dark brow rose and his mouth widened in amusement. "Then by all means, let's move to shallow water."

She swam away from him, stopping when the water was just below her breasts.

"Do you feel you have the advantage now?" he queried drolly, apparently willing to humor her.

"Almost. We have to make an adjustment," she said seriously, eyeing him.

Her eyes skimmed across his chest. Grinning, she refocused her attention on his face.

"A catch?" he asked mockingly.

"No, but because of your height and weight, we should make it equal." She squinted at him. "What do you say, are you up to making the odds equal?"

He began to look wary.

"Not backing out, are you?" she taunted.

"Do your worst. I'm all yours," he intoned softly, bracing his feet.

She prudently chose to take his words at face value. "If you want to even the odds, close your eyes."

She saw his momentary surprise, but he complied.

She stared at him for a fraction of a second, a mischievous smile curling her lips. "I have to make one adjustment," she said. Lightly, she touched her lips to his. "There," she said with satisfaction, "that's better."

She pushed his shoulder with hers and saw him smile. She pushed it again, harder. He leaned his upper torso toward her. She smiled in satisfaction. He probably thought she was going to body slam him or something.

"Ready?" she asked softly.

This time when she hit her shoulder into his and he braced himself toward her, she hooked her foot around his ankle and jerked him off balance, at the same time pushing his chest with both hands. He put a hand out in an attempt to steady himself, and with the other hand reached toward her. His eyes flew open.

She arched her body backwards, out of his immediate reach. "Sucker," she called out laughingly.

He regained his feet easily, slicking his hair back, a certain glint in his eyes.

"Fair play!" she cried, one hand out as she half-swam, half-walked backwards.

"You play dirty," he said, coming after her.

"Yeah, but it only works once." She lunged toward shore, her heart beating fast, expecting him to grab her at any moment. The anticipation of his touch was more than she could stand. On the other hand, she desperately wanted that touch.

As she ran to the pond's edge she was aware of her T-shirt clinging and wet. When she turned, expecting him to pounce, she saw him still out in the water. He dove and swam further out. Feeling a measure of disappointment, she dropped to the warm grass and squeezed the excess water from her shirt, then lay on her towel in the sun. By the time he joined her she was almost entirely dry.

Sitting up, she opened the basket and offered him a sandwich.

"So tell me where you learned that little trick?" he

drawled, taking a bite. Deliberately, he shook one arm over her and cool droplets of water hit her legs.

Shading her eyes, she let her glance skim over wide brown shoulders and narrow waist, down long, hair-dusted legs. Leisurely, she pulled some of the roast beef out of her sandwich and popped it in her mouth, then licked her fingers delicately. "If you recall I have four brothers."

"I'm surprised they didn't teach you an even more foul way to get even."

She grinned innocently. "Oh, they did, but I only use that on special occasions."

He shook his head. "I've been forewarned." He ate the remainder of his sandwich and moved closer. His body blocked out the sun as he leaned over her. "You never cease to surprise me, Jacie." A dark wing of hair fell across his forehead. Her fingers itched to touch it.

"I do what I can." She allowed her glance to skim the fine shadowing of beard along his jaw.

His cool mouth grazed her cheek, then the corner of her mouth. Heat infused her body and her stomach muscles contracted. She put her sandwich down on the wrapper and lifted her mouth to his. Gently, she touched her tongue to his bottom lip, and was rewarded with his groan.

Sloan gently pushed her back to the towel. His hands were on either side of her, yet only his lips touched her. She wanted to change that. She wound her fingers through his damp hair, enjoying its silkiness, her fingers tracing down the back of his skull. She arched her body up toward him, then away. His skin felt so cool compared to her sun-heated flesh.

He followed her down, heat burning wherever they touched. She wound her arms around him, her palms stroking slowly along his back. Their kisses became less restrained. She wanted to feel the slide of his skin against her. God! He went to her head, made her punch drunk, in serious danger of losing control. Losing herself.

She suddenly tensed, a niggling doubt creeping in.

Their eyes were mere inches apart. His voice came out gritty. "We're not teenagers. Unless we want to take this one step further..." his voice trailed off, but she understood his meaning.

Oh God, she thought, I'm intoxicated. Intoxicated on Sloan. Right now she didn't care if she ever sobered up, but did she want to take that irrevocable step? It would change both of their lives forever. She closed her eyes, trying to get her bearings. In the momentary hesitation he pulled away.

She felt her limbs tremble as the heat of moments ago drained down to her toes. She jumped to her feet and he put out a quick hand to steady her.

She smiled brightly, moving away from him. "I think you're right, neither one of us wants an involvement. It's physical attraction, that's all."

"We're adults," he muttered, "we know how to handle that."

She looked at him blankly and quickly nodded, anything to end this moment. "If we're going back, I'll get dressed."

"I think it's best. We have a good ride back and the sun will be going down soon," he murmured, frowning.

Moving away before she weakened and threw herself on him, she hurriedly pulled on her clothes, intensely conscious of the tremble of her fingers.

She thought fast. To her way of thinking she had reached the end of the line. She had two choices. Either she walked away or she went to him wholeheartedly, no restrictions. Both choices scared the hell out of her. Why would this choice scare her, she wondered frantically...she jumped out of planes, she was fearless, right? Wrong. He made her lose control. With the sexual haze still gripping her, she didn't want to think of tomorrow or the day after, but she'd been gullible before.

Straightening her shoulders, she knew she couldn't open herself to that vulnerability again, not without a lot of thought. Something deep inside her knew Sloan could hurt her worse than Brad ever had, just because the depth of emotion went much deeper.

It didn't take long to saddle the horses. At the top of the rise, Jacie cast a last look at the pond. She let her glance fall on Sloan, all too aware of the wistfulness in her heart.

Sloan was aware of Jacie, painfully so. He had called a halt down by the pond before it was too late, not that he had wanted to. He'd wanted her so bad he could taste it. He still ached with it.

He knew it was a risk, caring about a woman like Jacie. She was independent and strong, a woman with her own life.

He wondered if she would be happy here, if she even wanted to stay. Maybe this was just a summer thing for her. God knows a summer affair wasn't what he wanted. He was at a stage in his life he needed permanency and eventually a family. Maybe she was still testing the waters.

From all she had told him of her life, he figured a person like Jacie liked to move around. His mother had flitted in and out of his life for eight years, like a big sister or aunt. He didn't think he could live like that; he didn't want a wife that wasn't around. That kind of relationship would kill him. Damn! He was well and truly stuck between a rock and a hard place, and well aware he had put himself there.

∞ Chapter Eleven ∞

LATER THAT EVENING JACIE heard music drifting from the lodge. She leaned an elbow on the back deck rail, staring at the last rays of light as the sun was pulled back down the mountain. Very quickly, darkness fell. Another day ending at Timber Falls. Her stay was almost half over. At the end of the month she would be leaving.

The timed light on her deck flickered and came on, bathing her in an eerie purplish white glow.

Jacie couldn't get Sloan out of her thoughts.

The music stopped. The parking lot was crowded with cars tonight. She lifted her face to the breeze, warm and cool at the same time. That's what she felt like, she mused, hot one moment, cold the next.

Where did she stand with Sloan? Did she want to run scared, something she had never done or find out where a relationship could lead between them? God knows she wanted to trust him and herself, but she felt so muddled with emotion.

She walked around the front of her cabin, stopping as she reached the graveled drive. For a moment, she was startled to see a man's silhouette. For just one second, she thought it was Brad. She blinked, he moved and the light overhead shone on his face.

Sloan.

Her heart pounded and her palms began to sweat. She licked her lips as she walked toward him.

"Jacie." Her name on his lips was a sensuous stroke across skin. She trembled, shuddering as if his hand had caressed her.

"So tell me," he said conversationally, "who is he?"

"Who?" She stopped in her tracks.

"The guy who's ripping at your insides," he muttered. "The one who's keeping you from me. Stop running."

It's you who's ripping at my insides, destroying my hard-won peace of mind. "I don't run away," she breathed anxiously, her fingers curling.

He moved closer. "The hell you don't." His eyes were a dark gleam as if he searched out the pain. "I'm wondering if you look at me and see someone else."

"It's not something you feel every day," she muttered defensively, turning aside. "This thing between us is pretty unsettling."

Hard fingers trailed against her cheek, pulling her chin around, but ever so gently. If he had been demanding, she would have resisted. As it was, there was no resistance, just bone-melting heat, until she met his eyes once more, then it was worse. The grimness on his face, those hard lips...her remembrance of their gentle touch—she was lost, her stomach protesting his nearness with a quivering of feeling, a sensuous, all-over ache. It was almost a physical hurt, the wanting.

"What is it you want from me?" She couldn't contain the question.

"I'm just a simple cowboy." He looped his arms around her waist. "I think you know what you want, Jacie, but you won't admit it. I get the feeling every now and then I'm getting closer, then you back up two steps."

"Maybe I want to be normal like the rest of the world."

"What's normal?" He laughed.

She nodded in agreement as one of his hands reached for hers, his fingertips sliding slowly, sensuously along her palm before taking firm possession.

He brought her one hand up to his shoulder and then reached for her other hand, gently urging her closer to the hardness of him.

"Sloan, I don't think—"

"That's right, don't think," he said, ever so gently.

Self-preservation held her frozen as she looked into his eyes, so deep and compelling in the dim lighting.

Her nostrils twitched. She could smell his aftershave. It was subtle, weaving around her, coming into her mouth with each shaky breath.

She was unable to muster a defense, her mouth for once silent. He was so damned attractive, rugged and hard as nails. God help her, this emotion she felt hurt worse than anything she had ever experienced. She knew she would never recover if she fell in love with Sloan, she sensed it with every bit of her emotion. But Lord! How she wanted to say the hell with it. How she wanted him.

"What are you doing to me?" she protested half-heartedly.

"Shh, relax, let's dance." His lips touched the top of her head, lingered.

He gently led her into a two-step. "Listen to the music."

Her body followed his, entranced by his nearness. They fit together so well. She stared at his mouth, that wanting curling through her stomach. She should make short work of this attraction, but she just kept wanting more. She leaned into him, testing his strength, enjoying his mouth as they burned across her cheekbone, then feather-soft toward her lips. She turned her head away slightly, avoiding that final contact, met those eyes so close to her own. God! She could drown in those thick lashed eyes.

Her emotions were caught in a slow spiral, a freefall different than anything she had ever known. Excitement clenched her stomach muscles and made her tremble.

"Sloan."

"You sound worried." His husky voice came against her lips.

She nodded.

"Me, too," he said, showing a flash of his teeth. "Try to relax. I promise not to have my way with you."

A laugh gurgled in her throat.

"That's it, ease up."

"I don't want—" she broke off, calling herself a liar. She did want. She wanted Sloan.

She could see the dark shadowing of hair beneath his shirt. Her fingers strayed there of their own accord, unable to resist touching him. She groaned, but pushed back from him. "I need to know something. Do you always romance your lone female guests?"

His reply came without hesitation. "No, I make it a practice to stay away from the female guests. In fact, up until you came, it was a hard and fast rule. I prefer my life the way it is." He paused, one brow lifting. "I should say the way it was. Since you arrived, life hasn't been the same."

"So tell me why me?"

"You don't give yourself much credit. Take a look in the mirror, sweetheart...I won't lie. It's what first attracted me to you. There's a basic attraction I can't deny, but I'm afraid it goes deeper than that."

From the first moment she had been attracted to him, the maleness of him, before she'd even had an inkling of what he was about. Now, she knew this attraction went beyond physical, there was so much more to this man. There was caring, strength and humor.

"Relationships involve vulnerability, openness...I don't know if I can do this," she admitted truthfully.

"I'm in the same boat, sweetheart," he admitted huskily. "I was almost engaged a few years back, someone I knew from my city life. She couldn't handle the lifestyle here."

"That's the least of it right now," she muttered. "I admit I'm all torn up inside. We have to figure out where to go from this point."

"You're one hell of a woman, Jacie."

"Does that bother you?" She made her voice light, yet her entire body tensed. "It's the way I am. I value my independence, although I admit it's taken a real shot in the arm this past year."

"You're spontaneous, untamed in everything you attempt...you hold back nothing. I admire you for it."

"But?"

"There might be some reservations, but that's my problem, not yours."

"My family credits my leap-before-you-look attitude to the fact I was born during a twister," she murmured.

"How does your father deal with your mother skydiving?"

"He loves her," she said simply. "Along the way they found common ground. I've been spoiled, you know. Seeing my parents together, knowing how much they love each other, you tend to want the same thing."

"When you leave will you forget about us, Jacie, the

nights, the days, the spell of the Catskills?"

"I can't believe I would, though I am a city girl in and out." She mused. She stepped forward, impatient with the distance between them. "I won't forget Sloan. Not the mountains, their beauty, or...or you. You bother the hell out of me, Sloan Wright."

His arms pulled her hard against him. She pressed her face into his neck, and her voice was softer when she admitted, "I don't know why, but you do. Don't you dare laugh," she warned.

"Scout's honor, I wouldn't dare."

"You're laughing."

"Am not."

"You think I'm crazy."

He nodded slowly, his lips barely brushing across her lips. "Without a doubt. Crazy, impetuous, bold, brave. Need I go on?"

"Why stop?" she slurred, overcome with feeling. "You sound like you're just getting warmed up."

"You certainly do that to me. You're soft and warm and I find myself wanting to know more and more about you. I think you're pretty brave for a woman who's all soft inside."

She stepped back, pushing his hands away. "Why do you have to say stuff like that?" she demanded.

"It's true."

"There's nothing soft about me." She shook her head emphatically. "Nothing. I'm not like that."

"Really?" he drawled, dropping a kiss on her mouth. "I'll have to watch you more closely to find the real you."

She groaned, giving in to her wants and needs. His arms, his closeness just made her want more. She might be making herself vulnerable but she didn't care. There was something special touching her where this man was concerned. She couldn't let him walk away.

She grabbed his wrists and looked down at those calloused, capable-looking hands, then lifted her glance and smiled, she couldn't help it.

"You're shivering," He ran his palms over her arms.

"Reaction." Her laugh was nervous, sounding more like a hiccup.

"I promise I don't bite." His dark head bent towards her, his lips teasing at hers. "At least, not very much."

When he leaned into her, her fingers caught in his hair, urging him closer. It was a heady sensation, kissing the man she desired. Her brain felt in a fog as desire clutched at her.

"Come to my cabin," he murmured, his lips hot along her mouth.

"My place is right here," she said, not wanting to think beyond the moment.

Jacie closed her eyes as Sloan's fingertips brushed the hair back from her cheek. Passion held in check glinted at her from dark-lashed eyes.

Tenderness touched her, causing restless fingers to move in exploration across hard and muscled shoulders. She explored the flesh covering his ribs, tracing bone and muscle curiously.

His stomach was hard and flat, his waist narrow. Dark hair ran down to the button of his black jeans.

She stared at him, her mouth dry, afraid, yet excited.

He ran his thumb along her bottom lip, pulling slightly, coming to rest on her chin. "God, you're beautiful. So beautiful."

She turned her head, met his lips in acknowledgement of their mutual passion. Her hands crept higher, cradled the back of his head, her fingers splayed through the silky strands. Her body rested against his, the trust implied. On their outing by the pond she had known this moment was not far off.

She heard his groan and rolled her head back, letting him take her full weight as she clutched at the supple, muscled skin of his back. Blindly, she learned the contours, her fingers kneading his warm flesh. Lord, he was hard all over.

"Come to me, Jacie." His voice was deeper than she had ever heard it.

She pushed upwards, pressing her body to his. He was above her, his weight on his elbows. She wanted to feel him on her, his heaviness against her, all the hardness of him. His hand splayed across her stomach, making the muscles tighten.

"Easy, Jacie, there's time."

"There's never enough," she said raggedly, knowing she must grab the moment. "Things change, this opportunity might not happen again."

"Now that I've got you, I'm not letting go."

Sloan stiffened and went still.

"Sloan?" Vaguely, she heard the squeak of the door.

"Well, isn't this cozy," a jeering voice interrupted.

A hammering began in Jacie's head. Her entire body jerked, then tensed. She looked past Sloan's shoulder at the man in the doorway to her bedroom.

"Brad!" she exclaimed hoarsely.

Brad carelessly dropped his jacket on a chair. "If I'd known the plan for tonight, I'd have arrived earlier," he remarked insolently. "Luckily, the girl at the bar directed me to the right cabin. Looks like I'm just in time. I see you got someone to stand in for me, Jacie." Wearing a tight-lipped smile, he pushed his fingers through his sandy colored hair, eyes dark and cutting in his handsome face.

She jerked her T-shirt into place and sat upright, then realized Sloan's body shielded her from Brad's view. Brad had not moved from the doorway.

"Who the hell are you?" Sloan growled.

"Ask our Jacie," Brad said carelessly. "You shouldn't leave doors unlocked if you don't want people walking in," he went on, apparently unperturbed by Sloan's anger.

"Brad!" Angry and frustrated, she said loudly, "Get out!" Why had he shown up now? She'd told Bonnie not to come. What had begun so magically now felt sordid.

Sloan was on the bed one moment, then standing threateningly before Brad in the next instant. Jacie blinked uncertainly.

Brad backed up a step, then stopped, his jaw mulish. Jacie felt momentarily paralyzed. The two men stood face to face, both about the same size.

She swung her legs over the side of the rumpled bed. She hated her position in this. The silence was thick, waiting.

"Forget it, Sloan," she whispered, then cleared her throat. "I can take care of this."

He glanced over his shoulder at her, his mouth a white line. She could see the muscles in his back tense. Walking over to him, she touched his shoulder, the skin warm under her fingertips. She curled her fingers against his warm shoulder. Regretfully, huskily, she said, "Please, I'll talk to him."

Without a word he leaned down and grabbed his shirt, pulling it on as he walked from the room.

The screen door swung back into place with a thud.

"What the hell's going on, Jacie?"

She turned from the sight of Sloan walking away, aware of the dull, heavy ache in her chest. She turned to Brad, outrage sharpening her voice, "You don't have the right to ask me that, especially in that way. What do you think you're doing, coming into my place like this?"

He took a deep breath, putting out his hand. Carefully, she turned away and avoided the contact. Right now, she didn't want anyone touching her.

"Look—" He expelled his breath harshly, waving a hand, "-- I'm sorry, I was out of line. I shouldn't have stuck my nose in. I'll go after him and apologize."

"You had no right...have no rights where I'm concerned."

"I know," he agreed, throwing himself into the chair on top of his jacket. His mouth turned down. "I just lost it, I guess. I couldn't believe..."

She felt the color rising to her cheeks. She turned to look out the window, trying not to imagine how it looked to Brad walking in on them. How it was. "You had no right to barge in here."

"I know, I know, I wasn't thinking. Truth is, after I talked to you the other day, I was worried about you. You sounded so distant. I admit I didn't handle things well after the accident—"

"Brad, please." She put her fingers to her temples, rubbing the skin soothingly. "Let's not go over this. Right now I can't handle a post mortem on the past." Not after watching Sloan walk away.

"I know, but I have to...I-I feel like I have to make it up to you. I know I let you down."

"Forget it. As you said, it was a shock. People react differently in shock."

"No, I should have seen the whole picture. I was wracked with guilt, fear, a claustrophobic feeling," his voice thinned. It made her uncomfortable to hear it.

"That day at Angel Falls, I should have let you take the time to check your parachute once more. I make no excuse for it. I can't forgive myself, much less expect you to forgive me.

"That time I came to the hospital, Con wanted to kill me, he would have if your father hadn't gotten between us."

"Leave them out of it," she said tersely. If not for her father, her brothers would have had a free-for-all with Brad. "You can't expect my family to feel otherwise about you."

"I regret walking out on you."

"I got over it, it's time you did, too. I want you to leave right now."

"I can't forget it, I feel like it's there between us, this insurmountable wall."

"There is no wall," she said sadly. Then, more strongly, "There is no us."

"Jacie, please, give me another chance." Strangely, she sensed a real desperation in his voice. "I still love you."

His words shocked her, made her hesitate. She walked to the door. "Brad, don't do this."

He came to his feet, his handsome face hard and determined. "You can't say it's over. We had something really great, we clicked, how can you say you won't even consider trying again?"

Irritated now, she spun to face him. "I lied Brad. It did hurt, your rejection. I don't trust you anymore. I feel like I never really knew you. I thought we would get married and at the first sign of trouble, you bolt."

"You can't turn me away. I won't let you. I'll wear down your resistance," he said urgently. "I'll show you how much I care. I'll never let you down again. Say you'll at least give it a chance."

"Brad, you're going to leave now. I don't want to be pushed, and that's what you're doing."

He put a hand up, immediately backing off. "Fine, fine. I won't push. I've got some time off, I'm. . .er. . .in between jobs, maybe I could stick around for a bit—"

"No!"

"I won't get in the way. This place looks interesting. Hiking, swimming, riding. I haven't ridden since...since I was a kid. The place is big enough, you'll have your space." He paused, then back-pedaled and said, "What's with you and the cowboy?"

"Leave." The hackles rose as he referred to Sloan as "the cowboy."

"I'd just like to know where I stand."

Disbelieving, she stared at him incredulously. "You and I stand in the same place now as that last day I saw you," she told him baldly. "There is no us." Her words sounded hollow, even to her. What was the matter with her?

"Okay, okay. If I can get a room here for a couple days, can we just go easy, part as friends, at least?"

She wanted to finish this part of her life, once and for all. "I don't care what you do."

"If they don't have any empty rooms, how about I bunk down here?"

Letting out an exasperated breath, she said, "No!" She walked through the atrium door and stepped out onto the deck.

"One more thing, Jacie." He stopped in the doorway. He was jangling the change in his pocket, something he did when he was tense. Her ears perked up.

"Bonnie, uh...she's out in the car. She didn't come in because she figures you're really mad at her, considering your earlier conversation."

She muttered an imprecation, closing her eyes. Her stay at the ranch was turning into a three-ring circus. "Gee, I can't imagine why she would think that." He didn't move from the open doorway, but the change jangled furiously in his pocket. "Bonnie called early this morning and said she was already on the way here, so what took you so long?"

"Oh, you know Bonnie. She had all kinds of stops to make," he said vaguely. "Listen, I'll catch you later, babe, okay?"

She heard the front door close and she leaned against the railing. She had suddenly landed in the vacation from hell.

Walking around to the front of the cabin, she saw Bonnie's dark blue sedan parked out front with the motor idling. As she stepped in front of the headlights, the driver's door opened and Bonnie stepped out.

"Jacie." Bonnie's voice was low, hesitant, quite unlike her usually confident tones, yet she appeared perfectly groomed as always, her blonde hair tied in a knot on her shoulder, a burgundy silk coat hanging from her shoulders.

Bonnie moved forward to envelope her in a hug, but Jacie stepped back. The other woman halted and frowned, her fingers pulling nervously on the chain around her neck.

"Jacie?"

"Bonnie," she said coolly.

"How are you?"

Jacie sighed. "Come inside." She led the way.

In the light of the living room, she surveyed the hectic flush coloring Bonnie's cheekbones. Curiously, she wondered about the nervous energy driving Bonnie.

Bonnie put her hand out, then let it drop to her side. "I'm sorry about this mess." She pulled a packet of cigarettes from her pocketbook and lit one. "I saw the owner, what was his name? Sloan? I saw him come out of the house after Brad went in. He didn't look too happy."

Jacie gritted her teeth and motioned Bonnie to the couch. The other woman perched on the edge of the cushion.

"As I said earlier, I wanted to make sure everything was okay with you. You know I've been worried, especially since I talked you into this whole skydiving job.

You sounded so distant on the phone, almost angry. I really did think I was helping by bringing Brad here."

"I told you not to bring him."

Bonnie moved to the kitchen, ran the water and extinguished her partially smoked cigarette. She turned around, her back to the sink. "I'm sorry. You look great," she said quickly. "When you're ready, say the word and I'll come and get you."

Abruptly, Jacie turned and walked back toward the door. "I'm not sure what I'm going to do yet. Who knows, I might stick around here. Where is Brad?" she asked.

Bonnie waved her hand in the air. "He said something about lodging."

Jacie made no attempt to conceal her rising anger. "I can't believe you did this."

"You're mad...but what else could I do? He feels so bad and you said the police needed to speak with him."

Jacie shook her head. "Something else is going on."

Bonnie, in the act of lighting yet another cigarette, paused. "I don't follow."

"You're a nervous wreck."

Bonnie tossed her lighter back into her purse and stood up, her face now looking pinched and tired. "You sound like you need a longer vacation, Jacie. You're getting mad at the wrong person." She walked toward the door, then paused with her back to her. "I'll leave. Sorry I intruded. I never meant to hurt you." Bonnie half turned toward her, the words spilling from her lips. "I admit Brad caught me at a bad moment. Yesterday was crazy and hectic. I let him persuade me to drop him off here. His luck hasn't been the greatest lately, not that he'd tell you. His car is at the bottom of a lake, and his apartment's been burglarized."

"What are you talking about?"

"There are people after him. He didn't say why."

"And you bring him here?" she said incredulously. "I'm trying to get my life straight, not borrow more trouble."

"Bottom line is, he's been haunting my office day and night, he wants to make up with you." Bonnie turned back to her. "He really feels bad about you two splitting up, he says it was the best time of his life."

Mouth tight, she said, "Bonnie, this is none of your business." Taking a deep breath, she said, "In the future, I don't want you patching anything up. He left me, for God's sakes. Do you think that feeling of inadequacy just goes away?"

Bonnie's eyes widened. "God, I'm so sorry. I thought maybe you were over that by now."

"It goes deep, Bonnie. How would you feel about a man who took off when you were hurt?"

"I'm really sorry."

"I don't like what you've done." She turned away. As far as she was concerned, the conversation was over.

∞ Chapter Twelve ∞

AFTER A SLEEPLESS NIGHT, Jacie walked into
the lodge early in the morning to find Sloan wasn't
anywhere around.

The way they had parted last night left her with a sick
feeling inside. She needed to speak to him to set things
right but she didn't know what she would say. How do
you explain your old boyfriend just happened to turn up
at a most inopportune time? Would he believe her if she
said their relationships had been over for a year?

She saw Renee when she returned to the stables.

"Renee," she said. "Have you seen Sloan?"

"He left before first light. He and Donny are bringing
in the herds that have been pasturing all summer on the
other side of the ranch. It's a full three hour ride out."

"Thanks, Renee."

She decided to take a short hike. Maybe some
physical exercise would help still her rioting thoughts.

She had called deputy Bryant earlier and told him
Brad was at the ranch. She couldn't help thinking if Brad

hadn't shown up, she would have awakened this morning in Sloan's arms. The thought caused a trembling to begin in her hands. Damn! Nothing ever went smooth. She turned onto a footpath and concentrated as she climbed a steep incline full of roots and stones.

"Jacie! Wait up."

Brad ran up the hill behind her.

"Are you following me?" she demanded.

"I saw you leave the barn."

Brad wore a dark T-shirt, jogging shorts and running shoes on his feet. Apparently, he had packed several items with the intention of staying. She kept walking. He was the last person she wanted to see now.

He kept pace with her. His dark hair was brushed neatly back from his forehead where hers was wild and damp. That was the difference between them and Jacie supposed it always had been. While he remained cool and in control, she was disheveled, her emotions flying off in tangents.

"You know, Brad, I never thought about it before, but how do you always manage to look so...I don't know, never a hair out of place?"

He looked surprised, but then smiled as if she had paid him a compliment. "Habit, I guess."

She shook her head. "Even during the filming on Angel Falls. The wind was blowing, mist swirling through the air, and yet you looked the same. Look at me, I've probably never had a hair in place my entire life." She knew it was a minor difference, but it underlined all the bigger differences that had made their relationship fail. How had she gotten involved with him? Had she been so caught up in the image he presented that she forgot what was important?

"You're always beautiful," he said, his eyes sweeping appreciatively over her. "I've never seen you otherwise."

She shrugged and walked on again. "You'd be better off with someone like Bonnie."

Brad looked startled, then he frowned. "Why would you say that? Bonnie's a dragon. She'd try to rule any man dumb enough to fall for her. Anyway, I don't want her, I want you." He grabbed her arm and pulled her closer.

"Don't." She knew her protest wasn't as strong as it could be.

"I thought I'd let you know I've got a meeting this afternoon with someone from the sheriff's department." His voice was low.

She tried to shrug nonchalantly. "Fine." She stepped back, jamming her hands in her back pockets.

"Are they trying to open an investigation again?" he asked curiously.

"It's just routine questioning. I've had a couple accidents and they want to make sure the incidents aren't related."

Brad narrowed his eyes. "What do you mean by accidents?"

Jacie started to explain and then paused. "Actually, I'm probably not supposed to be talking about it. I guess you can ask the deputy to fill you in." She hurried her pace.

"Where are you off to?" he asked. "Maybe we could meet up later and have a picnic for old time's sake."

"Bonnie told me about your car and your apartment," she said bluntly.

Losing his smile, he looked up at the trees sheltering them. "I've had some tough luck."

"She told me about those guys chasing you." He started to deny it, but she shook her head. "Are they after money?"

His shoulders slumped. She noticed the tired lines beside his eyes, the faint touch of gray in his hair.

"Yeah. Oh, Jacie, I'm in a bind—"

"How much?"

"Eighty thousand."

She could hardly believe what he'd just said.

"I was so sure my next movie would be a hit, I just needed a little more backing."

"So you let that loan shark back you again, just like before?" she asked incredulously.

He nodded. "Only the movie was a flop, and now I'm basically in hiding."

"Maybe if you talk to them—"

"I've stalled them as long as I can, it's the end of the road." His voice took on a new note of urgency. "Jacie, come away with me."

"What?" she asked incredulously.

"We could live out of the country, have a good life together. I've got contacts down in South America." He tried to take her hand, but she backed away, shaking her head.

"I've been to South America, remember? It wasn't something I want to repeat. We're totally different, Brad. Maybe that's why things worked out the way they did. You go for the pomp and splendor and don't care if people get hurt along the way."

"The camera loves you, Jacie. We made a winning team. We can work together again."

She shook her head, the specter of too many shadows between them. "You take too many chances," she said somberly.

"Let's forget the past. Who says we can't? I know I've made some mistakes."

"I have to wonder where this change of heart comes from."

"It was a shock seeing you hurt so bad. I was suffering feelings of guilt over the accident. I've always loved you."

He reached forward and jerked her into his arms. The suddenness of his action knocked the air from her chest. His dark head lowered. Jacie stared at his mouth, so close, the past sucking her in. Brad's mouth covered hers, and she breathed him in. Like a whirlwind, their past flew through her thoughts. The good times, their fun times. . ..

Jacie stepped back, breaking the contact. "I don't love you anymore." It was the truth.

"Jacie," he said quickly, his eyes alight, "it could be like it was before. We still care about each other."

"It's so easy to see now what I missed back then," she said, ignoring what he'd said. "I was so busy being angry and bitter, I missed the most important part. Everything you do is for show, it doesn't mean anything. I don't mean anything to you."

There was a mottling of red on his cheeks as he cleared his throat. "You know how we clicked, we were good for one another. Remember those nights before the jump? We talked about marriage—we went out and got a special license?"

"Which we didn't use. I got hurt before that."

His eyes narrowed. "It was an accident—a terrible accident. You were in full control when your chute opened."

"Was I?" Jacie frowned. "I wake up at night sometimes, thinking I've missed something. There's a blank there where my memory should be. If only I had the chute so I could look at it. Those shroud lines shouldn't have failed the way they did."

"Are you saying someone messed with your parachute pack?" he asked angrily.

"I feel like I missed something."

"We'll never know what happened. In the hurry to airlift you out the parachute was left behind. It was nobody's fault, least of all yours. Stop worrying about the past. We owe it to ourselves to think about us instead."

"Us..." She shook her head. "I'll never forget the look on your face that day in the hospital, the way you didn't come back. I guess I'm not a forgiving person."

"Do you think this cowboy you're hooked up with would be any different?"

Without hesitation, she said, "Sloan would never leave me hurt and alone in a foreign country. He would do his best for me no matter what he felt personally. I have to know one last thing. Did you use that last scene in the movie?"

He had a harried look on his face. He spun around, rubbing the back of his neck. "Come on, Jacie, grow up. I had a lot riding on that film...it could make or break me. It was a chance to pay off those loan sharks, get out from under that debt. I couldn't just throw the scene away. Like it or not it was great footage."

"That was me in that tree, Brad. It was real, a situation gone wrong. I always did my skydiving drops to make them look like something more than what they were, but I never took chances until that last day."

"You worked with your brothers. Of course they wouldn't want you taking chances. But if you're in this business and you want to succeed, you have to stand out and sometimes that means taking a chance."

"You don't do jumps that leave the end result to fate. That's where I made the mistake. I got sloppy that day."

"Come on! You're the one who was always willing to go that extra bit."

"That's right, after I'd determined the risk and weighed everything in. I don't get a thrill putting myself in unnecessary danger."

"Working with me brought your temperature up, you can't deny it."

She admitted softly, "No, I don't deny it. I liked working with you in the beginning. There's one flaw, though, all you wanted was the money."

"What else is there?" he fairly shouted in exasperation. "We could have a great life together."

"I guess that says it all. Maybe that's why you're on the run," she said sadly, walking away.

"Jacie!" he called angrily. "I won't let you walk away!"

She shivered, even though the air was warm. "I already have." There was nothing else to say. She was finally free of the past. Free of her own demons.

The afternoon was almost gone when Sloan drove the last of the cattle through the gate. He rotated his shoulders back, trying to ease an ache that had grown steadily throughout the day. He figured he could finally call it quits. The entire herd was in the pen and everything was under control.

Everything except his life.

He'd had a lot of time during the night and the long day to think. A lot of time to reflect about Jacie. It irked him that Carlton had checked himself into a room at the lodge. Sloan didn't know for how long.

"I was right on one account," he muttered, his voice causing his horse's ears to twitch. "That Jacie is trouble." He pulled his hat off and dropped it onto the saddle horn. "She's trouble," he drawled, "but damned if I don't care. I'm not letting her go."

He knew he couldn't let her walk out of his life. It had taken him a while to come to that conclusion, but he had to at least give them a chance.

He unsaddled his horse, fed him and turned him out into the corral. He left the fading sunlight of the day and entered the barn. His eyes adjusted slowly to the shaded interior. He spotted Jacie sitting on a chair against the wall. Could he hope she was waiting for him?

"Hi," he said, resting his saddle on one hip, thinking how good she looked. His temperature soared as her glance ranged over him head-to-toe and a slow smile appeared as if she liked what she saw.

"Hello, Sloan, I was hoping you'd come by."

He dropped his saddle on an empty saddletree, then turned toward her, eyes narrowed. "Really? Where's Carlton?" he asked casually.

"Gone, I hope," she replied idly, tipping back her chair to rest her feet on a bale of hay.

He moved in closer. "He checked into the lodge last night." He sat on the bale next to her feet and encircled one of her slim ankles above her sneaker. "It was him, wasn't it, the guy who hurt you?"

She nodded, touching the toe of one foot against his leg. She let her attention drift to the right where the open doorway let in the last bit of sunlight. "The sun's setting. From where I sit, this is a front row seat on the world. The mountains seem on fire."

"It's the same most days," he told her. "This scene never changes. The season's maybe, but not the mountains. A person could get bored seeing the same thing day after day." He had to issue the warning. If anything came of a relationship between them, she had to know these were his roots.

She met his gaze unflinchingly. He knew what she was seeing. He had been out all night, hadn't shaved and dark stubble covered his cheeks and jaw. He saw her eyes change, almost sensed her breath quicken. Wanting curled inside him. He needed to wrap her in his arms and not let go.

He slid his hat from his head and rested it on his lap. He put his arm up to wipe the sweat from his forehead as he continued to watch her. For the first time since he had met her, he thought she looked relaxed, as if her life was finally on the right course. He wondered if Carlton showing up had brought about the change he sensed in her.

"Is Carlton an old boyfriend?" he finally asked.

"Yes. But it's been over for a year." She hesitated, then added slowly, as if for emphasis. "I wasn't sure it was over, even though I kept telling myself it was. I was afraid I might still love him. Today, I finally put it all to rest. There's nothing I want or need from Brad. I'm free."

He digested that. "He brought your friend Bonnie with him," he said.

She nodded. "Actually, Bonnie let Brad thumb a ride off her."

He frowned. "Is she trying to get you and Carlton to patch things up?"

"I disabused both of them of that notion. We didn't part on the best of terms—but he knows where I stand."

He stood up and turned his back to her as he looked toward the empty paddocks. "What's her stake in any of this?" he asked flatly.

She came to stand beside him, close but not touching. He could feel the heat of her body, smell the scent of the flowery fragrance she wore.

"Bonnie's the one who introduced me to Brad last year. She thinks we should try to at least talk but I told her she's wasting her time. She left right away."

"Tell me about last year," he said.

"About a year and a half ago my family did business with a new car rental company owned by Bonnie.

"Back then my contact with her was casual at best. About that time Brad rented a vehicle from her. When he mentioned he was looking for a skydiving company to do aerial jumps, Bonnie told him about our business."

He was highly aware of her fingers playing with the snap placket on his shirt.

"I usually work with my brothers, but they were out of town on a long-term job. I let Brad persuade me to work for him. He had some backers to produce an adventure film. The initial shots were done in New York. I guess I pushed to the back of my mind that his methods sometimes bordered on carelessness."

Her fingers began to knead the fabric of his shirt. It was driving him crazy so he caught her fingers with his.

"You were seeing each other?" he asked.

She nodded. "Yes. I soon found out Brad had everything tied up in this movie. It wasn't long before people came on the set hounding him for money. He was banking on it being a success...literally.

"Things went okay until the last day of filming...the last scene..." Her voice grew hoarse.

He touched her cheek. "Listen Jacie, just go easy, if it's too much..."

She cleared her throat. "No, it's okay." She threaded her fingers together and looked up at the ceiling. "The scene was shot in Venezuela. It took us four days to reach the site. It was hot, almost steamy...the bugs were terrible." She grimaced and rushed on but he could feel the tension emanating from her. "I felt...uneasy." More softly, she added, "I had a bad feeling, although I couldn't pinpoint why. The night before I couldn't sleep."

"You said it took you four days?"

She nodded. "An entire day to travel by canoe, then we had to scout the falls, check out the terrain."

"Angel Falls?"

She nodded. "We were dropped by helicopter on a practice run. It was a thirty-two hundred foot parachute drop from the top of Angel Falls. A freefall. Strange as it sounds, even with what happened afterwards, I can still feel the initial rush as I leapt from the cliff top into the mist.

"I had done it a few years back with my brothers. It's the extreme in skydiving freefall. Anyway, Brad was getting in deeper and deeper. Two men followed the crew to Venezuela."

She drew a heavy breath. "Brad wanted a really dramatic, heart-stopping shot." Her voice dropped, grew husky. "I must have overlooked something. I waited until the last possible moment to open my chute."

He began to get that sick feeling in his gut, the same feeling he'd had watching the video of her jump. "But something went wrong," he said.

She frowned. "Some of the parachute lines failed. To this day I don't know what happened. Sometimes I think I should have gone over everything again. I packed the chute myself, checked it."

"Did someone sabotage the chute?"

"I don't know."

"Maybe Carlton rushed you..." he said tightly.

"Con said much the same thing. When I worked with my brothers, they always inspected and double-checked everything after I had checked it out.

"Brad told me we were off schedule, the light was failing. I shouldn't have jumped without checking my pack again. My brothers had drilled the rules of survival into my head. I was as much at fault."

"Your chute never opened?"

"The pilot chute—that's the first small one, it pulls the larger chute out—it opened, but the shroud lines holding it to my harness broke free. It collapsed. I had to manually open the main chute. When you're in a freefall, you can do acrobatics. That was the plan, a course of acrobatics to make it look like I was out of control.

"When the chute opens, you pull on the shroud lines, they call it spilling air, and you can control the direction of your landing. I think some of the lines on my main chute were faulty, too, but everything happened so fast.

"I had the barest minimum of control, just enough to land in a belt of trees. I must've slammed my leg on the way down, but I don't recall. My chute held me fast. I was up there awhile before they airlifted me out."

"Take it easy, Jacie."

As tears spilled down her cheeks he pulled her down with him onto the bale of straw. He wiped her face with a handkerchief. She gave a loud sniffle and drew away from his chest. "Sorry, I guess it's still a bit close to home."

"Don't apologize."

She took a deep breath. "Actually, I feel better. I haven't talked much about it, not even to my family." She leaned her head against his shoulder, a grimace contorting her face. "God, I've shut them all out."

"Sometimes when you're hurt, you shut out the ones who want to help."

"While I hung in the tree all I could think about was how Con was going to get on my case big time. He's always the first one to say 'I told you so.' My family didn't care much for Brad."

"And did he?"

"Get on my case? No. He never said a word. One day I woke in the hospital in Venezuela and Con was there. He held me and didn't say anything."

"What about Carlton?"

"He came to the hospital once. He was scared worse than anyone. I could see it in his eyes. He was sweating bullets." She took a shaky breath. "I understood some of that fear, I felt it myself. I was hurt pretty bad, I was in a foreign country. No one spoke English. Brad never came back. He wiped out any trust I had in him. When I returned to the States, the production manager of Brad's company sent a lawyer to my parent's house. They wanted me to sign a release saying I wouldn't sue."

He muttered a curse.

"I didn't sign it." She smiled sadly. "I guess I was trying to get back at him. I thought if I made him think I might sue, I'd pay him back. The company's insurance carrier settled a sum on me. It sits in the bank."

He hesitated, then let out a long breath. "Who else knows about the money?"

She shrugged. "My family, the insurance carrier and Brad."

"Maybe that's where we should look."

"Brad would have nothing to gain. If something happened to me, everything would go to my family, my parents. My settlement would pay off the debt hanging over Brad's head, but I can't believe he'd hurt me."

"There's something else you should know," he told her. "I spoke to the vet who was here last week."

"Is Dandy all right?"

"He seems fine, but they're monitoring him for liver damage." He paused, clenching his jaw, knowing he had to tell her the rest. "The horse was given a chemical which affects the central nervous system."

"They could have killed Dandy—"

"Or you," he added grimly, running a hand over the back of his neck. "Someone knew what they were doing."

She twisted around and lifted her fingers to his cheek and rubbed the stubble there. He pulled back with a groan. "I'm a mess," he said. "I've been out most of the night. The weather-casters were predicting a big storm and I wanted to make sure the livestock were sheltered. Besides that, I needed time to think."

"I wish you had let me know," she told him softly. "I'd have ridden out with you."

He raised a brow. "After what happened last night, I wasn't sure what to think. It wouldn't have been much fun for you, it drizzled on and off all night and the cows were pretty spooked."

"Well, it would have been worth it to be with you. I spent a pretty lousy night too, though at least I was dry and warm."

Slowly, he began to smile. "Next time I go out I'll make sure to let you know. How about I get cleaned up, and we go to town for dinner?"

"Actually, I'd love to do that, Sloan." She paused and ran her tongue over her lips. "Some other time, though," she added with a slow, secret smile. She stepped away from him and ran her fingers over the front of his shirt, circling the snaps one by one. "How about I cook dinner?"

"Can you cook?" he asked, his mouth dry as one of her fingertips traced a design on his skin.

"Some, not much. I know how to use a can opener and the microwave."

"I'd love for you to cook for me," he said.

"How hungry are you?"

He dropped his voice, seeing the desire in her eyes, feeling it in his own body. "I'm starved."

"Me, too," she said.

He reached for her hand, recalling with vivid clarity that first day they had met when she'd parachuted into the ranch. He had offered her his hand then also.

"I need a shower and change," he said.

"I'll walk with you."

Sloan savored the feeling of having her hand trustingly in his. He sensed the rightness of hanging onto Jacie. He couldn't think right now if it would last longer than one night, but he was willing to take a chance on them.

Unable to resist any longer, he put his arms around her, his fingers splaying across the slim bones of her back. "God! You feel good. I don't want to let go."

"Then don't," she said simply.

He cupped her face with hands that shook, his kiss slow and lingering. Her body felt on fire.

They left the barn just as the sun was setting, the sky a fiery red burst across the mountains. It felt like a whole new day.

∞ Chapter Thirteen ∞

JACIE ENTERED SLOAN'S HOME ahead of him as he held open the door. She walked across the cool blue and gray tiled entryway and let her feet sink into the plush carpet of the living area. She stopped by the enormous fireplace that held center stage, potted flowering plants on either side of the hearth. She turned to face him, and watched him push the door closed with the heel of his hand. He carefully hung his hat on a peg by the door and followed her.

She welcomed his hands as they moved up her arms like liquid heat. She thought she would burn up, she felt so wantonly hot.

"I knew you were trouble the first minute I set eyes on you," she murmured.

"Funny, I had the same premonition. I guess we were both right." He placed a provocatively short kiss on her mouth and pulled back. "Give me ten minutes." He walked toward one of the doors off the living room.

She looked around the spacious living room, instantly

liking the mellowed wood walls and floor. The kitchen, with light green walls was located off the living room, and surprisingly large. The stove, dishwasher and refrigerator were all a modern black color. Jacie realized Sloan wasn't kidding when he'd said he had a green thumb. Flowers were everywhere.

"There's something to drink in the refrigerator," he called.

Jacie sank to the couch, finding it incredibly comfortable. Resting her head against the back, she let her eyes follow the whirring of a fan overhead. She tried to relax but she felt incredibly keyed up. It seemed like she had been waiting for this moment forever.

It seemed only a second later that she felt lips gently upon her own. Nostrils quivering, she drew in a deep breath, touching her cheek to Sloan's newly shaven cheek. She smiled. "I must have dozed off."

Pleasure jagged below her ribs, her entire body tensed, a fire burned in her stomach. His shaving lotion rose to her nostrils, spicy, orange scented.

She murmured his name and looped her arms around his neck. As he drew closer, she cupped his shoulders and then grazed her palms along his chest. Just touching him created a pulsing, undeniable heat. "If I woke up like this all the time, I'd never leave."

"We can arrange it," he said, touching his lips to hers. He pulled her up and held her hand as he led her across the room, down a hallway and into a bedroom. A large maple bed occupied one side of the room with enormous windows beside the bed.

Jacie sat on the edge of the bed. He dipped his head to her, his knee sinking into the mattress beside her leg. "Are you sure, Jacie?" he asked huskily.

"Mmm. Don't ask questions." Her lips trailed across his check, his neck, moved hungrily to his lips. There was satisfaction in every line of her body as she pressed close. She craved his attention, his touch. Heat roiled through her, her feverish desire reaching out to him. It felt right, it had to be right.

Right now she faced one of the most important challenges of her life. Loving Sloan.

His hands were on either side of her face, one thumb caressing the corner of her mouth. His eyes were intense. She loved their lightness, the sensual sweep across her face. She sensed he liked what he saw.

She turned her head slightly, caught his thumb between her teeth, gently nipped it and then kissed it. Her hands came up, gathered his large hands between her own as she pushed him back against the pillows. "I promise I won't hurt you," she mocked gently, tenderly.

"You've relieved my mind." His mouth caught hers in a rush, hard and crushing. She met him ravenously, her hands pulling him even closer. She needed his warmth, the hardness of him.

He rolled over, taking her with him. Feverishly, she pulled his shirt apart, tugged it off his shoulders. It slid unnoticed to the pale gray rug.

Palms down, she spread her fingers, sweeping her hands over the hair on his chest, the pads of her fingers smoothing up over his shoulders. Soap and aftershave whirled about her. Drugged on his scent, she dipped her head, lips and tongue tracking a course across his body.

His face looked hard, eyes darkening as he watched her. She loved the feel of him. Gently, her lips roved over the flat of his stomach, his chest, sliding upwards to his neck and seeking the hollow behind his ear, his still-damp hair tickling her nose.

She kissed the curve of his jaw, down along his neck, lips and tongue caressing his collarbone. The man was all lean muscle. Her fingers splayed across his ribs, tracing a tiny scar, playfully working across his skin.

She levered herself up, looking down at him. "You're beautiful," she whispered tenderly, then laughed shakily and shook her head. "I can't help it, I love touching you."

"Touch away," he rasped. "But I get to do the same."

She pressed against him, her arm resting across his stomach. She inhaled deeply, trying to catch her breath. She felt as if she had run hard.

Her fingers rifled through his hair. His hair was so fine, the light and dark strands sliding through her fingers.

He turned onto his side to face her, dislodging her arm. His fingers found the hem of her shirt, lifted it upward, slowly, his eyes on her as warm palms moved along her ribs and up over her breasts.

It became even more difficult to breathe. Licking dry lips, she allowed him to pull the shirt off, felt his care as he released her hair. She wore no bra, she was naked from the waist up, as was he.

His mouth found her breasts, teasing her. Restlessly, she churned against him. She wanted him crushed to her.

His fingers worked along the soft skin of her stomach, the slight hollow of her navel, then the button of her jeans. His eyes met hers.

Her nod was slight, she could manage nothing more. Her stomach quivered with small convulsions as he undid the button, pulled the jeans down over her hips, leaving only her briefs in place.

Work-hardened hands ran gently, sensually over her legs, down her thighs to slim ankles. A large palm cupped her heel and pulled the jeans entirely from her legs.

She stretched against the cool sheets, an overall sensual ache sweeping to the core of her. The look in his eyes made her feel like the most desirable woman alive.

She caught her breath as his lips touched like a hot

brand on the faint pinkish scar that ran along her neck. She jerked her head back, moving to push him away. He forestalled her, catching her nervously trembling hand as he dropped another kiss on the scar, gently, carefully.

She placed a hand on either side of his head and pulled him to her.

Their bodies did a slow, sensuous dance, side by side.

"Sloan." She released his name on a sigh.

"Come to me, Jacie." He pulled her against him, imprinting her with every hard line.

She feared in that moment her heart would burst from her chest, it beat so fast. His mouth trailed across her jaw, caught her mouth, played with her lips, then followed the flush of pink across her cheeks. She traced his lips with her tongue, darting at him.

Her hips moved, and she felt his nakedness against her own, hardness touching softness. She ran an exploratory palm down his chest, over the flat rigidity of his stomach, her curiosity knowing no bounds.

Time skipped away, sensation took over, melting all worry, making her live for the moment. Nothing mattered but this man, her lover. She hurried him when he went slow, reacted to him, wantonly begging, without words, for more.

He caught her closer, enveloping her. She clutched fiercely at him, afraid she couldn't get enough of his heat. Eagerly she took him in, giving back in equal measure.

Sloan held her tight, elation gripping him. Wildly their flesh met, plunged, rose again. Sensation overcame everything; the touch, taste and scent of Jacie was imprinted on his mind. Excitement held them, flung them wildly, then shattered all around them.

"Sloan!" Her cry was soft, breathless, her fingers gripping him fiercely. He held her close, protecting, guiding her until she shook with the fever, then became boneless, defenseless. Satiated.

His woman, he thought, pushing the hair tenderly from her face. She had placed her trust in him and given him everything, letting down her defenses.

He buried his lips deeply in her throat and traced a path across her cheekbone, over lids blue-veined and delicate.

He knew he had committed himself big time, and he felt it was right. He and Jacie could make a life together. They could combine their two worlds. There was always a way.

She snuggled down against him. He kept his arm around her as she slept. He pushed her hair back with a feather-light touch, watching her. He recalled his father telling him that despite everything, he would never have given up knowing Sloan's mother. Now, he understood what his father had meant. When you loved someone, it was really that easy. Sloan knew he loved Jacie. When she woke, he would tell her.

Ω

Jacie walked into her cabin early the next morning, her mind racing over the night she had spent with Sloan. It occupied her thoughts to the extent of all else.

These past weeks she had learned about Sloan the man, now she knew Sloan as a lover.

An ache began deep inside.

You should have stayed beside him and woke him, the voice in her head chided. She had wakened earlier in Sloan's arms. She had relished the closeness, the memory of their lovemaking, however, part of her needed time to absorb the implications of such a step, so she had slipped out before he woke. She wondered now if she had made a mistake.

She started as the telephone rang. Disbelieving, she

looked at her watch, wondering who would call at seven in the morning.

"Hello?" She heard rasping breaths, as if someone were out of breath.

"Jacie, you're there! I've been trying to reach you all night. I'm sorry to bother you—"

"Bonnie! What is it?"

There was weeping on the other end of the line. "Oh, Jacie, I lost my necklace when I was out there...out at Timber Falls."

"Your necklace?"

"You remember, the one my father gave me, it's a family heirloom, irreplaceable. After I left—I was upset, you were so mad at me and I don't blame you. I stopped on the road just outside the ranch at a small pull-off.

"I couldn't drive, I had to collect myself. I got out to smoke a cigarette. I walked around for a bit and that's the last time I remember having the necklace. That must be when I lost it.

"Maybe it slipped the chain. I haven't been able to find it anywhere. I'm frantic." She spoke so rapidly Jacie had a hard time understanding her.

"Slow down, Bonnie."

"Our conversation had bothered me so, I'm so sorry..."

A stirring of guilt gripped Jacie. "All right, Bonnie, that doesn't matter now. Tell me where this place is."

"After you leave the ranch, there's a sign and a small pull-off. I'm sure that's where I must have lost it."

"I think I know where you're talking about. Is it right by a big pasture and along the dirt track?"

"Yes, yes. Oh, thank you, Jacie. If I don't recover that, I'd never forgive myself. I heard it's supposed to rain and I'm afraid it'll be lost forever. I'll drive back out."

Jacie sensed the relief in the other woman's voice. "If

I should find it, I can mail it to you. That's a long way to drive—"

"I couldn't drive last night. I got a motel room in a town about an hour away."

Jacie sighed inwardly. "Okay, I'll see you when you arrive."

Jacie hurried into the barn and almost collided with Renee.

"Good morning, Jacie."

"Can I use one of the horses?"

"They've all been fed, take your pick."

"Thanks, Renee, it's going to be a short ride."

"Is everything okay?"

"A friend of mine lost her necklace. She thinks it might have been just outside the ranch. I'm going to look before it rains."

"That's kind of like looking for a needle in a haystack," Renee said doubtfully. "Do you want some help?"

"I'll help you Jacie."

Surprised to hear Brad's voice behind her, she whirled around. "Brad! You're up early."

"I came to say goodbye. I'll ride out with you then I'm leaving."

Jacie looked at him a moment, then shrugged. "All right. If we find it, you can give it back to Bonnie."

As they rode out to the east pasture she kept thinking of Sloan. She shouldn't have left before he woke this morning. How could she think she needed to think further about what had happened between them? She loved him. She would look for the necklace and then go find him and make it up to him for leaving. That thought made her smile in anticipation.

∞ Chapter Fourteen ∞

"So THINGS SEEM TO BE going well for you, Jacie?" Brad asked.

Jacie looked over at him, having been lost in thoughts of Sloan. "Yes."

Brad didn't look like he'd had a good night's rest. He hadn't shaved and looked pretty rough. She felt a moment's sympathy but knew Brad's problems were of his own making.

"Here we are," she said with relief, casting a worried glance at the sky. It had gradually become overcast, the sky a sullen gray. "You start looking here along this area and I'll check over by the ledge."

She dismounted, dropped her horse's reins and walked over to the ledge. The quicker she began looking the quicker she could get back to Sloan.

She could see fog creeping up the wall of rock. She had never seen fog roll along the ground like it did in the Catskills.

After an hour, she was convinced they wouldn't find

it. It had been barely two hours since she had left Sloan, yet she hadn't been able to stop thinking of him, their lovemaking, the entire night of loving. Lord! How could it have been so wonderful, so perfect?

"There's no way we'll find anything out here," she muttered, looking around for Brad. Jacie suddenly noticed a figure appear out of the woods.

Bonnie walked towards her across the field. She had never seen her dressed so casually in jeans, T-shirt and hiking boots.

"Bonnie," she said, "how did you get here so quickly? Where did you park your car?"

"That's not important."

"We couldn't find the necklace."

Bonnie shot her a surprised look. "We?"

Jacie saw Brad climb up from a small ledge. "I looked down over the ledge," he said, "but I doubt we'll find it." He looked at Bonnie in surprise.

Bonnie said angrily. "Why is he here?"

"What's going on?" Jacie said suspiciously.

Bonnie stepped back from them and pulled her hand out from behind her back. She held a small gun.

"Geez! Bonnie!" Brad said, horrified.

Jacie stepped back, fear a huge tightness in her throat.

"You've ruined everything. I wasted months of my life on you," Bonnie spat.

Jacie put her head back, comprehension dawning. "It was you all along." She looked around quickly but the area was wide open, there was nowhere to run.

"You're both fools!" Bonnie said. She turned to Jacie. "You've jeopardized his life by bringing him out here."

Jacie tried to keep her terror in check. The hard, angry glitter in Bonnie's eyes held her transfixed. "Is this about the money?" She needed to buy time.

"I set it all up. I've got the withdrawal papers ready,

my passport, and you're still walking around."

"Angel Falls," Jacie said in a low voice.

Bonnie laughed. "You two! Taking stupid chances in a foreign country. You made it so easy."

"You weren't there," Brad said, edging closer.

Bonnie pointed the gun at him and he stopped. "I didn't have to be," she said contemptuously. "I had somebody on the inside."

"And they tampered with my equipment," Jacie said, realizing Sloan had been right.

The woman she had considered a friend gave her a cold smile.

"Even if you kill me, you won't get the money," Jacie said.

"Don't you worry, I've always had a talent for signatures. Did you know you'd made a Last Will and Testament leaving everything to your best friend?" She laughed. "It's going to show up fully executed in your belongings." Bonnie looked contemptuously at Brad. "We're a lot alike. You wanted the money too, but when they find you two dead, they're going to think there was a struggle and you tried to kill Jacie. If they ever figure out it wasn't him, I'll be long gone and a bit richer." She pointed the gun directly at Jacie. "Back up toward the ledge."

Jacie's stomach heaved with fright, but she didn't move.

"Do it," Bonnie snarled.

"No!" Brad said, lunging toward her.

The gun discharging rent the air, echoing around them. Bonnie and Brad struggled for the weapon, stumbling back toward the ledge. Another shot sounded.

Jacie heard Brad's grunt of pain. She ran to him as he doubled over and fell on the ground.

"Back away." Bonnie pointed the gun at her.

Jacie knelt beside Brad. Blood poured from his thigh. Turning her head, she saw the horses held their heads high in the air, startled and quivering. A low rumbling began, like thunder in the distance. A heightened sense of danger knifed through her. "It's the herd." She could see a rising cloud of dust just beyond a small knoll.

"Shut up."

"They're stampeding," Jacie insisted. "We have to get away from the ledge. We have to run toward the trees!"

Bonnie looked back at the approaching herd. Alarm finally registered on her face.

Jacie tried to get Brad up, but in seconds, she knew it was useless. The cattle were running full bore toward them now, the width and breadth of the herd making it impossible for them to reach the trees and possible safety. They would be caught in the middle of the stampede.

Bonnie darted past them, running across the field.

She pulled Brad closer to the ledge as the first animal raced by. She was conscious of the sheer drop a mere three feet from where they were. She looked out across the herd but she couldn't see Bonnie.

There was nowhere to go. The cattle edged closer, hooves pounding the earth. Dust rose chokingly.

At a certain moment, she knew death was imminent. There was nowhere to go but down, down over the ledge into the ravine.

With dread, she watched the cattle shift almost as one, pushing them further toward the edge.

Jacie helped Brad as he tried to rise. Almost in slow motion, he fell to his knees. She clawed at him as he lost his balance and slid part way off the ledge.

Landing brutally hard on her stomach, she managed to grab the back of Brad's shirt. Spots jumped before her eyes as she hung onto him. Brad's fingers clawed the dry earth, trying to grab onto something, anything.

"Hold—hold still, Brad—" Even as she gasped the words, she felt the shirt rip from her fingers. "Brad!"

He fell from sight.

Disbelieving, she closed her eyes. "Oh, my God!"

The ledge beneath her trembled, a portion of it crumbling away. When she realized she too was going to fall, she tried to scramble backwards. Shards of stone bit into her flesh as the ground gave away. She held on a moment, her arms on the sandy ledge. Her legs dangled as she attempted to find a foothold.

An awful emptiness filled her as time seemed to stand still. She felt herself falling.

Ω

Sloan looked into the office and found James inside. "Have you seen Jacie?" he asked.

Looking up from his paperwork, James looked at the clock on the wall. "She was in the barn this morning, about two hours ago. Renee said she and Carlton were going for a ride. I don't know if they're back yet."

"Jacie went for a ride?" Uneasily, Sloan thought it was odd. He hadn't been happy that Jacie was gone when he woke, but the note she'd left had made him smile and he knew he'd see her at some point that morning.

"I'll see if anyone knows their whereabouts." He looked at his watch, an unfamiliar twisting in his gut. He left the office and strode outside.

"Sloan! Sloan!" Michelle rode furiously across parking lot. Her horse slowed and he grabbed the animal's reins. Looking into her alarmed face, that sickening fear grew worse.

"I was riding along the road pasture...two gun shots...the cattle stampeded..."

An icy wave enveloped him. "I had them penned. Is

anybody out there?"

"I don't know, but two horses came back—"

Dread consolidated into a hard knot.

"—without riders," Michelle finished breathlessly.

He felt as if he'd been punched. "Jacie." He didn't know he'd said it aloud until he saw the alarm darken Michelle's eyes.

James appeared beside him and gripped his shoulder. "Sloan, what's going on?"

He turned to his brother. "You know how jumpy the herd's been, well somebody's been shooting and the cows have stampeded. Jacie may be out there...and Carlton."

He took off at a run toward the barns, James beside him. "Get in touch with the Sheriff's office and call around for extra help. You'd better set up a search party. I want every available horse saddled and ready to go."

At the barn he led his horse from the stall and quickly slid the bridle on.

"Sloan!" Michelle called, "Your saddle—"

"No time." Bareback, he urged his horse in a canter, his thoughts on Jacie. Nausea churned his stomach. He couldn't lose her. He had just found her. He couldn't lose her.

Ω

Jacie lay without moving, eyes almost closed as she faced the dull grey sky. Slowly, her brain assimilated information. She had fallen and so had Brad. A heavy damp fog hung everywhere.

"Help!" she called out. Her voice sounded weak as it echoed around the stone ledges.

Her face and clothes were damp. She felt chilled. All around her was a strange, ethereal quiet. Shards of rock and debris showered down on her. Moving carefully, she managed to sit up, groaning as every muscle in her body protested. Pain burned like a brand between her shoulders, but she was alive. What about Brad?

"Brad!"

She heard a sound, like a groan. Biting her lips, she pulled herself on her elbows to the edge of the rocky precipice.

Lying on her stomach, she could see a figure on a ledge below her. She could not see Brad's face. He lay unmoving and appeared to almost blend into the rock. Drifting fog made it almost impossible to see anything.

"Brad!" she called, "I'm above you." She rolled to her side, glad there was no pain to indicate cracked or broken ribs. She had been lucky, she decided, looking upwards. Sort of.

She wondered how long they had been here. She remembered the horses and felt a ray of hope. When they returned alone, someone would come. Except that no one knew where they were, except Bonnie. What had happened to her?

Sloan. She groaned. He would be worried. Why hadn't she stayed with him this morning? None of this would have happened.

Rain began to fall gently. She had to figure out a way to safety.

Brad could die from exposure. That thought made her stand up. She did so carefully, wondering if the ledge she stood on was secure. With the exception of an overall soreness, she didn't think she had broken anything.

Looking up, she scanned the ledge. Going down was impossible, she knew it was a sheer drop. The way out was up.

"Brad!" she shouted. "I'm going to climb out. I'll be back."

There was no answer. He had lost a lot of blood, he could be in shock.

She chewed her lip nervously. She had never attempted rock climbing without the proper ropes, and if she fell again, this time she probably wouldn't be so lucky.

All she knew was she had to get out. Blanking her mind to any fear, she flattened herself against the craggy rock and began to climb.

Carefully, she searched for toe and finger holds, prayer like a litany upon her lips.

Jacie lay a moment, hardly caring that her cheek rested against caked mud, glad of the bits of grass tickling her nose. It was a brief respite, she knew she must push on, but she needed just a moment to rest.

She wasn't sure how late it was. The day was dark and the fog looked to have enveloped everything. The air was so heavy it felt like wet wool clinging to her clothes. She rolled onto her side, conscious of her burning fingertips.

Brad.

She stood. It had been a long, hard climb out of the ravine; it had seemed a lifetime. She looked around and tried to get her bearings. Staggering, she started across the field. It was a muddy quagmire from the rain and what the cattle had churned up.

It had rained most of the day and she was past cold. Her throat felt raw from yelling. She had given up on that quickly, concentrating instead on not falling. The closer she had gotten to the top, the harder the climb became.

Bemused, she put a hand to her temple. The day had begun so differently. She had been so content and filled with thoughts of Sloan. . ..

God! He probably thought she had fallen from the face of the earth. With a grim smile, she conceded they almost had.

A noise broke the silence, startling in its suddenness. Twin beams of light cut across the pasture. She forced her legs to move as she waved her arms.

Bright light sliced across her and just as suddenly an engine accelerated. The lights jumped wildly as the truck raced across the uneven pasture.

Such enormous relief welled she couldn't stop the moisture burning her lids. Somehow, she knew it had to be Sloan.

Sloan brought the vehicle to a sliding halt in the slick mud. The lights pierced the fog eerily, silhouetting Jacie's filthy bedraggled figure in the arc of light.

He jerked the door open and jumped from the truck. In the next instant he enfolded her in his arms. It felt like forever since he had held her this close. She was shivering and fell into him.

"Sloan," she said hoarsely.

"Jacie! I've been out of my mind. We've been out on horseback all day. Since dark I've been driving all over, hoping to find a clue, anything. We didn't know where to look. Did you get caught here when the herd spooked?"

She pulled back and tugged him toward the edge. "Brad's down there, Sloan. He's still down there."

"Sweetheart, come sit in the truck before you collapse." He urged her over to the truck and the open driver door. She slid onto the vinyl seat. Jerking his sweatshirt off, he placed it over her head and pulled her arms through the armholes. "You're frozen." He pulled a wool blanket from behind the truck seat and wrapped it around her shoulders.

"Thanks, that feels wonderful."

He picked up his cell phone on the dashboard and quickly dialed the rescue number, all the while keeping an eye on her. She leaned her head back against the headrest, her eyes closed.

Suddenly, she lifted her head. "Brad's down over the edge," she said, her voice stronger. She jumped down from the truck seat and he gripped her arm.

"Hang on. Where are you going?"

"We have to get him out, he's been shot."

"Shot!"

She squinted in the dim light at her watch. "The crystal's broken. I don't know how long, since this morning."

Sloan put his arms around her shoulders, feeling like he couldn't get her close enough. He felt the tremble in his own arms. "What the hell has happened and how do you know he's down there?" He put her at arm's length and ran his glance over her more thoroughly. The mud on her shirt was soaking through the sweatshirt and her jeans had holes in the knees.

"What happened to you?"

"We both fell down the ledge."

"You fell?" He lowered his voice, knowing it wouldn't do any good to start yelling. "How did you fall. . .how did you get out? It's almost sheer ledge."

"The herd."

"I've been out of my mind, wondering where you could be. I couldn't pick up a track with the rain. I don't want to tell you the things going through my head. I don't want to go through that hell again."

She gripped his arm tightly. "It was Bonnie all along. She was after the money. She came back here expecting to find only me. Brad tried to get the gun away from her and she shot him. The shots spooked the cattle and our horses took off. The ledge beneath us crumbled—"

Sloan tried to follow the rapid words.

"Brad fell and then I fell." She took a deep breath and her voice evened out a degree. "I managed to climb out, but that's not important now, we have to get Brad."

"It damn well is important. This isn't over," he promised with a growl.

"What can we do?"

"I called search and rescue. I'll notify James we found you and have the police come to this area. Where did Bonnie go?"

"She must have made it across the field before we were forced to the edge."

"They can track her down later. It will take at least fifteen minutes for a rescue team to arrive."

"I'm worried about Brad. The rawness of the air...it's getting colder. Can we lower a rope, maybe make a sling?" she asked hopefully.

"I'll tie a rope to the truck winch and lower myself over the edge."

"No. He unconscious, you'll never find him. We can save precious time if I go back down. I can cover him if you have a blanket. When the paramedics arrive I can show them where he is."

"No."

"Yes." Urgently, she grabbed his sleeve. "I have to. I know where he is. Besides, we're wasting time arguing."

"You look as if you've been through hell. You might be suffering a concussion. I won't chance it."

"I can do it," she insisted fiercely. "I came up over the top without any lines, I can go back down with a rope. If you're worried about concussion, check my eyes, whatever, but hurry."

He swore, but shone the light in both her eyes. He snapped the light off with a muttered curse. "Dammit, Jacie...I'll come with you."

"I need you to guide the rope over the ledge, it's razor sharp where it broke off, and somebody has to run that winch."

He banged his closed fist into his thigh. She glared at him, not saying a word. Clenching his jaw, he unwound the coil of rope and began tying knots. After a moment he secured the rope about her waist, back and upper thighs. Tension coiled inside him. He was afraid for her. He had almost lost her once today.

She gripped the rope, but he forestalled her. "Let me secure this to the winch."

He started the winch motor. The truck lights dimmed momentarily, then the motor began with a low whirring sound and he pulled the steel cable out several feet from the bumper. With several knots he secured the rope to the winch's hook.

Sloan crouched beside her to check the rope about her waist and thighs. "Here," he said tersely, handing her a pair of gloves. "They're big, but they'll protect your hands." He handed her the blanket she'd had on her shoulders. "You can use this to cover him."

She pulled on the gloves. He helped her stuff the blanket between her stomach and the ropes. She looked at him and he saw the longing and unspoken tenderness in her eyes. He rubbed the pad of his thumb along her jaw. "You swear you can do this?" he asked tersely, a terrible ache in his throat.

"I know I can."

"I'm going to trust you, Jacie," he muttered.

Grabbing the ropes, she turned to face the truck. He checked the ropes again, and then helped her lower herself over the edge.

"Jacie." He held her by the upper arms, her legs dangling in the air. "Bad timing, but I love you." He pulled her upper body to him, his arms catching her in a bear hug.

"What a coincidence," she whispered back. "I feel the same way. I love you too."

He stuffed a small flashlight in her back pocket, gave her a quick put his hand behind her head and gave her a kiss, then he lowered her over the edge.

"I can do this," she insisted quietly.

He wished he felt the same calm certainty. "Be careful, dammit."

"That's romantic," she quipped and then she disappeared over the edge.

∞ Chapter Fifteen ∞

JACIE DROPPED BELOW the outcropping of rock she had landed on earlier, the night dark and quiet all around her.

Her eyes strained the shadowy blackness, her hands feeling along the rock face as she dropped further into empty air.

"Brad!" she called. Surely she must be near the ledge where she had landed.

"Jacie?" Tremendous relief flooded her as she heard Brad's voice below her. She had feared he was unconscious.

"Jacie, are you all right? Where are you?" His voice sounded weak.

"I'm fine." A little further and she touched a jutting ledge with the toe of her boot. "Hang on, Sloan's up on top."

Digging her fingers into crevices, ignoring the stinging pain from earlier scratches, she pulled herself on her stomach onto the ledge.

Remembering the flashlight in her back pocket, she gripped it and flicked the switch. Nothing. With a muttered curse, she hit it against the heel of her hand. The light came on and she quickly swept the area. Brad lay in an awkward position, blood pooling beneath one leg, an arm twisted at an odd angle. Willing herself to remain calm, she touched his shoulder.

"Jacie? Are you all right?" he asked weakly.

"Of course. Sloan called for rescue, they should be here soon."

She was surprised he didn't mention his arm. Perhaps he was in shock. "I have something to cover you."

She pulled out the blanket wedged between the ropes and her stomach and laid it over him.

"Jacie, I'm sorry for all that's happened."

She couldn't quite make out his face in the fog. "This isn't your fault," she said. "You did your best to keep Bonnie from hurting me up there."

"You should have left me down here the way I left you," he said bitterly. "But nothing scares you, does it Jacie?"

"It's over with."

"I know, it's all over, and I'm sorry for all that went wrong."

The rope around her waist jerked. Looking up, she could now see several bright lights above them, but the outcropping of ledge over them prevented anyone on top from seeing her.

Rescue members outfitted with ropes and equipment soon dropped to the ledge where they waited and immediately began to work on Brad. With relief, Jacie felt her rope begin to tauten and she was pulled upwards.

As she neared the top, she was so tired that she lost her foothold against the rock face and began to whirl in the air. She closed her eyes, suddenly overcome with dizziness.

Finally, the rope moved again and hands reached down. Someone grabbed her belt loops and pulled her the rest of the way over the edge. She landed against Sloan, her face buried in his neck. She lay still, thankful to have made it.

"Don't ever do that to me again," he said harshly.

She lay on top of him in a tangle of ropes. "Doesn't this remind you of our first meeting?" she asked with a small hiccup of a laugh.

"I'd rather do that ten times over than ever let you go down there again," he said fervently.

The rescue team hoisted Brad to the top. As they carried the stretcher past them, Brad reached out and gripped Sloan's sleeve.

"I wish we'd met under better circumstances," he said. "Good luck." Sloan dipped his head in acknowledgement and then they placed Brad in a brightly lit ambulance. The vehicle drove off with an eerie wail, red lights a short-lived beacon in the dense fog.

Someone with rescue squad insignia on their arm carefully pushed the hair back from her face. Gently, fingers probed her temple and forehead.

"Are you all right, Miss?" the woman asked. "You should be checked out at the hospital."

Jacie shook her head, her fingers twisting in Sloan's shirt. "No thanks, I feel fine. Just fine," she whispered softly. "Just tired."

He supported her sagging body. "Get a stretcher over here," he barked. He insisted she lay down on the stretcher and he covered her with a blanket.

Almost immediately, her shivering subsided.

"I'm having you taken to the hospital to be checked out." His voice brooked no argument.

"Where's Jacie?" A new voice was added to the chaos

around them. "Is my sister okay?"

She jerked upright and then fell back against Sloan where he knelt beside the stretcher. Her legs were still curiously numb from the tightness of the rope. Pins and needles tingled as the blood began to circulate.

"Con?" she squeaked.

"Jacie, I just heard what happened. Are you okay?" her brother asked. "I'm not here ten minutes and I find out the sirens and police involve you," her brother said, pushing a hand agitatedly through his short-cropped hair.

"I'm okay, why are you here?" she asked.

"I just got back in the States. Sloan had the sense to call me."

Sloan twisted around to face her brother and extended his hand. "Glad you got here so quick," he said quietly.

As they shook hands Jacie saw her brother take note of Sloan's arm around her. Eyes narrowing, he said to Sloan, "I guess you didn't tell me everything that was going on here."

Sloan looked him straight in the eye. "Some things you don't go into over the phone."

"I owe you," Con said.

"Well, I'm glad to see you two are bonding," she said tiredly. Closing her eyes, she lay flat.

"Sloan, we've found a body," a voice said behind them.

Jacie bit back a cry, shocked by what the officer had said. It was Deputy Bryant.

"At the edge of the woods," he continued. "It's a woman. I've notified the coroner. Looks like she might have been caught in the stampede."

"Bonnie?" she whispered, her stomach churning.

The deputy tipped his hat to her. "Ms. Turner, I'm going to need a statement." He turned his attention back to Sloan. "We also found a pistol, looks like a .22 caliber." He hesitated a moment. "I need someone to identify the body."

"Can we take care of that tomorrow?" Sloan asked. "Jacie needs to go to the hospital."

"No," she said.

"Yes," said Officer Bryant.

She turned to Sloan and gave him a tremulous smile. "I'm really okay. I just want to go back to your place."

He put an arm under her legs and behind her back, lifting her as if she weighed nothing. She felt the exhausted tremble in her limbs, but protested at him carrying her.

He held her close. "I'm not letting you go. Let's get you home." He turned to her brother. "I'm taking Jacie to my place. I'll call the doctor from there. He makes house calls. You're welcome to come along."

Reading the possessive look on his face, she ceased her protest. The man had had a difficult day, let him do what he wanted.

Ω

About mid-morning the following day, Sloan nudged the door open, careful not to make any noise. Looking toward the bed, he studied the woman who lay there. Jacie's hair swept across the pillows and the bedcovers were twisted about her.

Untamed and brave, Jacie was special. That's what he loved about her. That's why he'd be a fool to let her go.

Her slim white back was exposed to his view. Sloan's lips tightened grimly as he surveyed the angry purplish bruises on her shoulders and spine, the scratch running the full length of her back. And her hands...he swallowed, closing his eyes, thanking God for keeping her safe.

It had been an awful risk letting her go back down

that ledge. He felt as if he'd aged ten years while she was down there.

He placed the tray on the bedside table as she began to stir. She stretched and then groaned.

"Don't move," he said. He knew he sounded incredibly bad-tempered. Jacie, of course, rolled over anyway and groaned again. She looked down and made an attempt to pull the bedcovers up over her breasts.

"Too late," he said grimly. "I've seen it all. You're a mess."

She lifted the covers and looked down at herself, then dropped the covers again. "God."

"Yeah," he agreed.

"What are you looking so furious about?" she asked in confusion.

"You. I should never have let you go back down."

Her mouth relaxed and a warm concern entered her eyes. She lifted a scratched and bruised hand and ran her fingertip along his cheek.

"You've had one heck of a worry, haven't you?"

"You're covered in head-to-toe bruises. I've never seen such a body."

"Thanks, glad you noticed." She grinned at him and stretched languidly, apparently not adverse to showing him more of it.

He tried to look annoyed, but his lips twitched.

"You're not getting out of it that easy." He indicated the tray. "I brought you water for tea. But first you should get into the tub, take away the sting of those bruises."

"The tea will get cold."

"It'll keep. Come on."

She sat up and pulled the covers with her. "Awful bossy, aren't we?" she queried mockingly. "However, I will let you have your way for the moment."

He picked up a large blue robe and turned to her. "By the way, the rest of your brothers showed up early this morning."

"All of my brothers are here?" she squeaked. "Did they give you a hard time?"

"Nothing I couldn't handle," he assured her.

She arched a brow at him, opening her eyes wide. "You handled my brothers?"

"That's right. I understand your parents are already on their way here, too. Come on, I've got the bath ready." Without looking at her, he held out the robe and she slipped into it and followed him into the bathroom. The small room was steamy, the floor-to-ceiling mirror fogged. He turned to leave, doing his level best not to look at her. She needed time to heal.

"Sloan, wait." She was looking at the over large bathtub, a doubtful expression on her face. "My legs are terribly sore." She pulled the robe aside and exposed a bruise high on her thigh. "I don't know if I can get in by myself."

He muffled a curse. "I'll help you," he said grimly. Again, he reminded himself she was bruised and he should put his lustful thoughts aside.

He almost lost his control when she dropped the robe off her shoulders, down to her waist, and finally to her feet. He groaned, and tried to cover the sound by clearing his throat.

She lifted her hair from her shoulders with both hands and threaded her fingers through it as she stood naked in front of him. She glanced at him over her shoulder. "Can you help me?"

He grunted in response, it was all he could manage.

She leaned heavily against him as he helped her into the bath. The water was warm. With a moan, she leaned back and closed her eyes.

"Okay now?" he asked as he backed away. He didn't know how much more he could stand of this.

"No, my hair...it's going to get all wet and it'll take forever to dry." He frowned at her. He had never heard her whine before. Her eyes were closed as she plucked fretfully at her hair. "Could you help me? My fingers are sore."

"What do you want me to do?"

"Tie my hair back. Do you have a rubber band?" She lifted several strands where they had fallen on her breast. His mouth went dry. She peeked up at him. "Please?"

With an almost inaudible groan, he sat on the edge of the tub. "Turn around."

She twisted slightly so he had better access to her hair. He looked at the curve of her neck, its slender arch. The lightly tanned skin of her back begged for his lips, as did the delicate shaping of a rounded shoulder as it curved down to her breasts.

He looked at the wall, ignoring the tightening of his body. She shivered and he couldn't help but notice the goose bumps spread down her arms.

"I have goose bumps," she said, a laugh in her voice.

His hands went still in her hair as his eyes ran over her body, seeing every single goose bump.

"Are you through?" she asked breathlessly.

"I don't have any rubber bands."

She ran her fingers over her collarbone and between her breasts. He stood. He'd had enough.

"This bath feels so good," she said softly. She swept her hand through the water and splattered him from his neck to the floor. "...doesn't it?" she added.

He saw the mischievous smile on her face and knew she had been playing him all along. If he hadn't been so preoccupied with not looking at her...

"Here I am trying to be a nice guy." Slowly

unsnapping his wet shirt, he tossed it into the corner. Standing on one foot, he removed first one boot, then the other. "I'm not usually so slow, Jacie."

Her gaze openly admired him. "Took you long enough," she jeered softly.

He hooked his thumbs in his belt loops and jerked. The jeans landed in a crumpled heap. His boxer shorts followed.

"My word," she said, fluttering her lashes.

"Lady, you better hope this thing is big enough for both of us," he warned as he slid into her arms. The water sloshed dangerously close to the tub rim.

"I think we've already established that," she said coyly.

Ω

Sloan handed Jacie a cup of steaming tea and sat on the couch beside her. She took a sip, then leaned her head back against his chest. His heart beat steady and strong, like him, she reflected.

"I was trying to be considerate," he murmured. "I put you in the guest room when I saw the shape you were in." He'd helped her undress the night before and it was all he could do to keep his mouth shut at the bruising she had taken. He lifted one of her hands. "And your hands, they're a mess."

"I'm fine." She placed her cup on a table behind the couch, then trailed her fingers across his jaw, liking the rasp of his whiskers.

"I wanted you to take it easy today."

"I didn't need consideration or gentleness earlier. It's a sorry thing when I have to seduce you."

"I enjoyed it." He cupped a bruise in the hollow of her shoulder and frowned. "This is serious, when I think of the risk..."

"Sloan," she said gently, "please stop. It's over." She sat up. "Brad is okay, right?"

He nodded, his mouth grim. "Yes, you were both damn lucky. They set his arm and operated on the gun wound."

"I'm relieved he's okay. He prevented Bonnie from shooting me."

His palm slid down to her wrist and his mouth touched several scratches on her neck. Heart racing, she arched forward, letting him pull her gently against him.

"I think it's time you told me everything about Brad and Angel Falls." His beautiful eyes were on her.

"The helicopter pilot should have been on standby, but Brad had released him prematurely. They radioed him back, but it took four hours. While I was in the tree the wind came up and I thought I'd fall before he got there. They got it all on film." She clenched her hands. "Brad used that footage."

"I watched the video," he said grimly.

"I've never seen it."

"What about Carlton?"

"I never saw him." She clenched her hands. "I have to let it go, it's past history. Brad's been history for a long while. It just wasn't right. I have him to thank for cutting it off a year ago." She grimaced. "If he had hung on, I might have settled for a lot less. I'm not happy admitting that either."

"Abandoning you, you mean?" he cut in, a hard line to his jaw.

"Whatever..." she shrugged. "It's over, before it began, really. I still can't believe after the last year, Bonnie's friendship was nothing more than a way to access my private information."

"Apparently, you're not the first person she's run a scam on. They don't even know yet if that was her real name."

"I guess it's lucky I'm weak," she said smugly.

He raised his brows skeptically. "You?"

"When Brad walked out, I told myself not to trust in any man's smile again. It took me a while to sort out the difference between you two. Good thing I've got a soft spot for cowboys."

"Make that cowboy and I'll agree," he said with a grin.

She stretched. "Well, it's over and done with. It's a great release."

"Does this mean you're going back to your family's business?"

She opened her mouth, but he forestalled her. "Wait, let me get this out. I might not be crazy about your line of work, but I know how important it is to you. I'll work through it. Somehow, I was seeing you and my mom in the same mold...risk-takers, period. I know now that's not true. You're a responsible adult and you're good at the job you do. God knows I don't want to talk you out of staying, Jacie, but this is a pretty quiet place, not much happens here."

She raised her brows. "You're kidding, right?"

"Let me put it this way, quiet until you arrived." He smiled and then sobered. "I won't ask you to walk away from skydiving because it's not on my agenda. I don't want that spilling over into our relationship. If skydiving is what you have to do, then I'll be there for you."

She blinked hard, emotion closing her throat. Sloan was a man who wanted stability, maybe a family life. He thought he would have to forego that, thinking such a step was necessary to make her happy. "I've had that career, still have it, if I want it. The idea has gone over pretty good right here. The thing is, I'm not willing to forfeit you.

"When I hung upside down in that tree, I saw every

small detail of my life, like a video rolling. I've done a lot of things, been a lot of places, and yet I never really belonged.

"They say I was unconscious; I don't remember. I could have died, but I didn't. My whole life is ahead of me, the possibilities are endless. Life doesn't add up to much if you don't share it with someone special," she ended fervently. "If that's all I've learned, I count it as the most important."

"You're one hell of a woman, Jacie."

He wrapped her close, then loosened his arms with an apology.

Having none of that, she pulled him back. "I've told you, I'm tougher than I look, even though you once said a strong wind could blow me away." She poked her fingers through the opening of his shirt.

He grabbed her fingers. "That first night I came to your cabin you looked like death warmed over when I turned your light on."

"So it was you."

"I wouldn't let anyone else over there, not even James." Ruefully, he shook his head. "When I caught you coming out of the shower, I was lost."

"Don't be misled. I am tough."

"You don't have to be tough with me. Just be Jacie." He set her away from him. "There's one last thing we have to clear up," he said brusquely. Before she could get alarmed, he continued, "We have to get married. My reputation is at risk since a lot of people saw me bring you in here last night. Not to mention your family knows you're staying here. The most important factor, of course, is that I love you."

Jacie wanted to laugh and she wanted to cry. He looked so serious, this man she loved. "Pretty sure of yourself, aren't you?"

"No, just desperately optimistic."

"Well, you're in luck. I'm a romantic at heart, and I can't envision a better happy ending than marrying the man I love." She looked at him with raised brows. "By the way, where are my brothers? I'm surprised they're not knocking down the door."

"My dad convinced them to help him round up the herd, which is by now scattered far and wide."

Jacie started laughing. "You're really in trouble now."

"I kind of figured that when my Dad started giving your brothers instruction on which side of the horse to mount. I think we'd better drive out and break the news to your family before there's a serious injury."

Jacie pressed her mouth to his. "Okay," she murmured, "but I need another kiss before we leave. I'm feeling neglected."

Sloan grinned. "You realize, of course, I won't stop at one kiss."

"I'm counting on it." And she was right.

∞ Epilogue ∞

"RELAX," JACIE SAID.

Some part of Sloan's brain heard Jacie's raised voice above the noise of the plane's engine.

"Don't think about the distance to the ground, just think about soaring on a current of air. You'll love it. I won't let go of you."

He looked at the ground far below them, knowing he would love it once he was on terra firma. "I can't believe I'm doing this. I can't believe I'm doing it in a tuxedo!" he yelled as together they jumped from the small plane. Immediately, her satin wedding dress billowed up to her waist, exposing her skin-tight white spandex leggings. They held hands as they spun slowly in the sky, first one way and then the other.

He released his chute and they were pulled upwards. Their landing was effortless, right on target in the midst of cheering family, friends, and the minister who waited to marry them.

Jacie looked at Sloan, noticing that although he

seemed to have made a good landing, he was now sitting on the grass, hands on his knees and staring at the ground.

She bent down and looked into his face. "Sloan, are you okay?"

He looked up at her and gave her a slow grin. "I sure am, sweetheart, although I think I've got grass stains on my tux. Call the pilot back, we'll have to do it again after the ceremony."

∞ *THE END* ∞

Women of Character Series

Excerpt Once and Always

Memory could be gentle. At other times it left scars.

Anna Barlow had read those words this morning and somehow they felt like a reflection of her life. She stared out over her ranch's fields now, trying to shake off the cobwebs of old memories.

Newly warmed earth and northeast temperatures collided, creating ground vapor as the sun fought its way through heavy clouds. She shivered, brushing at the cool morning mist that settled in her hair. Her mare stood unmoving beneath her, her nostrils blowing gently from their run. Anna patted Spirit's neck, wishing she could forget she was barely hanging onto the ranch. . . her home.

Every tree, stick and grain of dirt of the Double B Ranch belonged to her. The barns and dilapidated fences . . . the makeshift corral. She couldn't walk away from her only real home. Her grandfather Martin Barlow had brought her here at the age of fourteen. Now, everyone she'd ever loved was gone. Martin. Tyler.

Restlessly, Anna nudged her gray mare toward a well-worn dirt path that led down to the barns and house.

She'd survived worse. Somehow, she'd get through this too. Anna touched her right cheek and curled her fingers against the scarred flesh, her fingers tracing the faint ridges almost absentmindedly. Her face had once been her biggest asset. Now it brought her only anger and at times self pity. She hated feeling sorry for herself, but God Almighty she was only human.

Giving in to a reckless edge of emotion, Anna urged her mare into a bone-jarring trot down the hillside. When they reached level ground, the spring wind tore against her as they loped across open pasture. She inhaled the clean air into her lungs, reveling in the familiar thunder of hooves beneath her. Gradually, the sting of failure lessened. Self-absorbed and prideful these last two years, she'd allowed the fire that ruined her face to take over her life.

She had to live with her mistakes, but somehow she'd find a way out of this mess.

Excerpt Wishing on a Rodeo Moon

Someday, that bull would kill someone. Tye Jenkins just knew it. She straddled the top rail of the bull chute as old Hit Man moved restlessly from side to side.

Tye let her gaze roam the rodeo yard. Her heart jumped like a young colt on a brisk morning as she stared, transfixed, at a dark-haired man. Jake Miller. He stood close by, a cocky look of assurance on his lean face. He was a head taller than most of the men around him, a stranger in business clothes among mud-spattered cowboys. His suit looked expensive, not the most common attire down by the pens. She had never before seen him dressed like that, yet he carried it off with nonchalance and elegance. He stood, feet planted on ground churned up by countless boots and three days of rain, his dark head bare to the falling mist. Tye didn't try to stop the smile spreading across her face. Only Jake could pull off a suit at a rodeo in the drizzling rain.

She hadn't seen or heard from Jake in ten years, not since that terrible night she'd left. He'd showed up now, the night she planned to remember for the rest of her life—the night she'd make the rodeo finals. With the bittersweet knowledge of the past firmly in her mind, Tye sensed it was fitting Jake should be here to see her triumph.

Even knowing she was short on time before her ride, she continued to stare at Jake. Why was he here? What was that expression in his face—a mixture of pain and want? Tye wiped the mist from her eyes, knowing she was wrong. She drew a deep breath.

He had changed, matured, yet something in his eyes remained the same. How long had she loved that strong face with its wide cheekbones, no-nonsense jaw touched by the faintest shadow of beard and deep-set eyes of the lightest blue? Her seventeenth summer she had loved him with a young woman's vibrancy. They'd spent endless time together, planning, talking, dreaming. Back then, Tye had thought Jake could do no wrong.

She drew a deep breath and looked around. Why was he here? It wasn't to see her! He was already drawing attention: she could see some of the girls nudging each other. Her throat dry, Tye drew a deep breath and then pressed her lips together. There were a lot of handsome faces like Jake's, but he had a presence. He always had. Jake was special, that's why she had loved him so much, until she had walked away.

Excerpt Echoes From the Past

A woman, a man and a child with nothing in common but their respective troubled pasts. Three wounded souls determined to survive alone until they realize all they need to heal is each other.

On the verge of a nervous breakdown, Christie reacts by running away, emotionally and physically. Down to her last twenty dollars, she's determined to fulfill her dead sister's last wish—to locate their sister Judith who left home twenty years before. Her quest brings her into the lives of Garrett, Judith's husband, and the emotionally fragile Hannah, Judith's daughter. Christie is devastated to learn Judith died two years before. When Christie insists on getting to know her niece, Garrett agrees on the condition she doesn't reveal her identity. He hires her to work at his horse farm but what he doesn't count on is the turmoil and hope Christie brings into their lives.

Christie's own emotional journey forces her to come

to terms with her family's alcoholism and her perception of herself.

¤ ¤ ¤

Women of Strength Time Travel

Once Upon a Remembrance: Book 1. Photographer Isabeau Remington travels to 1894 Virginia and falls in love with a man she must ultimately leave behind when she returns to her own time...but things are not always as they seem.

Modern day photographer Isabeau is pulled from the present time and thrust back into the year 1894 in Virginia. She must help save Hawk Morgan, a man threatened by a killer, a man endangered by his own erased memories. Hawk must survive in 1894 so his present day ancestor Pierce Morgan, will be alive in Isabeau's future.

Isabeau begins to fall in love with Hawk Morgan but with both their future's uncertain and a killer on the loose, neither one of them may have a tomorrow to look forward to.

Soulmates Through Time: Book 2. Thrust from her own time in 1822, Elise has been separated from the man she loves for 24 years. She has adjusted to modern times, raised a daughter, and become successful in her own right. When she stumbles upon the way back, she must make the decision to step back into that time.

Will Darien still love her and will Elise be able to turn back the clock and regain the love they once shared? Does she want to turn back time?

Treasure So Rare: Book 3. Erik Remington Captain Erik Remington has been haunted for three years by a black haired sea witch. They spent seven glorious days and nights before she vanished as mysteriously as she appeared.

In 1850, when his ship is pulled into a strange vortex, he ends up in middle ages England. Forced to assume another's identity, Weinroof of Camdork, he travels to the home of the man's affianced, the Lady Iliana. This world is nothing like the England of history books. Danger lurks everywhere, even the skies. As Camdork, he meets the Lady Iliana and instantly recognizes her as the woman who's haunted him.

Iliana wants nothing to do with Camdork and will defy her Queen to not marry him. All she sees is the man known as a murderer, whose attack four years before on an innocent maiden haunts her memories.

Iliana has her own secrets, but her unwavering mission is to find the perfect green gem and restore it to her people. Camdork stands in her way, so she must kill him if she ever wants to see the return of her old life.

¤ ¤ ¤

Romantic Short Stories

Two Babies, a Cowboy and Sara: Short, sweet romance, 24,000 words. When Sara is appointed co-guardian of her deceased cousin's infant girls, their father Lucas is glad to accept Sara's help in caring for the twins. For Sara it's a labor of love and also a dream come true since she can't have babies of her own.

For Lucas, having Sara on his ranch is a reminder of how his life could have turned out so very differently, if only he'd met Sara first.

Deception

Short, sweet romance with a hint of suspense. Trey's boss is old, sick and his days are numbered; and he wants to see his missing granddaughter Katharine before he dies. Trey will do almost anything for the old man, even if it means having artist Sacha Fortune pretend to be Katharine.

Sacha is forced to assume the other woman's identity, because if she doesn't comply, Trey will expose her criminal past to the art world which has so recently embraced her art.

But Sacha has more to lose than Trey could ever guess.

Thanks for reading!

Faeries Lost Series Coming soon!

Visit my author page at www.GraceBrannigan.com to read all my contemporary, time travel, faerie stories and short romantic stories.

Grace Brannigan